TREASURE OF THE MAYAN KING

ISBN: 978-0-615-27549-9

Published by
Arcani Arts

Visit us at:
www.arcaniarts.com

DEDICATIONS & ACKNOWLEDGEMENTS

There is a saying: ‘No man is an island’ and how true that is with the making of a book! This literary work never would have existed without the assistance of my dear friend **Dyego Alehandro**, who I must say is an awesome author in his own right. Special thanks to him for assisting me in rewriting certain passages of this story as well as the awesome computer artwork.

To my wife, **Anita Zabala**: for her love, patience.

Greta Bishop & Ellie Jerauld: for their invaluable literary mentoring.

Timothy Rivadeneyra: for his ink drawings.

Joel D Canfield: for editing the first draft and his keen insight in assisting me in book mentoring. Visit him at: http://joeldcanfield.com/

To **Tom Bentley**: for editing the final draft of the manuscript. Visit him at:
The Write Word Writing and Editing Services http://www.tombentley.com

-Alex Zabala

AUTHOR'S NOTE

In its heyday the Mayan Empire ranged from Guatemala to the Yucatan Peninsula. Archaeologists, paleontologists and other scientists pursuing the study of the Maya (Mayanists) report there are still many undiscovered pyramids and temples in the area begging to be unearthed and studied. However, due to the encroachment of tropical vegetation and/or lack of funding, it may take many years to do so.

This work of fiction is based on an actual event that occurred after a tropical storm ripped through the jungle of Guatemala in 2001. An uprooted tree exposed the hidden steps of a Mayan temple. After the storm, scientists were excited to discover one of the longest hieroglyphs known to science. This discovery and the subsequent translation of the hieroglyphs have shed light on the ideas, culture and political organization of that lost civilization.

Having spent many hours in exhaustive research to bring to life the events in this book, it was my intent to present this fictional work with current knowledge and understanding. However, as with any theory, the interpretation of the Maya culture has been and will continue to be subject to debate and revision, especially as more sites are cleared and studied.

In addition to the scientific research for this book my travels throughout Mexico, including an eight-year residency, aided me in developing the characters and storyline. Initially, this novel was written as two separate books. In time I made the decision to divide the story into three small integrated "books" as indicated in the table of contents. Each book has its own pitch, pace and unique narration all three come together in the finale. The intention of this story is to bring an exotic and much wondered-about world into the reader's imagination. Enjoy!

– Alex Zabala

PROLOGUE

The sun was shining, with few clouds casting their shadows upon the jungle. The wind was blowing softly, the birds were chirping, and thousands of laborers carried the spoils of war upon their backs.

It was a good day to celebrate.

King Chac stood proudly atop his grand pyramid amidst the jungles of Palenque, Mexico. The colorful plumage of his royal costume glittered slightly in the afternoon breeze. The gold and silver of his garment contrasted with his dark brown skin and the mass of clothing weighed heavily upon his thin, muscular frame. Thousands of slaves carried the booty from his recent conquest of the Lowland Maya. Today the festivities were honoring his brilliant strategy and military cunning.

The smoke from many incense-burning urns wafted skyward, dancing in slow circles in tune to the wind. The staccato of drums, the whistling of flutes and the singing of songs seemed to propel the smoke's dancing as much as it did the performers. Dignitaries and their wives sat on exquisitely designed benches in the royal court, smiles on their faces and drinks in their hands as they observed the festivities. The priests were also present, attending to their myriad duties, invoking the favor of the gods.

The general populace stood at a distance, also observing the procession, content with the knowledge that their gods were looking down favorably on recent events. After all, was it not obvious they were a blessed people? They were the Highland Maya, and were enjoying such riches and glory as never before. King Chac had been nothing but successful in his conquests it seemed as if the entire Yucatan Peninsula had been subjugated under him.

The king smiled as he quietly observed the treasure pile grow to a phenomenal size as the workers continued to file into the courtyard, each one depositing his load of the riches before disappearing. All these, the precious artifacts of gold, silver, jade, obsidian, and other exotic materials, had been taken from the deposed kings. The jewels glistened, their many colors morphing in the sunlight as clouds passed over. The sight of so much wealth in one place was mesmerizing, gripping and taunting the minds of all the observers with such vast fortunes.

King Chac was now supreme ruler. He was aware of his new status and he had made it a priority to ensure that his fame, power, and riches were known to all the inhabitants of the Mayan world. He had commissioned the construction of great pyramids, making sure that his name was inscribed in the grand edifices by the hands of only the most masterful stonemasons.

His fame had reached its zenith, and the treasure of this Mayan king was now the largest ever acquired. There, before his very eyes, the mountain of riches continued to rise and swell to outstanding proportions, a testimony to his military success.

The next day the king's wife, Cihuatl, entered her husband's royal chamber, a grand room with rich and vibrant murals. Large benches rested against the walls while in the middle, upon a raised dais, sat the throne of the king. Near the throne was a small urn in which burned incense, giving the entire room a hazy atmosphere.

As was the custom, Cihuatl slowly walked into the room with her head bowed. Once she approached him, she raised her head to gaze at her husband, and nearly recoiled as she saw the king's face contorted with misery and grief.

"What is the matter, my lord?" she asked, worry evident in her tone. "Why are you so distraught?"

He did not answer. He just sat there, his eyes unfocused and his head downcast. When he continued to be silent, his wife made an effort to reach him.

"This is not a time for sadness, my king, but a time for great rejoicing! Are you not the greatest king to ever walk our land? Do not the gods smile upon your endeavors? Surely they must, for look at the treasure that has been deposited at your very feet!"

King Chac did not look at his wife when he spoke. "Yes ... yes, I am well aware of this magnificent mountain of treasure and the extent of my fame. That is what worries me."

"But why?" she asked.

He raised himself from his throne and walked slowly around the chamber, his eyes gazing at the many decorations. "I worry that sometime, somewhere, somehow, someone is going to find my treasure and plunder it! Then all will be lost, my treasure, my glory, my fame—yes, everything—will be gone. I must find a way to keep it for all eternity!"

"Who would steal it, my dear husband? We have many loyal subjects who guard the treasure and who guard you with their very lives."

"Yes, I am aware of that," he said with a heavy sigh as he walked around. "After I pass away, what guarantee is there that my treasure will not be plundered and stolen? No! That thought is too much for me to bear! There must be a way to secure my treasures and conceal them from my enemies."

"What do you propose to do, my lord?"

The Mayan king stopped walking and turned to look at her for the first time since she entered. "I have been thinking of a way; I have a plan! I must consult with the priests first, however, for they can help me. I will find a way to guard my treasure forever."

Several days passed before Cihuatl entered the royal room again and found her husband sitting on his throne, two priests at his side, and a smile upon his face.

He seemed to be in a jovial mood. "Ah! My dear wife, do come closer, for I have good news for you."

"This is a welcome change," she commented, mimicking his smile. "Please, tell me what it is that has you in such good spirits."

King Chac was holding a scroll in his hand as he stood up. "I have thought of a way to solve the problem of securing my treasure! Beginning today, my workers will construct a grand pyramid, where my body will be entombed once I pass from this world. Most kings bury their treasure with them, but not I. No! My treasure will be taken somewhere else, somewhere secret. The workers involved in hiding the treasure will be sacrificed to the gods so they will never tell a soul of its location. But, upon the steps of my temple, there will be a great riddle, one to tantalize and perplex the people for ages."

"What is this riddle?" his wife asked.

The king answered: "The meaning of this riddle will never be explained to any mortal! Only my successors, the kings and the priests, will have the knowledge of this great secret, and they will guard it jealously. Forever will my treasure be secured, and forever will my fame live on!"

Book One

The Mayan Riddle

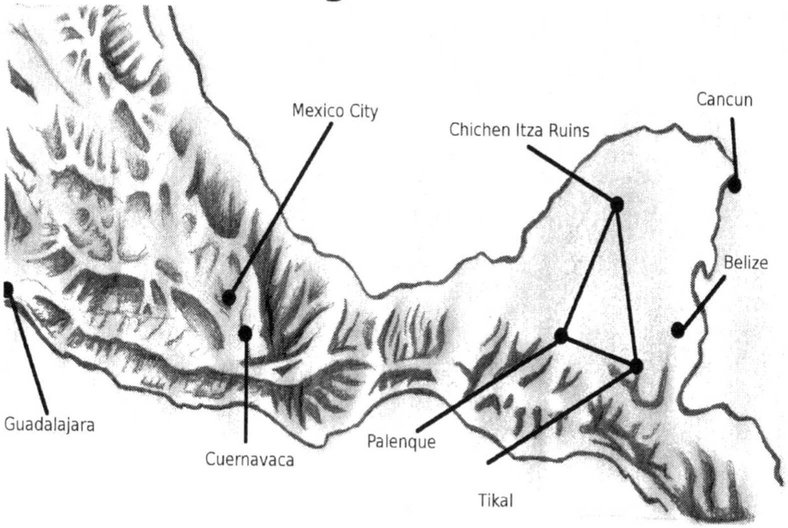

CHAPTER ONE

The jungle was noisy with animal sounds as he stood on the top of the steps of the small plane. Disdain clouded his face as he surveyed those gathered to meet him. He puffed the thick cigar clenched in his teeth, muttering in French as he disembarked. Dr. René Sova was no tourist visiting the Yucatan peninsula in Mexico for the climate. In fact, he considered any climate, hot or cold, dry or humid, simply a nuisance to be ignored.

"Ah, Doctor Sova," one of the men called out. "I am Doctor Joseph Lopez. Welcome to Palenque. Is there any way we may assist you?"

Yes, by getting out of my way, he thought. He hoped he wouldn't have to spend too much time with these fools. "You may direct me to the nearest vehicle and the pyramid," he said. His Spanish was excellent under the thick French accent.

"Certainly Dr. Sova, the blue SUV is yours, with a knowledgeable driver on hand. Shall I brief you?"

"At the site, Lopez, at the site," carefully not calling him 'doctor.'

Doctor Lopez stared the world-famous linguist: he was short, but not fat; his hair was thick but no longer showed any black at all. With that pointed goatee, it took only a bit of imagination to see a resemblance to a certain fast-food icon famous for his fried chicken. All present were well aware they had been completely ignored by their visitor.

Meanwhile Dr. Sova sat in comfort in the front passenger seat of a luxury SUV, thinking about what was waiting for him ahead. There was evidence all around of the damage nature was capable of. The hurricane had also revealed Dr. Sova's reason for being there. For decades, archaeologists suspected a certain large mound in the vicinity was, in fact, a pyramid. Busy with existing finds, they had neglected the area—but the winds of the hurricane had not. Uprooted trees and vegetation revealed the staircase of an ancient Mayan pyramid.

Mayanists were astounded to find an ancient message on the staircase. These anthropologists and archaeologists specializing in Mayan culture, unable to decipher the lettering, had called in Dr. Sova.

Idiots, all of them, he thought as the vehicle bumped and slid to the pattern of the road. Rough or smooth, it was immaterial as long as he got where he was going, and when he wanted to get there. Seeing the mound in the distance, he set about analyzing the passing jungle to keep his mind busy until they arrived.

The blue SUV came to a halt fifty yards from the pyramid. Ignoring the dust the SUV had caused, Dr. Sova quickly stepped from the vehicle to look at the work site.

Much of the debris had been cleared from the steps of the pyramid by the hurricane but there was still much to remove. *Those workers look like insects, yes, they remind me of ants.* Dr. Sova chuckled to himself as he perused the architectural design of the pyramid.

It was fairly typical of Mayan style. He couldn't be certain, for most of the structure was still buried, but it looked like it was actually larger than most, certainly quite a find. His eyes swept the surrounding vegetation and area, noticing several other mounds at a distance that he predicted might be pyramids as well. He would mark the spots for future study. His eyes continued on and looked at what the Plaza. This new pyramid was actually at the end of a long roadway that led to other pyramids, all of them previously unearthed and studied.

He knew manpower was scarce, but it was beyond him as to why this pyramid had not been unearthed before; it was located so close to a well-known Mayan find.

Doctor Lopez came up next to him, his right hand shading his eyes from the glare of the sun as he gazed at the pyramid. "Quite a beautiful thing isn't it?" he asked.

Dr. Sova actually agreed with him. "Yes indeed. What is the synopsis?"

"Basically what the newspapers have been reporting; a tree topples over and reveals Mayan glyphs. As for the writing ... well, we're not sure what to make of it. It is obviously Mayan hieroglyphs, but there is much about the translation that makes us wonder if we have it all wrong."

Which you probably have, Dr. Sova thought with a slight smile on his face. Being at the pyramid had improved his mood, and he was willing to humor these dull-minded colleagues for the time being.

"Well let's see what I can do about correcting your translations, eh?" Without waiting for a reply, he walked briskly toward the pyramid, eager to begin his work.

After a cursory study of the initial results from the professionals, Dr. Sova had concluded that the translation had been wrong on nearly every level. Dr. Sova quickly discarded the previous work and began translations anew, working feverishly from dawn till dusk, and sometimes far past it. During the next few weeks it was not unusual to find him out during the night with spotlights and yards of paper, scribbling away furiously and talking to himself in the strangely beautiful Mayan tongue, almost chanting as he walked up and down the steps. These strange "conversations" would occasionally be interspersed with cries of discovery or grunts of satisfaction as his guesses were proved correct and he added another piece to the puzzle.

The other archaeologists avoided the linguist entirely, which was not difficult because the doctor avoided them too.

He ignored the low murmurs in the camp—he knew they were talking about him. *Let them have their little talks*, he thought more than once. *They will know who the true Mayanist is before long. They will be forced to recognize my genius.*

He rarely spoke to anyone, but he was always talking, always muttering some peculiar phrase; sometimes in Spanish, sometimes Italian or French, but mostly in Mayan. He was comparing the dialects, finding equivalents in other tongues. It was amazing how idiosyncrasies in one language would find a companion in another language, if one knew where to look.

And the doctor knew where to look. The writings were making sense, as he linked words and phrases back and forth, erasing a meaning and then penciling it back in his notebook, changing his mind and erasing it again as he stared at the engravings in the steps, the beautiful word pictures linked mysteriously to meanings. The language had peculiar differences from most Mayan. The message seemed to be a poem and at the same time a description. This contrast more than once caused him to rip up entire days of work and start again.

And then, one day, it was over. Everything finally made sense, and Dr. Sova nodded. *Sneaky devil*, he thought silently of the man who had had this engraving made so many centuries ago. *Devious devil indeed!*

He stood up and triple-checked his translation, reading the words first from the staircase and then from his notebook. After at least half an hour of examination, he was satisfied. He knew exactly what the hieroglyphs said, and it was time the world knew as well.

He descended the staircase shouting to Dr. Lopez, "Call the media. I have a special announcement to make concerning the Mayan glyphs!"

Dr. Sova had orchestrated the event to its full potential. The press conference was being held in a hotel lobby in Merida, most of which was filled with a life-sized plaster replica of the Mayan staircase, complete with hieroglyphs. The media was eager to hear what the renowned Dr. Sova had to reveal to the world.

Dr. Sova knew how to handle himself in front of the cameras, and he enjoyed the attention. He walked to the lectern situated in front of the staircase replica and waved his hands, indicating he was ready to speak.

"Ladies and gentlemen," he announced in impeccable English despite his accent. "May I have your attention please? The time has come to reveal the mystery of the Mayan hieroglyphs we have found on what we now call Temple #22."

The lobby was quiet except for the sound of the morning traffic outside.

After having let the silence hang for a few dramatic seconds, he continued. "It is my pleasure to bring to you the explanation of the Mayan inscriptions. As you are all aware, the destructive nature of Hurricane Sheila was responsible for clearing away enough vegetation so as to expose an ancient staircase. This staircase has revealed the history of a formerly unknown ruler by the name of King Chac.

“As you can see here behind me ..." he said, and turned briefly to point at the plaster staircase replica, a gesture he repeated several times during his discourse. "King Chac lived in the post-classic period of the Mayan empire. What makes this discovery so fascinating is the fact that we had no record of this king: he was an unknown entity! For many years it was thought that all of the Mayan kings of the Quiche Maya had been accounted for." Sova, of course, had thought no such thing, but he figured that the simple-minded Mayanists had assumed the book of knowledge on the Mayan culture had been read from cover to cover.

"But now we can see, according to the glyphs that have been uncovered on the pyramid, we have a new ruler to add to our list. And much to our great delight, we also have reason to believe that this pyramid contains his remains. The work of clearing Temple #22 will commence shortly in an attempt to excavate inside the structure. It has been decided among my colleagues and I that this work will be accomplished by an international crew of archaeologists, all of whom will assist in uncovering the temple."

After the applause died down, he answered the many questions the media posed to him.

CHAPTER TWO

The sun was shining brightly on the small turboprop airplane as it made its final approach to the dirt runway. Trying to remind himself that the pilot was an expert, American archaeologist Chauncy Rollock sat with both hands tightly gripping the arms of his seat. Despite the number of times he had landed on remote, barely maintained runways, the deep blue eyes under his blond crew cut showed that it never failed to scare the daylights out of him.

"Come now, Chauncy," chided his associate Mack Estlund. "Surely you know they wouldn't let anybody but the best pilots fly us here."

Chauncy tried his best to appear relaxed and carefree as he turned to look at the taller, lankier man. "What are you talking about, Mack?"

Mack smiled knowingly. "I'm talking about the permanent indentations you are making in the armrests of your seat."

Chauncy felt his face warming as he consciously relinquished his grip on the armrests. "Let's just say I'm not overly fond of landing, Mack."

Mack smiled. "I know."

Chauncy ignored the windows at both edges of his vision. He could tell by the whine of the engines and the plane's angle that they were only seconds from landing and he found himself gripping his chair again. The plane touched down with a minimum of jerking. The cabin door opened and the pilot smiled at his passengers.

"Welcome to the Yucatan Peninsula, my friends. Please gather your carry-on luggage. My co-pilot will bring the rest of your gear. Thank you again, and may the rest of your journey be fruitful."

The pilot disappeared into the cockpit and was replaced by the co-pilot, who opened the hatch and lowered the steps. Chauncy and Mack unbuckled their belts and assembled their bags. The rest of their luggage was waiting at the bottom of the steps.

The co-pilot waved as he re-boarded the plane. Moments later it was just a speck among the puffy white clouds. Chauncy dusted himself off and looked around as he chuckled. "Well, Mack, how do you like being left in the middle of nowhere?"

Mack looked around in dismay. He stared for a long time at the place where the plane had disappeared from view, and then sat down on a sturdy piece of luggage. "What if the pilot made a mistake? What if this isn't the right location? What do we do?"

Detecting the rising fear in Mack's voice, Chauncy tried to calm him down. "Don't worry; this isn't the first time for me."

Mack gazed at the runway. "Yeah, well that's good for you, but I would rather be 'somewhere' and not 'no where' right now."

Chauncy adjusted his wide-brimmed hat and his sunglasses, surveying the area again. There was no sign of human life, but he knew from experience that the jungle was far from lifeless, no matter how still it seemed at first. If one only knew but to listen, there was much sound. It had been silent when the plane left, but now the silence of the jungle was broken by the sounds of wildlife. Screaming monkeys, an array of bird squawks and songs, hisses of unidentified origin, all blended together. Some would consider it noise, but to Chauncy it was like a beautiful melody.

The sun beat down upon them, and the humidity was well above what they were used to. Dark perspiration spots began to form on their clothes.

Chauncy wiped his brow before stooping to pick up his luggage. "We better start setting up camp and then look for Dr. Sova," he said as he made his way toward the shade under the canopy of trees. "If there really was a mistake then we have no reason to fear, Mack. We can always use my satellite phone to call for help. Of course it had better be an emergency—I'm sure you know how much it costs for each call."

Chauncy started to walk the perimeter of the airstrip, wondering how the landing had been as smooth as it had been. Calling it an airstrip was far too generous; it was more like a dirt road, a simple break in the jungle canopy. Perhaps if he looked hard enough he could locate a way out of the primitive landing area with the intent of finding a civilized area. Instead of joining the search, Mack just sat on his luggage, apparently wondering what to do.

The lack of a welcoming committee had obviously thrown him for a loop. Chauncy felt that talking to Mack would raise his spirits. "I've found two roads so far that go off into the jungle," he called out, picking his way carefully along the edge of the trees. "Neither appears like it has been used for a while ... no, wait ... here we go!" He smiled broadly, turning back to look at Mack. "There are fresh tire tracks on this one, my friend, all is not lost."

Before Mack could respond, the distant sound of a vehicle came to them through the jungle. Chauncy stood for a moment, his head tilted at a slight angle, identifying the sound. After a few seconds his smile returned. "It's definitely getting closer, and if I had to guess, I'd say it is coming down this road too. Cheer up Mack, I think our ride is here."

As Chauncy stepped back to the luggage, a large and luxurious SUV crossed the runway. A small man dressed in safari khakis stepped out of the passenger side. Chauncy immediately recognized the gray hair and white goatee of the famous Dr. Sova.

Sova walked toward the two men and introduced himself, even though he knew he wouldn't have to. "Good morning, Mr. Estlund, Mr. Rollock. My name is Dr. Sova. Please, you must forgive me for the delay—we were quite busy with another matter. I'm sure you understand."

"Think nothing of it," replied Chauncy as the chauffeur loaded their luggage.

As they drove slowly through the dust they generated along the bumpy road, Chauncy relished the cushy interior of the vehicle, since it was as far removed as possible from the environment outside. The leather seats were very comfortable, and the air conditioning was a welcome relief. Despite the jarring ride, Chauncy knew what mattered more than the environment or the condition of the road was their destination: Temple #22. Mack and Chauncy had been chosen as the representatives of the United States in the multinational archaeological undertaking. The only paleontologists, they had been invited because it was believed that the skeletal remains of King Chac would be found in the pyramid.

To fill the long drive, Chauncy took advantage of the privilege of speaking with the great Dr. Sova. They discussed the general state of the project, the overall mission, and the progress that had so far been made in clearing out the temple.

"We are making fine advancement indeed." Dr. Sova's voice was rich with professional excitement. "Most of the overgrown plant material has been cleared. Soon we will be able to make our ascent to the top of the temple and from there we will need to pry open the flagstone on the top floor in order to gain access to the tunnel."

He paused as the vehicle hit a rather large pothole. "You two are the last men I have invited to this project, and therefore the last to arrive. Once we have access to the tunnel we will then be disinterring the remains of King Chac, and I will need you two paleontologists to analyze his skeleton."

The vehicle came across another particularly rough spot on the road, and this time the conversation did not resume or a while.

It was almost exactly an hour later when they arrived at the foot of the imposing pyramid. As he got out of the vehicle, Chauncy couldn't help but stare at the muted grandeur of the place. The first thing that came to his mind was how vertical the structure was. He wondered idly whether any of the ancients had lost their foothold and fallen to their deaths while climbing the temple. It wasn't a pleasant mental image. He shook his head in an effort to rid himself of the thought, and gazed at the details of the pyramid.

It had the weathered and eroded look that was peculiar to buildings with centuries of neglect and abandon behind them. It was obvious to the paleontologist that at one time the temple was adorned with vivid, colorful paint, but dark and nearly indiscernible streaks replaced what had once been vibrant color.

It taxed the imagination to visualize that this place and other silent temples of the area had once been a thriving metropolis with a dynamic economy.

Dr. Sova led the way to a large courtyard, which had been improvised as base camp. Many tents had been erected and there was a large outdoor kitchen. Even from a distance, Chauncy could smell the food.

When they made it to the large open sitting area, Chauncy was surprised to see how many people there were. They were sitting on benches, chairs, or the ground, eating, chatting, studying maps and diagrams, plotting their work. Dr. Sova introduced the two Americans to the rest of the international crew, all of whom had already been working at the site for some time. The doctor did the introductions in at least four languages, which impressed Chauncy. The various professionals and workers offered their welcomes in their respective languages, with Dr. Sova translating for most before carting the two paleontologists off to show them their tents.

They arrived at Mack's tent first, and Dr. Sova recommended he get settled in before exploring. Mack agreed and exchanged farewells with Chauncy. Once Mack had disappeared into his tent, Dr. Sova motioned Chauncy to follow. The linguist immediately set off, Chauncy right behind him.

But instead of continuing down the line of small tents, Dr. Sova was making his way toward a very large white tent structure, one of the biggest in the camp. Chauncy felt his eyebrows lifting—was this the doctor's tent, or his own?

His question was answered the second they arrived. "This is my humble abode," Dr. Sova said jovially. "Please, come in."

Chauncy followed the doctor inside and was astounded to see modern conveniences in stark contrast to the primitive surroundings of the jungle. Chauncy could hear, and feel, an air conditioning unit and generator hard at work. The tent appeared to have several rooms partitioned with cloth doors. From where he stood Chauncy could see a full-sized kitchen with a microwave, refrigerator, and other modern amenities. He was obviously in the living room portion of the tent, as there were several plush chairs, a couch, and a coffee table.

Dr. Sova's personal chef was busy preparing a meal. The linguist called to the cook and asked something in French that Chauncy didn't catch. Moments later the cook returned with two glasses and a bottle of wine. He placed the glasses on the coffee table and poured the wine, leaving the bottle and returning to the kitchen.

"Come, sit down," the doctor invited, taking a seat himself in one of the chairs near the coffee table. He picked up his glass of wine and raised it in a toast. "Congratulations, Mr. Rollock!"

Chauncy sat down, perplexed about the whole situation.

"If I may ask, what exactly are you congratulating me for?"

Dr. Sova laughed before taking a long drink from his glass. He did not answer Chauncy immediately; instead he leaned back in his chair, crossed his legs, and took a cigar from a metal case in his vest pocket. Clipping the end off, he lit it and took a puff from it. As he exhaled the smoke he finally looked at Chauncy.

"You passed the test! You were the only one who did. The Russians, the Europeans, the Mexicans, the Canadians, even your American colleague—everyone out there in this camp, they all failed," he said as he waved his hand in disdain.

Chauncy was even more perplexed. He took a cautious sip from his wine, hoping he could figure out what was going on. "Okay. I give up. Why are you congratulating me?"

Dr. Sova unfolded his legs and leaned forward, a look of concentration on his face, his wine glass in one hand and the cigar in the other. "Please allow me to explain. What I am about to say is very serious. You see, I really wasn't late to pick you up from the airstrip as I made you believe. In fact, we were observing you, watching the both of you from a distance with binoculars."

Chauncy took another sip. "You were? Why?"

Dr. Sova's eyes flashed with emotion as he glared out at the camp. "What we have out there is no small, insignificant project! This is a very important and serious undertaking. It has been many decades since a burial tomb of a king has been discovered. The translation of the temple staircase has enlightened the world about this new king, but it has also enlightened me about something else. There are amazing things to be discovered from that temple, amazing things.

"The reason I have invited an international crew was for the purpose of finding one man, just one that I could take into my confidence. I intend on grooming that man to become my partner, and you, Mr. Rollock, are that man! I need a person that I can use in the continuation of this project. There is so much more that I have read on that staircase that I have not revealed to the world, as of yet." He leaned back in his chair, waiting to gauge Chauncy's reaction.

Chauncy couldn't believe what he was hearing. Dr. Sova wanted to take him under his wings and train him? He took another sip from his glass and let the wine sit on his tongue for a moment, as if the liquid would somehow wake him up from this dream. But it wasn't a dream; he had heard correctly. He took another sip, still thinking furiously.

This was the chance of a lifetime. What others would give to be personally trained under the tutelage of the great Dr. Sova! And now here he was, Chauncy Rollock, sitting and talking with the famed linguist himself, drinking expensive French wine in his tent.

"Why me?" he finally managed to ask.

Dr. Sova put his wineglass down, stood up, and began pacing the room. With the hand that held his cigar he tapped his temple. "Because you are a thinker Mr. Rollock. Oh, don't get me wrong, those men and women out there are fine, hardworking professionals, all of them. But you my friend, you are different, you are exceptional! I have observed every man and woman at the airstrip, including you. I had given orders to the pilot beforehand, stating that he would deliver the archaeologists and scientists and then leave immediately, not waiting for me or anyone else to show up, and that he would tell them nothing. I did that on purpose, Mr. Rollock, in order to observe them from a distance. Stressful situations are the most wonderful way to test people's mettle, to see how they think and react. You were the only one that used powers of perception and discernment.

"It was obvious to me that you are the analytical type. As soon as you realized that the pilot had left you and Mr. Estlund alone, you immediately set about finding a way to survive. Not Mr. Estlund! He simply sat down on his luggage, baking in the hot tropical sun. Meanwhile, you were busy trying to find a way out of your predicament. You found a place for your luggage in the shade, away from the harsh sunlight, and then you proceeded to examine your surroundings and find a way out. You are an analytical multi-tasker. Is my evaluation correct?"

"Well ... I suppose." Chauncy was proud that Dr. Sova had taken note.

Dr. Sova continued. "Yes, of course. Next point: on the way over here in my vehicle, I keenly observed that you were making mental notes as to where the temple was located. You were looking out the windows, keeping track of our movements. You even took out your notebook and drew a map, did you not?"

"Yes, that is correct." Chauncy replied as he pulled out his notepad and opened it to reveal the crude drawing.

"But your colleague, Mr. Estlund, was looking at the palms of his hands," Dr. Sova stated. "God knows where his mind was! What if my vehicle had broken down? You would have known how to return to the airstrip. Not him."

"You saw all of that?" Chauncy asked, surprised.

"That and much more my friend, when we arrived at this camp, your associate was too busy worrying about his luggage. You, however, were observing the details of the whole operation, your eyes missed nothing. In fact, I would venture to say that your notebook contains another map, one of the camp. Is that correct?"

Chauncy turned the page of his notebook, grinning broadly as he showed Dr. Sova the schematic he had drawn. "Could I dare take the liberty of making a suggestion? The latrines are upwind from base camp—not a good idea, if you know what I mean?"

Dr. Sova laughed out loud. "Very good, my friend, that was very observant of you and on top of that you are gifted with a sense of humor."

Becoming serious again, he said, "And yet none of those

people out there were able to see all of these details! Your brain, Mr. Rollock, you are using it. You are using your critical thinking abilities. The rest of those people just flow along a stream like dead fish in a river! They simply keep moving with the knowledge they have been taught in their books.... But they can't think outside the box; they lack that ability. You are different."

"Why, thank you." Chauncy said with a smile.

"However, there is one major fault with you!" Dr. Sova thundered in a stern voice.

Chauncy's smile evaporated. "Uh ... and what would that be?"

"I noticed on our way over here, while we were in the vehicle, that you took your wallet out, opened it, and rubbed your fingers over a picture of a woman who I am assuming is your wife. You seem to suffer from homesickness, my friend. That weakness can be your undoing."

Chauncy could almost physically feel his ego deflate. It was obvious the man had seen every subtle nuance; nothing had escaped his quick and discerning eye. "I ... well ... I guess you're right," Chauncy said.

"Ah! Do not fret, *mon ami*," the doctor reassured in a friendly tone. "I'm sure that we can work on that small detail."

Chauncy looked up, a smile on his face. He raised his wineglass and drained it. He felt not just respect, but friendship.

"Tell me something, Doctor, why did you decide to become a Mayanist?"

The doctor, still pacing, stopped and sat down. "I am a master linguist; my one love is the study of languages. Ah yes, now that is my passion! I quickly learned and then mastered most of the Latin-based languages. I was going to progress on to learn the Oriental languages next.

"Then one day during a visit here to the Yucatan I realized

my real calling in life. And what a marvelous undertaking it has been, to learn the Mayan language and decipher ancient writings from a lost civilization. It is truly a task for the mind and the imagination, two things that are most important to me. And now look where it has brought us. That temple out there, that grand pyramid of the past, is just waiting for us to uncover its long-held secrets. Who knows what wonders await us? It is very exciting!"

Dr. Sova's eyes sparkled as he spoke; his voice had an unmistakable fire. It was evident his whole heart was dedicated to his vocation. He began pacing the living room again, his face serious.

"There was another reason I decided to become a Mayanist. It is because of the people of this world."

"What do you mean?" Chauncy asked.

Dr. Sova stopped pacing and looked directly at Chauncy. "I'll put it quite simply: I do not suffer stupidity. The majority of the people in this world are imbeciles, Mr. Rollock. They are morons. It's that simple."

At first Chauncy thought he was jesting, but the frown on the doctor's face erased any doubt.

Dr. Sova continued. "Our modern society is run by foolhardy politicians and judges," Dr. Sova said. "Men spend more time in prison for killing a dog than for the murder of another human! What an outrage of injustice! Pure stupidity! The masses of humanity have been brainwashed by the media—everything is pre-packaged, pre-edited, and pre-digested for them. They no longer need to think or reason; instead it is all done for them. Like blind, stupid sheep they follow."

Dr. Sova sat down and took a deep breath, his agitation leaving him slowly. He cleared his throat and spoke, visibly and audibly more relaxed; his voice soft, almost gentle. "Ah, but out here in the jungle, I am a free man. I am not burdened by all the madness out there; instead I am liberated by the simple laws of nature. I do as I please and think as I please without the restraints and irritation of useless bureaucracy and management. I have these Mayan hieroglyphs to occupy, soothe, and challenge my mind. The brain, my friend, is a wonderful thing. Use it! Use it wisely and you too will be liberated."

Chauncy sat back slowly, his mind racing as he thought about everything Dr. Sova had said. The doctor's dissertation about society and his general dislike for people left Chauncy feeling a little shocked. It was obvious this man had a remarkable mind, one of the finest, but he also had a very low tolerance for human folly. Chauncy struggled to comment.

"Well ... I hope I won't disappoint you."

"That's why I have surrounded myself with professionals like you, Mr. Rollock. I have a tendency to insulate myself from idiots."

"I'd rather you call me Chauncy."

Dr. Sova chuckled as he rose from his seat. "Come now—we have much work to do."

The work on the temple progressed swiftly. The international team worked with few snags, each one accomplished in their specialty. Except for the paleontologists; they waited on the sidelines for their opportunity to analyze the Mayan king's skeleton, if and when it was found.

In the meantime, Dr. Sova spent much time with the translators as they attempted to decipher the writings on the temple stairs. It was evident to Chauncy that the relationship between Dr. Sova and the other translators was anything but amicable. They frequently engaged in heated discussions regarding the proper translation of the Mayan glyphs.

Chauncy noticed a distinct change in the doctor's disposition. He began to distance himself even more from his colleagues more and more as the days passed.

Chauncy tried to follow the discussions, but he quickly lost track. All he could get out of them was that Dr. Sova insisted his translations were more accurate than those of his colleagues. During one particularly heated debate, while they were in Sova's' tent, Chauncy was about to make a quick retreat when the fabric of the conference tent shuddered and a worker ripped apart the opening flaps and entered.

"Dr. Sova, we have located the flagstone covering at the top of the pyramid!"

Immediately the team of translators forgot their argument. They all knew what that announcement meant: they now had access to the bowels of the temple.

It took only moments to get to the temple. Their excitement was held in check as the workers slowly lifted the flagstone.

The flagstone cover was lifted up and placed aside; the workers raised their arms triumphantly as they yelled in a victory cry that reverberated throughout the camp. One of the archaeologists atop the pyramid, a Russian, shined his flashlight inside the dark opening as cheers erupted from the crowd. Their cheers were short-lived, however.

"Arrgh," Dr. Sova exclaimed. He was looking down the tunnel alongside the Russian worker, Chauncy beside him. The triangular tunnel was small, barely large enough to fit a human. But that wasn't the problem. The problem was the abrupt stop a few feet down.

"How do you like that?" Dr. Sova continued. "The ancient Mayas filled the tunnel with debris. How inherently rude of them! It will take quite some time to remove this material from the temple."

He then turned to Chauncy. "Due to the new state of affairs, the project has been woefully delayed. I'm afraid there isn't much for you to do here. I want you to come with me to Merida for a week or so."

"Merida? Why do you want me to go up there?"

Dr. Sova chuckled as he spoke softly so as to be out of earshot from Estlund. "I own a Hacienda there and my wife will fix us some good meals. Besides, there is something very important I need to explain to you. Don't worry about these men—they have much work to do here. As for Mr. Estlund, as far as I am concerned, he can sit here and examine his hands. Come Chauncy, let us go!"

CHAPTER THREE

Through the plane's window the lush green jungle far below contrasted beautifully with the clear blue sky. With a bit of imagination, the land far below could have been a gigantic stretch of green carpet interrupted only by occasional columns of smoke wafting skyward from the fires of local farmers. Up here with the air so clear and the land so far below one could almost feel free from the constraints of civilization.

All too quickly reality rushed back upon Chauncy as the plane started its descent. The sky gave way to rapidly approaching ground. Chauncy spotted the small dirt runway as the plane banked toward it and a familiar feeling crept into his stomach. He hated landing. Thankfully the landing was uneventful. Stepping from the plane Chauncy saw a building near the end of the runway partially hidden in the jungle. As they walked closer he could see it was a large colonial-style house.

Dr. Sova smiled as he guided Chauncy along, the pilot trailing behind with the luggage. "I bought this home a few years ago, when I first became interested in the Mayan language. I figured this would be a good spot from which to conduct my studies: close enough to several large temples yet secluded enough to allow me peace of mind. The original structure was built sometime in the late 1800s but it had fallen into disrepair. I have refurbished it and retrofitted the building with all the modern amenities, the best that money can buy."

"I would expect nothing less of you, Doc," Chauncy joked.

The ancient trees towering over the hacienda swayed majestically in the afternoon breeze. A cobblestone roundabout connected the patio to a dirt road that led to the airstrip, then disappeared deeper into the jungle. In its center a three-tiered waterfall gurgled and splashed. The breezes and the splashing of the waterfall created an effect of absolute tranquility. Chauncy's survey of the landscape was interrupted as two young Mayan men approached smiling graciously. Dr. Sova introduced them. "Ah, Chauncy, these are my gardeners, Lucio and Jose."

Lucio and Jose greeted Chauncy softly in Spanish with a humble demeanor. Continuing toward the house Chauncy and Dr. Sova ascended a short flight of stairs to a veranda, an empty hammock in one corner. A closer look at the house took Chauncy's breath away. In the muted sunlight beneath the jungle canopy that surrounded it, the place looked like it had been lifted straight out of a fairytale. The ancient stone construction, the wrought iron railings, the various pieces of pottery artistically strewn about—it was perfect.

As he was looking around, Chauncy spied an old Mayan Indian sitting under a large tree out in the garden.

"Who is that?" he asked.

Dr. Sova turned and focused on the old Indian. "Oh, that would be Miguelito. He feeds the animals, watches the house while the other two men are gone on the weekends. The poor old chap is simple, but he is cheap labor. By hiring him I have saved myself a few pesos a day. Don't waste your time attempting to converse with him. He can't speak a word of Spanish; only understands the Mayan tongue."

Surprised, Chauncy asked, "You mean you hired someone who is mentally handicapped?"

"Economics, Chauncy, I hate those who do not make full use of their brains, such as the morons of society. Those who cannot use their brains to full capacity, however, I do not hate. They do not understand because they simply cannot.

There is a difference."

Chauncy nodded. He didn't agree but he understood the man's position. As Chauncy watched, Miguelito rocked slowly in a dilapidated chair. His wrinkled face was contorted in a permanent smile, and it appeared that he was talking to himself. How sad. *What a pity. At least he has a job*, Chauncy thought consolingly.

Chauncy noticed that Dr. Sova had promptly he forgot about Miguelito as he called out for his wife. "Marie? Marie, *Oue vous* Marie?"

A frail-looking woman came out and greeted Dr. Sova. Nearly the same height, she looked younger than the doctor. The flecks of gray just beginning to show in her hair did nothing to diminish her beauty. Something in her demeanor troubled Chauncy; something in her eyes that seemed to belie her smile.

Marie moved over and kissed her husband, who introduced her to Chauncy. They all walked together into the spacious, expensively furnished living room. At Dr. Sova's invitation, Chauncy sank into one of the recliners and for a moment feared that he would be devoured by the cushions. He couldn't recall a single piece of furniture that had ever been so comfortable. A butler appeared and made drink requests in the French language.

As they sat and chatted, he admired the impressive house; the Spanish colonial furniture, the soft terra cotta and brown of the walls. Chauncy was comfortable here.

An hour later, they sat down for a sumptuous dinner of quail and wild turkey with vegetables. Servants kept serving generous amounts of expensive French wine. Chauncy found it hard to resist the excellent food and fine wine. When they finally finished and returned to the living room, Chauncy was certain that he would fall asleep in his chair.

By now Chauncy had learned that Dr. Sova hated to be trapped in small talk; mundane conversation bored the doctor.

Chauncy had seen him abruptly walk away in the middle of a conversation if a fellow archaeologist had changed the subject to trivial matters. If deep thinking was not involved the doctor would take his leave. So Chauncy was not surprised when Dr. Sova began pacing the room, immensely preoccupied, as he had in the tent.

His steps grew increasingly faster and more agitated until he finally blurted out, "Chauncy!"

"Yes, Doc?"

"I want to show you something in my study—it is extremely important."

Marie stood and announced that she would retire for the evening, and said goodbye to her guest. Chauncy thanked her for the fine dinner and followed the doctor down a long hallway, and Dr. Sova's wife disappeared down another.

Halfway down the hallway, Dr. Sova turned and opened a door. He stepped inside and flicked on the lights before inviting Chauncy in.

Chauncy's eyebrows were raised in surprise: he had expected something grand, but the magnitude of the doctor's study went even beyond his expectations.

Dr. Sova, ever the dramatist, walked around in the study with his arms extended and a bright smile upon his face. "Welcome to my humble study! It is here that I do my studies of the Mayan language. Before the gathering of the international crew to Temple #22, I spent much time in here, attempting to decipher the hidden messages of the steps."

A large window, almost an entire wall, let in the fading sunlight. In the middle of the room was a table so large and thick Chauncy thought it looked like a good candidate for Dr. Sova's runway. Set upon this table were pieces of ancient blocks, barely discernible Mayan hieroglyphs carved into them. A few knives and brushes lay beside the stone, thick dust and debris from the chipped blocks littered the table and floor. On one wall there was a large diagram with many sketches of hieroglyphs, most of which had handwritten notations and equations next to them.

Surrounding the doorway they had just passed through was a bookcase completely packed with books. Chauncy tilted his head and read some of the titles out loud. “The Toltecs, the Aztecs, the Olmecs, the Mayans.” Chauncy turned and observed that the last wall was taken up by a bank of computers. On the wall above the computers were many photographs of Mayan temples and pyramids. “What a fantastic reference library and laboratory you have here!” Chauncy exclaimed as he walked around the room, touching and examining everything. “This is very impressive indeed!”

There was a strange look in the doctor’s eyes as he spoke. Chauncy noticed he was trembling slightly. “I have spent much time here, examining the writings of this ancient civilization. As I have mentioned, I fell in love with this profession. But until Hurricane Sheila came a few months ago and exposed those steps, well, perhaps I spent a little too much time in here. My studies of the Mayan glyphs have become an obsession. The steps out there on Temple #22 … they contain some wonderful information, information that is so astonishing that I tremble with excitement just thinking about it!"

Continuing to examine the room Chauncy asked, “Are you talking about King Chac’s tomb? Well, maybe we will find his remains in the temple.” He leaned down and looked closer at a piece of stone that displayed an engraved jaguar’s head.

Indignant, Dr. Sova objected, “No, no, not maybe! King Chac’s remains are in the temple. I know because I am the only person that translated the Mayan writings correctly! Soon you will see that to be fact. But that is not what I am referring to.”

“Then what are you referring to?” Chauncy asked. He set down a stone he had been examining and turned to the doctor. “I would venture to say that finding the remains of King

Chac, an unknown Mayan deity, would be earth-shattering news, but you speak as if there's something more fabulous out there."

Dr. Sova's eyes glistened as he continued his explanation. "I want you to listen to me, listen very carefully. I have told no one else what I am about to tell you, not a single soul. It is the reason you are here." He walked toward Chauncy and waved a finger at the window. "On the steps of the Mayan temple, Temple #22, I found a secret code, a Mayan code. It was very subtle and I almost missed it, but once I knew what to look for there was no doubt in my mind. It was hidden within the syntax of the other message, the one revealing the details of King Chac and about his entombed body. It is simply art! It was so well hidden that if one read the normal message, the reader would not have a clue of anything amiss unless he dug further.

"What we do know about this king is that he amassed a gigantic treasure from his many conquests against his rival kings. After his final victories, he became fearful that someone would steal his treasure, so he went and hid it out in the jungle. That is what I found on the temple steps, Chauncy, the location of that immense treasure!"

"Come on, Doc! Stories of buried treasure are all over the place, rarely are they ever true, you know that. Besides, if it was that simple, why not just go and get it yourself?"

Dr. Sova chuckled. "I never once said it was simple, my dear Chauncy, did I? The location is disguised as a blasted riddle, of all things. Allow me to demonstrate it for you."

Dr. Sova walked to a small desk in the corner of the study, leaned over and pressed a button on the side of the desk. A panel dropped in its front revealing a secret drawer. He gingerly took a large scroll from within and walked over to the large table in the middle of the room. Moving aside some of the debris, he carefully unrolled the scroll, placing some of the hieroglyph-carved stones on its edges.

“These are the inscriptions from the temple steps, the entire description of King Chac’s dealings. See here the genius of King Chac’s code. A simple reading of this description yields no clue that anything is amiss, but look, look!”

Pointing excitedly to a hieroglyph, he continued, “This appears to be part of the regular description, right? But it is not! It is a number, but it is a head glyph number. Mayans used dots, dashes and shells to represent numbers, but they also used glyphs that looked like the glyphs for certain deities. This number here uses a head glyph that looks like the one for the Mayan sun-god!”

Chauncy had the impression he was expected to comprehend and be excited. Failing on both counts, he admitted sheepishly, "I don't get it."

Dr. Sova read the glyphs slowly. “Allow me to simplify it. I translated the major Mayan words on the temple steps. The names of three major gods of the Mayans were clearly visible as follows: *K’ inich Aha, Quetzalcoatl, Xibalba.*”

“Keep talking,” Chauncy prodded.

Dr. Sova continued. “*K’ inich Aha* is the sun-god, *Quetzalcoatl* is the Winged Serpent. However *Xibalba* can have various meanings. It can mean the god of the underground or a cave.”

“Which one is it?” Chauncy asked.

“I am not sure yet. Once I translate the words in between the names of the deities I should have the complete translation. But the biggest clue is the word 'treasure'. It is clearly found at the end of the riddle. In other words, the riddle is leading to his immense treasure!”

“Okay, but where do I come in, why are you telling me these things?” Chauncy inquired with a mesmerized expression.

“I need your assistance.” Looking Chauncy straight in the eye, Dr. Sova continued, “I want you to help me translate this

Mayan code. That is the sole reason I had you come here to my hacienda. I want you to assist me. If you can aid me in deciphering this riddle we will have cracked one of the greatest of the Mayan mysteries. Imagine that, we will be the heroes of the archaeological world!"

Chauncy swallowed hard. "But Doc, I know almost nothing of Mayan hieroglyphs. I'm a paleontologist. Don't get me wrong, I love the idea of helping you, but it would take years of dedication and study to be able to catch up with you. I would only slow you down. Why not use one of those professionals in Palenque? What's wrong with them?"

"Idiots! All of them!" Dr. Sova bellowed as he waved his hand in a disdainful manner. "They are trying to fit square pegs in round holes."

Embarrassed for his colleagues, Chauncy asked, "What do you mean?"

"Surely you have heard all the arguments that we have had? The main problem is that they have come from the university with preconceived ideas, Chauncy. They cannot see beyond what their books have taught them, they will not use their God-given brains. Believe me, I have argued with them to no end. They say I am not translating the writings properly. They claim the entire descriptions of King Chac are merely poetic and that few of the details should be taken seriously. Bah, imbeciles! No, I tell you, King Chac's remains are in that pyramid, and there is a fantastic treasure out there, and I will prove it. You see, the majority of archaeologists out there working in the jungles are not translating the Mayan hieroglyphs properly, only I am."

"What makes you think that you are the only one doing it right?" Chauncy asked pointedly.

Dr. Sova tapped his temple with the hand that held his cigar. "I told you already, I am a master linguist—that is why. I learned the Mayan dialect and lived with some Mayan people in their village for a while. Their priests and shamans have handed down a fantastic oral tradition that somewhat contradicts what the archaeologists are translating and teaching in the universities. By using my powers of deduction and comparing both schools of thought, I have come to understand the complex Mayan dialect and their meanings in a way that no university-taught linguist can understand."

"How did you manage to gain entry into their village and become their friend? That's next to impossible."

Dr. Sova replied, "Of course, I had to lie to the Mayan Indians; they thought I was an anthropologist. They believed I was there to help them and their cause. You realize how downtrodden the Mayan people are in our modern times? Well, I pretended to be a liaison between them and the outsiders. Once they found out I was a Mayanist they kicked me out of their village. They have little regard for Mayanists or any outsiders for that matter. But I had learned enough to look at these temple writings from a different perspective, a different angle. That is one reason I have become successful in my understanding of the writings. Soon, you will see what I mean."

Chauncy shook his head. "Well, well, look at this! Pardon my boldness, but you Mayanists remind me of Bible scholars of different religions who claim they know the proper translation of the scriptures while others do not."

Dr. Sova's eyes lit up as he lifted his index finger. "Precisely my point; that is an excellent analogy, Chauncy, but let me ask you a question. Of all the Bible scholars, there must be one man, yes only one who has the proper translation, one that truly understands what the Bible writer meant to write! Do you agree?"

Chauncy smiled. "There is a possibility, but ...."

"Of course there is!" Dr. Sova interrupted. "Surely you do not think the God of the Bible would let God-fearing men remain in a state of confusion regarding His own word, would you? But what He does is weed out the idiots and mental midgets who do not want to spend their energies to figure out what the scriptures really mean, therefore they fall back to believing false ideas and doctrines that are not taught in the Bible—and the same can be said of the Mayan riddle. I have spent my mental energies figuring out how to unlock the secrets on the temple steps, while the other scholars are playing it safe by not going beyond what they have been taught in schools. Soon you will see that I am telling you the truth. But, alas, this task is too great for one man; I cannot do it alone. I need your help, Chauncy. You are intelligent enough, my friend. You have an uncluttered mind when it comes to these matters, you can learn quickly, especially under my tutelage."

Chauncy was overwhelmed. What the doctor was asking of him just seemed too much; the reason for coming to Mexico was to inspect the bones of ancient Mayan kings, not to start a new vocation. It just seemed all too unrealistic to him. Chauncy wondered if Sova was making a rash decision or perhaps the doctor's intellect was being superseded by his excitement of finding a candidate suitable for training. Whatever the case, Chauncy was still unsure how to respond.

With his hand on Chauncy's shoulder, the doctor pleaded, "Please, I ask you—will you assist me? Not only will I double your wages, but imagine how this exciting find will change your life forever."

Chauncy took a deep breath to calm his nerves as he looked around the study. He was here, in the very lair of perhaps the most intelligent linguist alive. Every scroll, every rock, every book in this room spoke of the time and energy Dr. Sova put into his work. Perhaps the doctor really was onto something. Perhaps only he knew the secret behind the Mayan riddle, something that others were not aware of. What did he have to lose anyway? Even if the doctor was wrong, Chauncy would be properly compensated, in addition to having the bragging rights of saying that he had been mentored by the famous Dr. Sova.

Chauncy heaved a sigh. “Okay Doc, you win.”

Dr. Sova clapped his hands together. “Good, good. Tomorrow we start your language lessons.”

“But wait!” Chauncy protested. “How will I ever learn the Mayan language in so short a period of time?”

“There is a method I developed after much research that can help to expedite your abilities. It is the same system that I applied to myself, so I know it works, as I am now fluent in French, Spanish, Italian, Portuguese, English, and two different Mayan dialects. The brain is a powerful tool, Chauncy, but first I must teach you how to unlock its potential. Now let us get some rest, for tomorrow will come quickly.”

A sudden realization hit Chauncy. “Wait a minute! Just one minute! You … you knew that the shaft of Temple #22 would be filled with debris, didn’t you? And you knew it would take a few weeks to clear out all the rubble before Mack and I were even needed to look at the skeleton of the king! And now by having me here early, you were hoping I would be convinced to join you! And now Mack is going to be out there in Palenque examining his hands and scratching his nose while you teach me how to read Mayan hieroglyphs. Am I right?”

Dr. Sova chuckled, his eyes twinkling. “Ah, yes! Now do you see why I chose you? You are—how do you say it in America? Oh yes: you are *'one smart cookie'*.”

The following morning, bright and early, the first day of class began in earnest.

Dr. Sova was sitting in his study when Chauncy arrived; there was a new item on the wall that Chauncy had not noticed before. It was a large poster of the human brain was on the wall behind the doctor, various regions clearly marked. Dr. Sova instructed Chauncy to sit down in a chair that was opposite him, and then stared into his student's eyes.

Dr. Sova was in good spirits, but when he spoke his voice betrayed none of his own eagerness. Instead, he spoke slowly and methodically. "Before I begin teaching you the Mayan dialects, I shall reveal to you the secrets of how I learned so many languages. Years ago, while attending a university, in France, I would routinely visit a nearby morgue for experimentation. Despite my particular science, I was fascinated with the human brain, and I performed many an experiment on a corpse's brain, most of them extremely esoteric and unusual. I wanted to understand exactly how the brain was responsible for human speech and language comprehension. As you can observe from the poster behind me, scientists have already mapped where the brain handles speech, but that did not satisfy me. I wanted to answer the question of 'how?'"

The doctor paused, exhaled slowly as he crossed his legs and then continued his story. "If I could solve the mystery, then I would be able to concentrate my energies and stimulate just those particular brain cells in my own head, thereby wasting as little time and energy as possible. As you may know, the brain is composed of approximately ten billion neurons, and each neuron has over one thousand synapses that act like bridges between the cells. Studies other than my own have shown that when the neurons are regularly hyper-stimulated, a phenomenon occurs in which the synapses actually become stronger, allowing more information to travel in an easier manner. The challenge for me, then, was to spend all of my energies hyper-stimulating the brain cells related to language. If I could accomplish this, the learning of languages would be expedited."

Chauncy was puzzled. "But what use would dead brain cells have to your research? Unless the dead can talk, that is."

Dr. Sova chuckled. "That is a good question, and one I asked myself! I could slice and photograph and dissect a thousand dead brains and it would still get me nowhere. What I needed, then, was a live human to experiment on, one into which I could inject a radioactive solution and observe the dendrites, axons, neurons and synapses at work. One day I went to visit a good friend of mine who was studying to be a surgeon. I casually mentioned the problem I was having concerning the human brain. Despite the risks and the questionable legality, he allowed me to perform my experiment on him by injecting a small bit of solution into his neck and then taking pictures via my X-ray camera while he read various paragraphs I had prepared for him. The results were exactly what I hoped for."

Chauncy leaned forward. "And what were the results?"

Dr. Sova swiveled around in his chair and pressed a few keys on the nearest computer. After a few seconds he pointed to the monitor. "See for yourself."

Chauncy stood up to get a better view over Dr. Sova's shoulder. He could clearly see the dark outline of a man's head, along with some lights that were pulsing up his neck toward his brain.

"You see the lights moving up the neck? That is the radioactive solution I injected. In but a few seconds it will light up my friend's brain neurons like Paris at night. However, once he starts reading the material I prepared for him, the neurons that control speech light up even brighter. See?"

Chauncy noticed that a particular portion of the lights had indeed turned brighter and were rotating in a semi-circle near the left temple of the head. The lights were actually very colorful, shifting patterns as he watched. Blue, orange and crimson all eventually wound together.

"Now, however, observe what happens when I have him continue reading and attempt to juggle three balls. Notice this challenges his brain cells to the limit."

Indeed, it was hard not to notice, and Chauncy could not

help but feel awestruck as the same semi-circle moved even faster and got even brighter. "Amazing!" Chauncy gasped.

"Now watch what happens when I have him read a paragraph in English, which is not his native tongue and is a language he has difficulty with, while he continues to juggle."

Suddenly, another swirl of lights began to form next to the original swirl. Chauncy stared in fascinated delight. "So there is a different 'compartment,' so to speak, for each language the brain tries to comprehend?"

"Yes. The main purpose of the exercise, however, was to determine what exactly would lead to hyper-stimulation of the cells." Dr. Sova pressed a button and the computer screen went blank. "And that is exactly what I discovered. I have formulated at least seventeen different teaching techniques that hyper-stimulate the brain cells, specifically those related to language. Fascinating, is it not? You see why I do not waste my mental powers on trivial stupidity? Let us get started and you will understand."

CHAPTER FOUR

Chauncy stared at the hieroglyphs for the fifth time that morning, trying desperately to juggle a few paperweights at the same time. "So you've assigned the jaguar head to the letter A, and the serpent to B, but this tree thing here is not a letter but a sound? Is that what you mean?"

Dr. Sova nodded. "These are, of course, not the literal transliterations but for our purposes they will do. Even a cursory study of the code, however, would reveal the simple substitution of symbols for letters, which is why I have taken our Mayan code a step further."

Chauncy dropped a paperweight. He picked it up and continued juggling. Chauncy sighed and stared at the glyph again. It made a certain sense, of course, but that didn't mean it was coming very easily. "Let's return to the real hieroglyphs, shall we?"

Dr. Sova chuckled. "As you wish, I've taught you the first group of twenty. Read it for me. Come on!"

Suppressing a grimace, Chauncy turned to the wall, where a duplicate of the scroll had been posted. Squinting at the hieroglyphs, he began to read. "Here lies the great King Chac, supreme and trusted ruler of fifty-three lands and the richest monarch of all."

"Your memory is certainly good enough, Chauncy, but that is not what we are testing here, now is it?"

Chauncy couldn't quite suppress his grimace this time. He was hoping Dr. Sova wouldn't notice that he hadn't read the glyphs but had simply recited the sentence from memory.

"No, I guess not," he managed to reply.

Dr. Sova chuckled, then extended his pointer and rested its edge against one of the glyphs. "What does this symbol mean? Tell me!"

Chauncy immediately recognized it, despite his lack of familiarity with the Mayan language. "That is the head glyph of the sun-god, here combined with dashes and dots to represent the number fifty-three."

"Excellent! That was too easy. Now what glyph is this?" The doctor pointed at one glyph past the familiar territory of the first block of twenty, and Chauncy could almost feel the neurons in his brain try to catch up. It looked familiar, as he glanced between that glyph and the first twenty. He desperately tried to remember what the glyph meant.

And promptly let out a curse when one of the paperweights he was juggling slipped from his grasp and landed squarely on his toes.

Dr. Sova glanced at him quizzically. "Sorry, but there is no Mayan translation for that," the linguist said with a hint of humor.

Chauncy dropped the other paperweights and grabbed his foot.

"Take a seat and rest a bit. You're doing quite well." Dr. Sova said.

Chauncy sat down, still trying to rub his injured foot. He looked up at the doctor. "The word is 'Supreme'?"

A smile broke out on the doctor's face. It was obvious that he was both pleased and impressed. "Indeed, that is what the glyph means! You are catching on very quickly."

Chauncy stared at the poster. "How much of my speed is linked to my natural intelligence compared to this brain cell hyper-stimulation of yours?"

Dr. Sova sat down across from Chauncy. "I would have to say that it is probably an equal ratio. You are naturally a very quick learner; I am only helping you to focus that natural ability on one particular area, so it all works out in the end."

Chauncy glanced out the window. The shadows were at the opposite angle from when he had last looked. That meant it was past noon; they had been here through the entire morning. He stood up, his brain too worked up to rest at the moment, the pain in his foot forgotten. *This is going to be harder than I had imagined. What was I thinking*? Chauncy thought.

As the days passed and Chauncy learned Dr. Sova's Mayan Code, he transferred that knowledge to help decipher the actual Mayan hieroglyphs. He could now pick out words and even compose simple sentences. He and Dr. Sova pored over the Mayan riddle every day, seeking to find patterns that would give more clues to its secret.

Thus far, the only thing they could find was the three references to the deities. They continued to mix training with the reading of the actual riddle. By the end of the third week, Chauncy could read King Chac's message in its entirety and write most of it as well.

In the fourth week, they found it.

"I knew that devilish king had something up his sleeve!" Dr. Sova shouted as he excitedly copied the glyphs onto a separate piece of paper. The two of them hunched over the scroll and double-checked their findings, their wild guesses, and their measurements.

There was no doubt. They had finally cracked the code hiding King Chac's message. The only problem was that they now had a riddle *within* a riddle to figure out! The text read as follows: *"Sun god follows the winged serpent, winged serpent points to the gods of the underworld where treasure is to be found."*

Dr. Sova sat down and heaved a sigh. "He is taunting us."

"How so?"

"It is all about *Xibalba*."

"Explain that again to me."

Dr. Sova looked at Chauncy. "*Xibalba* is the cosmos of the Mayan underworld, the place of fright, the place of legends! According to Maya mythology, a great battle of twin brothers occurred. They were skilled at playing a traditional ballgame. Their raucous noise disturbed the gods of the underworld, who then challenged them to a contest. The gods, of course, defeated the twins easily and subsequently had them sacrificed, their bodies buried under the ball court and their heads hung on a tree. Eventually, a goddess named *Xquic* went to see the tree for herself and became impregnated by one of the heads that spat in her hands. She gave birth to the twins *Hunahpu* and *Xbalanque*, and they became known as the Hero Twins.

"As time passed they became ball players like their father. Soon, though, they returned to *Xibalba* for revenge. After performing many tricks in front of the underworld gods, the twins contrived an ingenious trick: *Xbalanque* beheaded his brother *Hunahpu* and then made him whole again. The gods were so fascinated by this display that they begged to be sacrificed and revived in the same fashion as *Hunahpu*. The twins were more than happy to oblige, so they proceeded to dismember the gods but refused to restore them to their original condition, thereby defeating them once and for all. Good triumphed over evil and the earth was now prepared for the dawn of human beings. The Hero Twins emerged from the underworld as the sun and the moon and each day they reenact their journey to *Xibalba*."

Chauncy tilted his head to the side. "That is a very fascinating story, Doc! You'll forgive me, however, if I don't see what it has to do with our riddle."

Dr. Sova laughed. "The mention of *Xibalba* is the clue and I think I can venture to say that I may have figured out how the word was meant to be understood."

"Okay, tell me."

"*Xibalba* is not only the god of the underworld, but the

underworld itself. The Maya believed that caves were the entrance to the underworld, and the same word, *Xibalba*, was used to refer to both of them. So our sly King Chac used a double meaning once again, this time to point to the destination. King Chac's vast fortune is hidden inside of a cave!"

"So, have we found it?" Chauncy mused with a slight hint of sarcasm.

Dr. Sova laughed again. "I wish it was that easy. Do you know how many caves are in Palenque? Tens of thousands, even hundreds of thousands! An army of men could spend their entire lives digging and searching and would not be able to uncover them all, let alone find the right one."

All Chauncy could manage was a deflated, "Oh." They had been so close.

"But fear not, my good friend. The key to the cave is right here, in this riddle! Somehow we must figure out how the sun-god and the winged serpent point to the right cave, and we will have discovered King Chac's treasure! We must study the entire message again and see if we can find any more clues."

Days passed, and Chauncy was indeed becoming fluent in the Mayan language. When Dr. Sova would occasionally leave the hacienda on business, the two of them would communicate via hand written letters in their own Mayan Code they had invented. The code consisted of picture-graphic Mayan symbols. Chauncy found it sharpened his abilities to distinguish the difficult shapes of the Mayan hieroglyphs.

He was consistently amazed by Dr. Sova's extraordinary mental abilities. It seemed that the doctor's mind never rested, and regardless of the time of day, Dr. Sova was always alert, always "on," analyzing everything, never missing even the smallest of details. He had an excellent grasp of science, history, and of course, languages. Every morning he would keep himself abreast of the current events of the world via the Internet, and afterwards he would immerse himself in the study of the Mayan hieroglyphs that had been discovered on the steps of Temple #22.

However, as with all men, Dr. Sova had faults, which eventually came to light. Chauncy noticed several idiosyncrasies and habits that were beginning to irritate him. First of all, there was the constant cigar smoke that hung around the house. Chauncy, a non-smoker, was finding it hard to breathe inside the hacienda. Then there were the daily disparaging remarks about his fellow man. According to Dr. Sova, the majority of mankind were fools and buffoons, especially the uneducated and poor.

Chauncy found this highly offensive, since he felt everyone had their place in human society. As long as they did no harm to one another, he had no problem dealing with all types of people in an amicable manner.

But of all the doctor's failings, one would be his undoing: gambling. Chauncy found it difficult to understand how such a brilliant man could even consider it. Many times, in between teaching sessions, the man would disappear from the hacienda for many days.

And when confronted by Chauncy the arguments always ran on the same theme. Chauncy would berate him. "Really, Doc! How could you fall for such folly, you of all people?"

And Dr. Sova would answer in the usual manner, throwing his hands up in a disdainful manner. "Bah! You do not understand, Chauncy. The mind needs diversion."

"But the odds are stacked against you! Every casino is rigged in their favor!"

"I understand your argument my friend. But I do win at times. Let's just say I'm addicted to dopamine."

Chauncy never won the arguments. Dr. Sova's distraught wife would mope around the house, for she was well aware of what was occurring. It was the same gloomy expression that Chauncy had noticed when he first met her. However, now he understood the reason.

One day, when Dr. Sova was off on one of his gambling forays, Chauncy was coming back to the hacienda from one of his regular meditative strolls in the jungle. He had developed the habit of taking leisurely walks to refresh his mind and practice the Mayan language. Something about the area was conducive to thought. Perhaps it was the presence of nature everywhere around, with no cars or smog to befuddle the mind.

As he approached the hacienda he spotted Miguelito sitting under the shade of a large Ficus tree. Chauncy felt the impulse to practice some of his newly learned Mayan words with the old Indian. He felt confident that he was now becoming proficient in the native tongue, enough to possibly converse with Miguelito.

However, when Chauncy got nearer to the old man, he came to an abrupt halt when he understood what Miguelito was chanting.

"K' inich Aha, Quetzalcoatl, K' inich Aha, Xibalba."

Chauncy felt a shiver run up and down his spine. "It's the Mayan code from Temple #22!" he whispered as he heard the words flowing again from Miguelito's mouth. "How in blazes does he know the words?"

"K' inich Aha, Quetzalcoatl, K' inich Aha, Xibalba."

"Where did you learn those words, Miguelito?" It was an effort for Chauncy to get the Mayan words out, but he managed it.

There was no response from Miguelito, so Chauncy switched to Spanish and asked him the same question: "*Donde aprendistes esas palabras*?"

"He has been eavesdropping on both of you!" a voice said from behind him.

Startled, Chauncy spun on his heel to see Marie Sova leaning on the railing of the covered porch, the same cheerless expression on her face.

"Ah! Mrs. Sova, you startled me."

"Miguelito has a bad habit of eavesdropping," she answered.

Chauncy thought it was rather ironic—he was going to comment how she *also* had been doing the same, but he decided to keep silent.

Mrs. Sova continued. "He stands by the study window while you and my husband discuss the Mayan language. We are not sure how much he understands, but I believe he simply likes to hear others speaking his native language."

Embarrassed for not realizing it Miguelito's presence himself, Chauncy turned to him and spoke to him in Spanish. "Shame on you, you should respect other people's privacy."

The old Mayan Indian simply continued chanting the Mayan code as spittle dripped down his chin. Chauncy immediately regretted speaking harshly to an old man who probably didn't understand the concept of privacy. Leaving him, Chauncy walked over to the hacienda.

"What is troubling you, Mrs. Sova?" Chauncy asked. He wanted to hear her side of the story, as well as distance himself from the encounter with Miguelito.

Marie turned to look at Chauncy, and for a moment he was taken back by the sheer sadness in her eyes. She spoke quietly, Chauncy straining to understand past her thick French accent.

"Oh, Mr. Rollock, my husband is in debt again. It's that demon gambling habit of his. It will be the ruin of him, and us!"

"Why is he so obsessed?"

"It is because he thinks he is Superman, that is why. He claims he can overcome anything. Oh, Mr. Rollock, please talk some sense into that man. I fear that his gambling is out of control."

Chauncy assured Marie that he would do what he could. But when Dr. Sova returned, it was business as usual. Once they became immersed in their studies, the subject was never brought up. And it wasn't due to any negligence on his behalf. There were many reasons for his reluctance in dealing with this problem. The chief one being that Chauncy was keenly aware of the futility of trying to argue with Sova. There was also the sticky situation of being involved between the two and having to take sides. Yet it bothered his conscience to remain silent, so he had made his mind up to reason with him one more time.

When Dr. Sova returned from another gambling foray, he found Chauncy in his study reading a book about the indigenous people.

There was a large smile on Dr. Sova's face. "Chauncy!" he nearly bellowed, "I have excellent news! The crew in Palenque has found the sarcophagus. It is now time to show the world that King Chac does exist. Did I not tell you that his remains would be within the temple?" Dr. Sova pointed to his head in his usual manner, with the same hand that held his cigar. "Yes! Now all will know the brain that they are dealing with. Pack up, we are leaving now."

Chauncy was thrilled. With all of their work trying to decipher the Mayan writings, he had almost forgotten the reason he had come to Palenque in the first place: to examine the skeleton of King Chac, if and when it was ever discovered. Well, now it was his time to fulfill that job.

He was packed and ready in minutes.

Their SUV broke through the jungle canopy and once again Chauncy was awed by the majestic site of the ancient temple, recently unveiled to this world. He felt like a college graduate all over again, full of expectations, ready for whatever came his way.

As Chauncy stepped out of the vehicle, he could feel his own excitement mirrored in everyone else. Many people came up to Dr. Sova and congratulated him. Chauncy watched the doctor closely. Despite Dr. Sova's disdain for these people, he showed none of it when they came up to congratulate him. Chauncy had expected the linguist to gloat, but he simply smiled and nodded. There was no doubt in Chauncy's mind that was seeing the many personality profiles of his friend. Today, Dr. Sova was acting as the gracious linguist.

The preparations to enter the pyramid were over shortly, and Dr. Sova motioned Mr. Estlund and Chauncy to follow him.

"Bring your cameras and flashlights, gentlemen, we are about to make history!"

The three climbed the steps of the temple, with various cameras in hand. Once at the top Chauncy took a quick look around them. From the apex, he could see jungle stretching out for miles beyond the nearby temples. It was truly a magnificent sight. But what was inside the temple would be the crowning glory of their time here.

They began their descent into the pyramid. It wasn't what Chauncy had expected. The tunnel was triangular in shape, it was very cramped, and it was very humid. After seven steps, the light from outside nearly vanished, and they were forced to rely on the heavy-duty flashlights they had brought along. The humidity seemed to make the air heavy and, somehow, ancient. The deeper they went into the tunnel and the stuffier the air became, the older it seemed. The beams of their flashlights flickered randomly off reflective chunks in the wall, adding a surreal sensation to their descent.

Dr. Sova was the first to break the silence as they slowly stepped down the tunnel stairs. "My crew is down there as I speak, attempting to lift the sarcophagus cover. Just a word of warning: it may be a little cramped."

When they finally reached the bottom of the stairs, two shirtless laborers were trying to lift the cover of the sarcophagus by means of a pulley system. Heavy perspiration ran down their bodies. They pulled and tugged on the ropes as the heavy flagstone slowly lifted. With the addition of three more bodies, the atmosphere became hot and stifling.

None of them cared. Anticipation was running high, for they all knew that they would be the first to set eyes on King Chac's remains. All eyes and flashlights were centered on the sarcophagus as its cover continued to rise.

"Look at that!" Mack exclaimed as the lights shined on a ghostly outline of a human skeleton.

"Wonderful!" Dr. Sova said with wide eyes. "Can you believe this, gentlemen? We are the first to see his remains after many thousands of years in obscurity!"

Chauncy swallowed hard and tried to remain calm despite the fact that his heart was racing with excitement. "Observe the jewelry and the other artifacts. His skeleton is so ... so intact."

The dust from the lid had filled the tiny chamber and it was rapidly becoming difficult to see anything in detail. Dr. Sova cursed and reminded the others that they would have to wait until the dust settled before they could begin their examinations.

Chauncy looked carefully at Dr. Sova, wondering why the linguist was telling the paleontologists how to do their job. It suddenly occurred to Chauncy that Dr. Sova was more annoyed than he sounded, in addition to being more excited. The doctor was simply used to telling people what to do, and in this brief lapse of action, he had reverted to his natural state.

Chauncy shook his head, suddenly realizing that he had fallen into the same trap that Dr. Sova had. He was so excited and awed that his mind was running along strange channels.

He had simply not voiced his thoughts like the doctor had, but he was basically doing the same thing. The atmosphere was charged with wonderment and thrill.

Despite the heat, despite the dust, despite the humidity and the oppressive atmosphere, he was here, the tomb of a king! And not just any king, an unknown king, one who was rich and powerful, perhaps more so than any other Mayan monarch! He was one of the five to be the first to see this king after thousands of years, the first to see the regal skeleton in its resting place. It was simply impossible not to be excited.

Suddenly they heard a voice from the top of the stairs.

Dr. Sova yelled back. "What are you saying man? Speak up!"

The voice yelled again, this time a little louder, and all of them strained to hear. Chauncy turned to the doctor. "I think he's telling us to come up the stairs," he said, perplexed.

"What the devil for?" Dr. Sova's voice echoed in the tiny room. "Can't he tell that we are busy?"

Again the voice yelled, this time frantic. Mack was the first to understand what was being said. "I may be wrong, but it sounds like he's saying *'come back up quickly, we have a serious problem.'*"

"What the blazes is happening up there?" Dr. Sova angrily asked no one in particular.

Mack put his finger to his lips. "Sssh. Quiet everyone!" he strained his ears as he attempted to understand what the man was yelling.

Despite the dust and the darkness, Chauncy could tell that Mack had gone pale. "He said, *'Hurry or we are all going to die.'*"

CHAPTER FIVE

"What?" Dr. Sova asked in disbelief. Disgusted, he threw down the handkerchief he'd used to wipe sweat from his face. "This had better not be a joke. Come on gentlemen, to the surface!" He motioned for them to follow him up the stairs.

From the platform on top of the pyramid they could clearly see the entire camp surrounded by a motley group of machine gun-toting men. Most of their weapons were pointed at the workers, and more than one gun was pointed at the top of the pyramid.

The army fatigues worn by the men were old and tattered, torn and creased by years of exposure to the elements. The trucks and jeeps they had arrived in looked no better: covered in mud, dented, banged, and patched together with duct tape.

The international crew of archaeologists, scientists and laborers had been assembled in a courtyard near the camp. They were all seated with their hands either behind their backs or on top of their heads. A perimeter of men with machine guns prevented escape.

One of the laborers with Dr. Sova and Chauncy spoke in a trembling voice. "*Son los rebeldes*!"

Dr. Sova nodded as his eyes swept the situation. With another nod he turned to Mack. "Rebels huh? Let me do the talking; say as little as possible to these men. In fact, if you and Chauncy can keep your mouths shut the entire time, it would make things infinitely better." With a deep sigh the doctor pulled out a cigar from his case, lit it, and puffed a few times as he motioned the others to slowly walk down the temple.

Chauncy's legs were on autopilot as he descended. Trying desperately to think of a plan, anything that might get them out of this, he risked a glance at Dr. Sova and realized that the doctor was doing the same.

Because of the slow pace down the stairs, Chauncy knew the doctor's mind was rapidly analyzing and rejecting various scenarios of how to deal with the rebels. Despite the danger, Chauncy couldn't help thinking how comical Dr. Sova looked as he puffed madly on his cigar. It seemed as if the gears of the good doctor's mind were turning so fast that smoke was pouring out of his ears.

As the five men reached the final steps of the pyramid, the leader of the rebels approached. He was the only one with a new military uniform. His gun was also noticeably newer than that of his compatriots. He was a handsome young man, with well-toned muscles that did not make him any less thin. He was perhaps in his early twenties. He smiled before speaking in perfect English.

"Good afternoon, Dr. Sova. It is a great pleasure to meet face to face. Allow me to introduce myself, I am—"

"*Comandante* Solis," Dr. Sova interrupted with a scowl. "The rebel-rousing troublemaker of Yucatan."

"Oh, I see my reputation precedes me," *Comandante* Solis replied with pride.

"Yes, I've made it a personal hobby to study the lower forms of life in the jungle, hence my familiarity with you," Dr. Sova responded, and then he blew a stream of smoke in Solis' face.

Comandante Solis seemed as surprised by the insult as Chauncy himself. Chauncy stared at Dr. Sova, wondering if he was trying to force the rebel off balance.

Solis stepped back and pointed his gun at Dr. Sova's head. "And I make it my hobby to scour the jungle for intelligent life, and it is very obvious at the moment that I have not yet reached my goal. You are a fool, Dr. Sova! As smart as you claim to be, you couldn't figure out that some of the security guards you hired were actually working for me. They were charged with the job of informing me when the king's tomb was finally uncovered. That means that you, the great Dr. Sova, have unwittingly toiled for me! Soon I will sell the king's remains on the black market, and we shall make our millions—"

"And fund your revolutionary movement, I suppose?" Dr. Sova interrupted.

The *Comandante* smiled. "Of course, we live and die for *'La Causa.'* We fight to end all oppression of the Mayan people in Mexico. I will make sure of that. Today we have been successful, and it has become painfully obvious that I have outsmarted the self-proclaimed savant of the archaeological community in the process. What an idiot!" His laugh was echoed by his men as he translated the conversation into Spanish.

It appeared *Comandante* Solis was trying to humiliate the doctor. From the anger simmering in the doctor's eyes and the cigar tightly clenched in his teeth, Chauncy gathered that it was working.

Comandante Solis peered up at the sky. "It will be getting dark soon. Tomorrow at daybreak we will remove everything and be off before breakfast." He barked orders at his men who began directing everyone to their tents. Solis turned his attention back to the two in front of him.

"You will remain in your tents until tomorrow!" he ordered.

Chauncy walked with Dr. Sova to the doctor's tent. "I have some reading material that I want to pick up at your tent before I go to mine. By the way, who is this guy? He sure speaks good English."

Dr. Sova was walking with his head down. After a moment he replied in a whisper. "He is a fraud, a wannabe rebel. His real name is Raul Martinez. He grew up as a rich boy in a privileged family in Mexico City. His father wanted him to be an archaeologist so sent him off to a university in Texas, which is where he learned English. He was too stupid to get good grades, however, and eventually dropped out to become this, this jungle thug. He is hiding behind his '*La Causa*' philosophy as an excuse to rob and plunder archaeological digs for his own selfish gain."

They reached Dr. Sova's tent and Chauncy went into the small study portion to retrieve two books. When he came out into the living room, he stopped suddenly, surprised to see Dr. Sova sitting with a dejected look on his face.

Dr. Sova sighed heavily. "It is over with, Chauncy." His tone matched the expression on his face. "It is finished. Tomorrow you can pack up and go home."

"Wha ... what do you mean?" Chauncy's heart sank.

Dr. Sova raised his head to look Chauncy in the eye, his tone angry. "Your training is over! There will be no more Mayan Code. Those thugs know exactly why we are here. They are going to destroy the writing on the temple steps by wrecking all of the hieroglyphs and then they will remove the remains of King Chac. The riddle of the Mayan treasure will be gone forever. Your services are no longer needed. Hence, you may leave tomorrow."

"But, but Doc! Can't you figure something out? I mean, you—you must have a plan."

"Really?" Dr. Sova said. "Are you bullet-proof? I am not. What do you expect me to do? There comes a time when there is only so much one can do, you must know your limits. We should be grateful that he has not killed us." He waved his hand and looked back at the floor. "Just go. Leave me alone. It is all over. Let's face the facts, Chauncy—I know when I have lost. This rebel has got me."

Disappointment flooded Chauncy's thoughts. It was the first time he had ever seen the doctor without a plan. "Aren't you even going to try something?? Remember—the brain?"

"Get out of my tent, Chauncy." Dr. Sova turned away and buried his face in his hands.

Chauncy walked numbly to his own tent, barely noticing how dark it had become. Night fell and the hours passed slowly. Wide awake, Chauncy watched the glow of the campfires casting eerie shadows of the rebels on his tent wall. He could hear the quiet muttering of the men outside.

He lay there thinking how fast everything had come to an end. Here he thought he had a promising career with Dr. Sova and in a matter of minutes it was all over. The whole incident had crushed Dr. Sova's ego. He had seen it clearly on the doctor's face.

Chauncy's wristwatch showed it was past midnight. He was never up this late. Though he was exhausted, he still couldn't sleep.

Suddenly, he heard a strange noise that made him sit bolt upright on his cot. At first he thought it was one of the rebels, but they also became silent as the noise grew louder. It sounded as if an infant was crying, off in the distance.

The sound stopped almost as soon as it had started and silence descended again upon the jungle. Shrugging mentally, Chauncy lay back down. But the sound started again, louder this time. Soon it was a plaintive, wailing moan.

Chauncy leapt to his feet and unzipped the tent door with shaking hands. Expecting a rebel to shove a gun at his head, he peered through the door. The rebels guarding his tent didn't even look at him as he poked his head out. They seemed, instead, to be frozen in place as the sound grew to a painful howl.

The rebels started chattering excitedly. Chauncy could now tell that the sound was coming from some distance, off in the dark hills. He shivered at another loud burst of wailing. Something very creepy was going on. The rebels reached the same conclusion and began to shout in confusion.

One voice rose above the others. "*Es el espiritu del Rey*

Chac!"

It took Chauncy's befuddled mind a moment to piece together the Spanish words. *They think it's the ghost of King Chac!*

He tried to stifle a rising dread. He was not a superstitious man. He did not believe in ghosts.

But that sound.

Comandante Solis came running with machine gun in hand. "What's happening here!" he demanded.

"It's that strange sound coming from the hills. They think it's the ghost of King Chac," Chauncy answered.

The wailing began again in earnest.

Solis pointed his gun toward the hills and squeezed the trigger, letting loose a barrage of bullets. The rat-tat-tat of the gun echoed in the dark and eclipsed the wailing sound as he continued to shoot toward the hills at the unseen specter.

Dr. Sova rushed out of his tent flailing his arms, an angry scowl on his face. "What is the meaning of this shooting! You are going to kill us all if the bullets ricochet off of the temples!"

With a defiant sneer, *Comandante* Solis turned and looked at the doctor. "The men are descendants of the Mayans, they are very superstitious."

The wailing continued. The rebels chattered loudly, frightened looks on their faces. Puffing his cigar, Dr. Sova stepped a few paces toward the perimeter of the camp, straining to see past the glow thrown by the lights. Past that glow, however, there was only deep darkness out in the jungle.

"It is probably the death screams of some pitiful dying animal in the jungle. Tell your men to stop being so stupid." He then abruptly turned and walked back to his tent, grumbling to himself.

Chauncy secretly mocked the superstitious feelings of the native people, but later lying in the semi-darkness of his tent,

Chauncy replayed over and over again the eerie wailing from the hills. His mind kept drifting to the skeleton of King Chac in the sarcophagus, imagining a malevolent smile on its ancient features.

No one in the camp slept that night, despite the fact that no more wailing was heard. When the sun finally rose, Chauncy joined Dr. Sova as he went to the breakfast table in the outdoor kitchen.

Comandante Solis walked up to them, his machine gun in hand and a large grin on his face. "Well, it looks like the king's ghost gave up on us! Today we will take him away for good. As for you, my dear doctor, perhaps you will end up as a good tour guide in some museum. Ha-ha-ha-ha!"

Dr. Sova clenched his fist, but before he could answer a rebel came running up to the group.

"*Comandante*!" he yelled when he came to a stop, his face twisted with worry.

"What do you want?" Solis asked.

The rebel's face turned from being twisted with worry to being contorted with pain. He attempted to step forward, but his gun slipped from his fingers and he gripped his stomach. Within seconds he fell to his knees and began vomiting violently on the ground.

Comandante Solis backed away quickly in disgust. "What the—? Get this man away from me, now!"

Another rebel came to pull the sick man away, but he also grabbed his stomach in pain and began vomiting as he fell to his knees.

"You, too?" Solis yelled. He turned and ordered another of his men to move them, but that rebel also became violently ill.

The rebel looked up at his commander as he fell to his knees. "El espiritu del Rey Chac nos esta castigando Señor, por haber violado su tumba!"

Dr. Sova looked at Chauncy with wide, surprised eyes.

"Ha! He thinks the spirit of the king is punishing them for violating his tomb. That is impossible! Let us not panic, Chauncy, there is a scientific explanation for these phenomena."

Chauncy held his nose because of the stench of the vomit

Comandante Solis looked around with a terrified expression. He saw that, one by one, his men were succumbing to the mysterious ailment. His men were yelling and begging him to leave the site without King Chac's remains, lest the king's ghost kill them all.

"What is the meaning of this?" Solis shouted to no one in particular. A moment later a deep anger came to his eyes and he spun around and approached Dr. Sova.

Before he could speak, a look flickered across his face. Chauncy stared in horror as Solis began to cough. The commander tried to conceal his discomfort, but within seconds he, too, was on the ground vomiting.

Dr. Sova overpowered *Comandante* Solis and picked up his gun from the ground. "Chauncy, quickly, get a rope and tie up this swine!"

As they tied the commander's arms, Dr. Sova ordered the other archaeologists and laborers to bind up the rest of the rebels. Within moments, all of the rebels were sitting inside the courtyard with their hands tied behind their backs. All of the men were looking at Dr. Sova. The doctor was going to dramatically make an example of Solis.

Dr. Sova lifted Solis by his shirt collar, forcing the commander to stand up in front of his men. Vomit dripped from his chin to his stained shirt. His face was contorted with pain.

Dr. Sova plucked a small vial from his shirt pocket and tapped it on Solis' forehead. "You fool! Do you know what this is, Commander?"

Comandante Solis closed his eyes as the object was tapped against his forehead. Opening them again when the doctor had stopped, he glanced at the vial but didn't answer.

"It is syrup of Ipecac in a concentrated form. Do you know what it does?"

Solis glared and shook his head.

Dr. Sova laughed. "Are you having trouble figuring it out? Ha, ha! Well, I will indulge you. In mild doses, this syrup makes you nauseated. In strong doses, it gives you horrendous stomach cramps and produces extreme vomiting seizures. Understand now?"

Now the commander's expression would have melted ice. "So you are responsible for this?"

"Bang!" Dr. Sova said, clearly enjoying himself. "Did you hear that, ladies and gentlemen? *Comandante* Solis just had a flashing revelation! If you have not pieced the puzzle together yet, allow me to do it for you. I took advantage of your men and their natural disposition to superstition. All this time they thought it was the evil spirit of King Chac. This morning, via a bit of sleight of hand, I poisoned your water supply."

"But what about the wailing in the hills, surely you could not have done that!"

Dr. Sova laughed again as he pulled a small black object from his pocket. "This is called a remote control, in case you did not know that. And this ..." Dr. Sova held the remote in the air for all to see and then pressed a button on it.

Immediately a wailing sound cut through the air, reverberating from the hills.

"How did you do that?" *Comandante* Solis demanded in an incredulous tone.

Dr. Sova turned off the wailing sound and returned the remote to his pocket. "Many years ago I read an article about music therapy. It went on to explain how dairy farmers in the Midwestern United States would play music for their cows, such as Mozart, Beethoven, Bach and other classics. They noticed that the cows were actually producing more milk. So I thought to myself, why not do the same for my workers so they can be more productive?

"So when I first came to Palenque, I had special weatherproof wireless speakers installed in the hills that were linked to a CD player in my tent. I had planned to try playing classical music for them, but as time went on I became distracted with other matters and dropped the experiment. Last night, however, I covered my head in my bed sheets so as not to be overheard and I recorded these horrible wailing sounds. Even as I walked around the camp I was able to control the sounds with my remote—and *Voila*!"

A light went on in Chauncy's head. "So, you didn't mean what you said to me last night, Doc?"

Dr. Sova turned and put his hand on Chauncy's shoulder, a soft smile on his face. "Of course not, sorry *mon ami*, but I did not want anyone to know in advance what I was planning. There is another language that does not involve the mouth, it is body language. I had to have you believe the ruse as well, otherwise the rebels may have read in your posture that it was a ploy. I certainly could not risk failure, could I? You see, I had already formulated a plan before descending the temple steps to meet the commander. I heard that he was prowling this area and I had already anticipated his visit."

"Are you going to execute me?" Solis interrupted.

Dr. Sova turned to face the man. "No, of course not, that would only make you a martyr."

"Are you going to turn me over to the authorities to be arrested?"

"No, that would make you a hero."

"Then what are you going to do with me?"

"I'm going to expose you for what you are," Dr. Sova replied with a hint of a smile.

Jumping onto a dining table, he explained in a loud voice that *Comandante* Solis's real name was Raul Martinez, an imposter whose sole desire was to enrich himself by plundering archaeological sites. After a pause to allow that to sink in, Dr. Sova also explained that Martinez was not the least bit interested in fighting for the Mayan people because once he was finished with his plans he would abandon them and take the money.

Offering the rebels payment to help clean up the temple site, he explained that when it was completed they would be allowed to go free. In addition, he offered to have the Mayan priests bless the temple to rid the place of evil spirits and appease the gods in an effort to gain forgiveness for ransacking the tomb.

A large cheer arose from the camp when Dr. Sova ordered the rebels released.

With an angry expression, Dr. Sova turned back to glare at Martinez. "This is what you get for attempting to outsmart me! I hope you have learned a vital lesson, miscreant: nobody will ever outsmart me. Nobody! I will release you once we are done with this project. Do me a favor, will you? Take my advice, return to your parent's house in Mexico City, and go back to school. Get some good grades and maybe—just maybe—you *might* make a good tour guide in some museum."

Dr. Sova motioned to Chauncy. They walked in silence for a few minutes, watching the rebels begin helping reorganize the camp. The doctor paused and then spoke to Chauncy. "Let this be a lesson to you, as well, Chauncy. Use your brain to its maximum potential, use it fully and you will see that no man will ever outsmart you—ever!"

In time, King Chac's remains and artifacts found their way into the Museum of Anthropology in Mexico City.

A book entitled *The Mayan Mystery, Solved,* authored by Dr. Sova and Chauncy Rollock was shortly thereafter seen on bookshelves, recounting how King Chac's remains had been discovered; it quickly became a best seller.

They had promised each other that they would reunite to

decipher the mysterious riddle on the steps that would lead them to the treasure of the Mayan King. However, Dr. Sova was having personal and legal difficulties with the Mexican government, besides the financial problems and marital strife created by his compulsive gambling. Seeking greater control over archaeological projects in Yucatan, the Mexican officials desired to have more control and oversight at all of Dr. Sova's digs. Opposed, he insisted that he be allowed to work independently.

The result was a downward spiral of red tape, delays, bad temper and impatience.

Chauncy eventually became involved in his own projects. In time, Chauncy lost contact with the doctor.

Sova's colleagues abandoned the notion that King Chac had commissioned his workers to carve a riddle on the temple steps. Once the remains of King Chac were taken away to the museum, they closed base camp and left Temple #22 to be refurbished for tourism.

The jungle reclaimed the temple steps, growing over the Mayan inscriptions. Their meaning was lost as Dr. Sova ceased communicating with the outside world. Chauncy assumed that, fed up with the bureaucratic stupidity he so hated, he had simply chosen to vanish.

In the study of Dr. Sova's hacienda in Merida, deep in his computer files, lay the answer to the greatest riddle of Mayan history, forgotten.

Book Two

The Mayan Code

CHAPTER ONE

The sun's morning light over Guadalajara found its inhabitants already hard at work, driving, bicycling or walking in every corner of the growing city. The rich, the poor, and the shrinking middle class scurried about, surviving by sheer will the many adversities faced by the Mexican people.

Above the urban hubbub, a helicopter made its way toward the city's center. Since military aircraft crossed the sky almost daily, the citizens below paid little attention.

In the city's center was the infamous federal prison, *La Penitenciaria*, or *La Peni,* as the locals called it. It was well known that *La Peni* was currently host to Jose Padilla Madrid, leader of one of the largest Mexican drug cartels. The prison itself was a converted castle. A leftover from the Spanish conquest, the gigantic structure was as large as a city block.

The helicopter, bearing its prominent military emblems, changed course and moments later was hovering above the courtyard. Guards in the turrets, more curious than alarmed, shouted questions among themselves. Outside the prison street vendors and other passersby paused and pointed upwards.

The guards' questions were answered as two doors opened on opposite sides of the helicopter, and before they were fully extended, machine guns from inside opened fire.

Glass and concrete shattered as the helicopter concentrated its fire on the turrets. The frightened screams from the civilians below were barely heard above the ear-splitting burst of machine gun fire. While most of the guards fled, a brave few opened fire at the aircraft, their pitiful weapons drowned out by the helicopter's own arsenal.

A small object was tossed from the aircraft. When it hit the ground, a bright light was accompanied by a thunderclap of noise that boomed through the other sounds. The few brave guards who had been shooting at the helicopter tumbled to the ground, incapacitated by the flash-bang. Two smoke grenades hit the courtyard and within moments the area was blanketed in acrid smoke.

Unseen by anyone, a black-clad man rappelled from the aircraft. The instant his feet touched the ground inside the courtyard he was on the move, deftly maneuvering the rocket launcher he was carrying into firing position. He dropped to one knee and fired at the iron gates leading into the interior hallway of the prison. The helicopter had stopped firing, and in the semi-silence the explosion was ear-shattering.

The intruder was inside before the echo of the explosion had died away. Loading a second rocket into his launcher, another explosion ripped apart a second set of iron gates.

Strapping his rocket launcher to his back, he pulled out a pistol and sprinted to one of the cells blasted open by the last rocket. Kicking the twisted metal doors and removing a gas mask, he stepped inside shouting to the prisoner who had taken shelter beneath his cot.

"Are you Jose Padilla Madrid?"

"*Si*," the prisoner responded, smiling as he stood up. Even in prison garb his aura of power wasn't diminished.

"Come, Mr. Madrid. It's time to check out of this hotel."

Madrid donned the gas mask provided by his rescuer and followed him quickly into the hallway and through the haze in the courtyard. Less than five minutes after the helicopter had appeared over the courtyard Madrid was inside. The large guns rolled back, the doors closed, and the helicopter moved upward and disappeared from sight.

An hour later a black Ford pickup came to a stop not far from the prison walls, the lights on top flashing red and blue. A tall, thin middle-aged man stepped slowly and deliberately out. His olive complexion, thick graying hair and perfectly trimmed gray mustache were instantly recognizable to the onlookers, who moved aside as Captain Gustavo De Leon strode purposefully toward the gates.

Nicknamed "The Incorruptible," he had a reputation for refusing to bend to the drug dealers' wishes, even though he had been approached many times with lucrative—and very illegal—offers. His love for his country far exceeded any desire to attain riches.

A no-nonsense man who took great pride in his position, it seemed he always wore a scowl on his face. No surprise, for his job offered any reason to be happy. With serious crime increasing daily, he was broken-hearted that his country seemed to be caught in an evil vortex of violence.

As a captain of the Mexican military force, it was his responsibility to investigate the incident that had just occurred and assess the damage. As he neared the gates he shook his head, murmuring to himself. This was no small incident: in a matter of minutes the Mexican authorities had lost their most prized prisoner. The last thing he needed to hear was that the military had been involved in this operation.

The gates were opened for him and he entered the prison courtyard. He stood there for a moment, surveying the scene from behind his dark aviator-style sunglasses. He was amazed at the degree of damage. Fires were burning; smoke was thick in the air. Shattered glass, rock, stucco and other debris filled the courtyard. As he walked around the perimeter he looked into a hallway past a twisted iron gate. Water from broken pipes ran everywhere and would flood the lower levels before long, if they weren't flooded already. Cries and moans could be heard from the injured.

He glanced back over his shoulder. The crowd of civilians had probably been standing there since the word had spread that the shooting had stopped. The director of the prison, Martin Verdugo, came out to speak to Captain De Leon. The captain gestured, summoning the director to him so that they would be out of earshot of others.

His face grim, Captain De Leon asked, "How many are dead, Mr. Verdugo?"

"Fortunately we have no dead," the director answered, wringing his hands nervously. "However, there are at least eighteen wounded, two seriously, sir."

De Leon stared at the director for a moment. The man was in his mid-sixties, short and heavy. He was obviously nearing retirement, and just as obviously knew he was in the international spotlight because the whole affair had taken place on his watch.

"Are the prisoners under lock and key?" De Leon asked brusquely as he a made hand gesture.

"Yes, Captain, all is secure for now."

"Was there any structural damage?"

The director paused to swallow. "Currently there are still some fires out of control, sir. Two iron gates destroyed; we're standing by one of them. The other is deeper inside the prison near the holding cells. In addition, some of the plumbing and electrical has been destroyed or damaged. The lookout turrets were shredded and suffered extreme damage. Water damage, smoke damage to furniture, windows destroyed—oh, and there is much bullet damage to the walls, sir."

"Could you or anyone else identify the men in the helicopter?" De Leon asked as he looked around.

"No sir. Not only did it happen so quickly, but all of the men wore black gas masks and hoods."

The captain nodded slowly and thought for a minute. "The guards, Mr. Verdugo," he said at last. "I desire to interview them as soon as possible, especially those that were not injured. Do you understand?"

"Yes Captain, I will arrange that."

"Thank you for your cooperation, Mr. Verdugo. Do you mind if I look around myself?"

"Oh no, no, go right ahead! I'll be in my office." At once Mr. Verdugo scuttled off toward his office, relieved to be out from under the gaze of *The Incorruptible.*

Captain De Leon strolled slowly around the hallways and courtyard, surveying and scrutinizing every detail. Debris crunched under his highly polished black boots as he walked. Men ran to and fro around him, every one of them preoccupied with the business at hand. The smoke from the grenades and the fires lingered in the building, giving everything a gloomy, depressing atmosphere.

As he walked around the courtyard again, a glint on the ground caught his eye. Approaching it, he knelt to get a closer look. He picked up the piece of metal and turned it around in his hands, gazing intently at it, his forehead creasing in concentration. Picking up a few more pieces like the first, he shifted his weight on his knee, unclipped his radio from his belt and called his assistant.

"Arturo? Arturo, can you hear me?"

The radio sputtered and the voice of a young man came through. "Yes, Captain, this is Arturo."

"Come into the main courtyard and bring me a couple of plastic bags will you?"

"On my way, Captain," Arturo responded.

In a few moments he was at De Leon's side holding out the plastic bags. An academy graduate in his early twenties, Arturo was quickly learning this business of crime fighting in the metropolis of Guadalajara. Captain De Leon was comfortable around Arturo. He felt the young man was a promising candidate to move up the ranks of law enforcement. The captain knew that Arturo had not yet been reached by the greed to which so many of De Leon's peers had succumbed. Perhaps Arturo would eventually also gain the reputation as *The Incorruptible.*

He looked up at Arturo. "I have some interesting samples I want to analyze at the lab. Here, help me put them in the bags."

Arturo knelt and helped the captain put the fragments in the bags. "What have you surmised so far, Captain?"

De Leon glanced around, then spoke softly so as not to be overheard. "It seems it was an inside job, Arturo. Some of the guards must have known the helicopter was coming. They put up very little resistance! Also, can you imagine the amount of shooting that occurred in here? Those military Mini-guns are capable of shooting four thousand rounds per minute, and yet not one guard died. Not that I would have wished it, of course, but it does seem a bit odd, don't you think? There was a lot of property damage, though, as if to dramatize the event, yet so few injuries. Something doesn't look right."

"Sounds plausible," Arturo responded. "And these fragments, what do you make of them?"

"They look ... strange. That's all I'll say for now until a hunch of mine is confirmed. Here, take these bags to the laboratory."

They stood. De Leon zipped the bags closed and handed them to Arturo.

"I also want you to find out how many military helicopters were in the air in the last two days, whether in Jalisco or any surrounding states. Bring me the report tomorrow and put it on my desk. Now remember: not a word to anyone about what you just heard from me, understand?"

"Of course, Captain," Arturo said before briskly walking away.

Mr. Verdugo came scurrying out of his office again with the same worried expression on his face. "Captain, the media are outside the prison and they want to interview us!"

Captain De Leon groaned. The one thing he detested most

was the media. He hated the distortions and half-truths that they spun to the public; hated them with a passion. He knew he would be in the center of their maelstrom of blame, especially since his department seemed to be involved.

The media can never get anything right, he thought in disgust. How can they relay to an ignorant public in just a few seconds things that take months to investigate and explain? All they are interested in is sensationalism and excitement. It's all about selling and commercials.

De Leon shook his head in disappointment as he looked at Mr. Verdugo.

"This isn't going to be easy, director. Let me handle the interview first. Let's go outside."

As the two men exited, a swarm of cameras and reporters mobbed them. "Do you know why your military men kidnapped Jose Madrid?" "What do you make of this?" "How many men died in the prison?" "Where do you think Mr. Madrid is now?"

Captain De Leon stifled a curse and quieted the questions with a gesture. In as few words as possible he explained the situation as he knew it, and assured the press that he would do everything in his power to get to the bottom of the incident. Referring the reporters to Mr. Verdugo for further questions, he made a hasty retreat to his truck.

CHAPTER TWO

"Ahhh, Cancun." Anita Rollock's long blonde hair fluttered in the soft breeze as she sipped her drink. "Sandy beaches ... margaritas ... mariachis ... mmmm ...."

Anita and her husband, Chauncy, were taking a break from the hectic schedule that had nearly turned Chauncy into a nervous wreck. Sitting in a large ranch house in Wyoming while snow piled up outside had made it easy to choose Cancun as their vacation destination, at least for Anita. Where else would they go except where the sun shone all day?

Reclining in the beach chair next to her, Chauncy smiled and then sipped his margarita. He had been in the international limelight back when he had been working with Dr. Sova. But when the famous linguist had disappeared, Chauncy had become little more than a footnote in the entire Mayan episode, and he had returned to his normal archaeological expeditions.

He was pleased that Anita had also suggested bringing Marlo Gund and his wife Gloria. Chauncy admitted that the destination had been his wife's idea, but he later confided to Marlo that he missed the Mayan episodes. It had been a while since he had heard from the doctor, during which time he had never once ventured back to the spot where their adventures had begun.

"It was truly amazing, Marlo, to hear from Dr. Sova himself the explanation of the Mayan hieroglyphs, and to see his magnificent brain at work. Well, I'd like to go back to those pyramids and see what has become of them."

Now the five of them, including the Rollock's son Troy

were relaxing on the famous beaches of Cancun, the bright tropical sun doing its best to brown their complexions.

"You should have thought of this idea two years ago." Marlo's smiling face hadn't changed much in the three years since Chauncy had seen him. He was not as thin, and his goatee had been reduced to a mustache.

"Yeah, well, what can I say? It was my wife's idea; blame her for being late about it."

Marlo grinned again, knowing he didn't dare blame Anita for anything. Regardless of whether it was two days, two weeks, or two years too late, it still felt good to be relaxing on the beach, chatting and reminiscing with Chauncy.

After a couple of hours, they packed up and headed back to their hotel. Being eight, Troy wanted to stay at the beach the entire day, but his parents persuaded him otherwise. It had only been a few hours since they had arrived, and they had two weeks to enjoy the beach and everything else that Cancun had to offer.

They were nearing the hotel when they caught sight of the military personnel stationed at the doors. Chauncy privately wondered if there had been a break-in.

The guards ushered them in without a word. Their questions were answered as they made their way through the lobby. A large group of hotel guests sat in front of the large television screen, watching the news in English on CNN:

"We're reporting live from downtown Guadalajara," the reporter's voice crackled, "where the infamous cartel crime lord Jose Padilla Madrid escaped earlier today. Details are still sketchy, but we do know that casualties were at a minimum despite the massive damage done to *La Penitenciaria*."

The screen shifted to a bird's-eye view of a large castle-like structure, black smoke curling toward the sky. "We'll have more information as it becomes available," the reporter concluded.

The scene of the burning prison immediately cut away to a CNN reporter interviewing the American Embassy representative, George Hawkins.

“Mr. Hawkins, what do you make of the recent prison escape?”

Mr. Hawkins leaned toward the camera. “This is sheer incompetence as far as I am concerned. I will be meeting with the Mexican representatives to express the concerns of the President of the United States.”

“What a joke—as if he could do anything stop this from occurring again,” Chauncy muttered.

Gloria whistled, running a hand through her short brown hair. "That must have been quite the doing; they would have had good protection around an inmate like that!"

Marlo nodded. "Let's hope Jose Madrid won't be checking into our hotel anytime soon," he said.

They spoke to the clerk at the desk. "There will be many military roadblocks," she informed them in precise English. "I recommend that you stay here in the beach area."

The four adults agreed to meet in the lobby after changing their clothes. Once in their room, Chauncy walked over to the window and opened the curtains, looking out across the turquoise water. "Well," he said, putting his hands on his hips. "That incident will put a kink in some of my plans."

"In what way?" Anita asked.

Chauncy took a deep breath, gazing off at the horizon. "I was hoping to take us on a tour to the Mayan pyramids."

"We may still be able to, Chauncy. If we travel on a tour bus we shouldn't have any problem with the roadblocks."

"Yeah, I thought of that," Chauncy muttered as he pulled clean clothes from his suitcase. "Except that I wanted to rent a Hummer and just take our group, you know? To keep away from all the gringo tourists. Besides, I wanted to show you some ruins off the beaten path, where I was with Dr. Sova."

Whatever Anita might have said was interrupted when

Troy grabbed the remote control, flopped down on the bed, and turned on the television.

Anita turned quickly to him. "Hey, turn off that TV! We didn't travel a thousand miles just to watch that stupid thing."

"Ah Mom, I just wanted to see some cartoons."

Before Troy was able to shut off the television Chauncy and Anita noticed the network was still running the report on the escape from Guadalajara, and all three of them stopped to stare at the footage. The screen then shifted to an interview with the representative of the American Embassy again.

Chauncy shook his head. "They keep running the same scene over and over."

"Wow, look at all that smoke!" Troy exclaimed. "Dad, it must have been bad!"

Chauncy nodded. "Yeah, it must have. I wonder where the drug lord is now. You know, he could be anywhere in Mexico, or maybe even outside of it already."

Anita grabbed the remote from Troy and turned off the TV. "Come on, you guys, we didn't come here to listen to bad news. Let's have some fun, okay?"

Chauncy sighed again. "I guess you're right. Hey, I'm in the mood for some good Mexican food. Do you think this town has any?"

The sun had set but the air was still hot and humid. As it wafted through the open windows of the restaurant, flying insects of all sorts gathering around the white lights, writhing and moving as if they were dancing to the mariachi band that played loudly in the background. The low hum of traffic mixed with the boisterous voices of the cantina. The tension from the news was starting to fade as the group enjoyed the festive music and their drinks.

"Hey Chauncy," Marlo said suddenly. "This tequila is so different from the stuff we buy at home."

"Yes, I agree with you." Chauncy downed the last swallow

of his drink. "I believe they add cane sugar to the exported bottles. What a difference the domestic tequila is though. Amazing, isn't it? It's only here in Mexico where the maguey or *Agave Tequiliana* grows."

Marlo nodded. "It has to do with the soil. The soils in the state of Jalisco are permeable loams, rich in elements derived from basalt, all because of the volcanic activity that occurred in the area thousands of years ago."

Gloria giggled. "Listen to him. That's the geologist talking."

Chauncy stared into his shot glass. "Actually, the word 'tequila' is of Nahautl origin, the mother tongue of the indigenous people. They believed that the Maguey plant, or also known as Agave, was a divine creation, a representation of the female goddess, *Mayaheul*. Now the male god counterpart, *Petacatl*, was married to *Mayaheul* and represented various plants. He was believed to assist in the fermentation of *pulque*, the unrefined liquid of the Maguey from which tequila is derived."

Anita ribbed Gloria. "That's the wannabe anthropologist talking."

Marlo's brow furrowed. "Hey! Stop mocking us, ladies. I'll have you know I did intensive studies of tequila when I was in college."

"I'll bet you did," Anita said, laughing. "With all those frat parties you had."

While Marlo attempted to come up with a retort to Anita's comment, the mariachi band approached the table.

"Musica Señores?"

Marlo glanced at the bandleader. "Got any Van Halen or Metallica tunes?"

The musician gave him a perplexed stare. "*Que*?"

Chauncy laughed, then spoke to the bandleader. "*Musica romantica, por favor.*"

He smiled. "Oh, si, si muy bien."

The band struck up a melodious song, the Spanish words sung over the soft sounds of a violin.

Marlo took a long last sip from his shot glass and turned to Gloria with lusty eyes. "Kiss me baby," he murmured.

Anita smirked at Gloria. "And that's the tequila talking."

Gloria adopted a mock-serious expression and shook her head. "While they drink we better talk about our itinerary."

"Yes," Anita laughed as she lifted her own drink. "These guys are in no position to make those important decisions."

Gloria took a travel guide out of her bag. "Let's see, there's hang gliding, scuba diving, swimming, boat tours, deep sea fishing, oh yeah Jet skiing and—"

Troy interrupted them, a broad smile brightening his face. "Yeah, Jet skiing! That sounds awesome! Hey, Dad, let's go!"

Chauncy turned to look at his son. "Why not, sounds like fun. What do you say, Marlo?"

"That sounds good to me."

Anita smiled at them. "Well you guys can go ahead; I'll just stay on the beach and work on my tan."

"I'm with you Anita," Gloria chimed in. "Tomorrow's our first full day here, so let the guys do what they want first while we relax."

The following morning after breakfast, the five left the hotel and headed for the beach. From behind his dark glasses Chauncy watched the clear waters of Cancun shimmer and sparkle in the bright sunshine, making him very glad he had remembered to bring his sunglasses along. Puffy white clouds dotted the horizon; a warm breeze blew in from the ocean.

At the marina Chauncy checked out keys for three Jet Skis and walked over to Marlo and Troy. After showing Troy how to operate the watercraft, the three of them ventured out onto the water.

Gloria and Anita lay back on their beach towels, enjoying the warm tropical sun and talking occasionally. Eventually Anita dozed off on the white sand.

Marlo and Troy zigzagged on their skis, causing waves and splashing each other. Chauncy followed more slowly and admired the scenery. He didn't quite feel like racing; he had come here to get away from his hectic life. He just sat there, motor idling, bobbing up and down over the gentle waves. As boats full of tourists zipped past him, he gazed in at the shoreline and the greenery of the jungle. For a long time he let his mind wander back to his adventures with Dr. Sova in the Mexican jungles.

Eventually, Marlo motioned Chauncy to come over. "Hey, I say we go in for a rest; Troy and I are both low on fuel."

"I still have plenty left," Chauncy said. "Of course, I wasn't going as fast as you two. Go ahead. I'll be just a few minutes behind."

Chauncy had spied a cove in the distance that begged to be investigated. As he left, Marlo and Troy opened the throttles on their machines and began the journey back to the marina.

Half an hour later, Marlo scoured the horizon, his hand shielding his eyes from the sun.

"That's strange," he said. "Chauncy said he'd only be a few minutes."

Anita looked up at Marlo. "I think you'd better go look for him; I've heard that rental Jet Skis aren't always maintained properly."

Marlo nodded and ran to his Jet Ski, accelerating into the open sea, the water frothing madly in his wake.

Another half hour passed, and Anita was becoming increasingly worried. She walked out into the ocean until the waves slapped against her legs, her eyes scanning the horizon looking for any sign of her husband or Marlo. A few more minutes passed before she spotted Marlo at a distance, towing Chauncy's Jet Ski beside him. Her breath caught in her throat when she did not see Chauncy on the machine.

"Oh my God," she murmured, her hand over her mouth. A million scenarios ran through her mind: Was Chauncy pitched off the Jet Ski by a rogue wave? Had he been knocked unconscious somehow? Could a shark have come upon her husband?

Marlo ran his machine up onto the beach, an extremely worried look on his face. Anita, Gloria, and Troy were waiting for him, but he motioned them over.

Anita got there first. "Where's Chauncy?" she asked, her voice quivering with fear.

Marlo lowered his voice, more out of fear than anything else; the consistent lapping of the waves and other noises would have made eavesdropping impossible. "This is his Jet Ski, obviously, but he was nowhere to be found."

"What!" Anita exclaimed. "Oh my God Marlo, where's my husband? What do you mean he was nowhere to be found? Did you at least try looking for him?"

Marlo shook his head but remained silent.

"Why didn't you?" Anita said, trying desperately to hold her temper.

Marlo took a piece of waterproof parchment paper from the utility compartment of his machine. "I saw this note stuck on the handlebars. Perhaps you'd better read it for yourself."

He handed the paper to Anita. She read it aloud in a soft voice, a sinking feeling in her stomach.

"'If you want to see Mr. Rollock alive again, do not call the police.'" she began to shiver despite the heat from the tropical sun. "Oh no, Marlo, someone's abducted Chauncy—they know his name!"

Marlo stepped from his machine, and Gloria turned around to see if anyone was watching. "Let's go back to the hotel room you guys, I'm scared."

Troy looked out at the horizon hoping this was all a terrible joke. "Dad—where's Dad?"

The first thing Chauncy felt when he awoke was a throbbing pain in his right shoulder. The second thing he noticed was a matching throb in his head. He opened his eyes and immediately regretted it; the harsh light from two bare bulbs only made his headache worse. Keeping his eyes squeezed tightly shut, he groaned and tried to move. He still had his swimming trunks on, but someone had removed his life jacket.

Moving slowly, mindful of the pain in his shoulder, he sat up and almost crashed back down. His head swam, pain thumping through him with every heartbeat. Gritting his teeth he fought against the pain; fought to stay upright. After a few moments he risked opening his eyes again.

The light wasn't as intense the second time around, and he could take in the few details of the room. It was large, probably forty feet long by twenty feet wide. The bed was simple: firm but thin, a sheet, a blanket and a pillow. At least it smelled clean.

Raising his head he opened his eyes completely and then stood on wobbly legs. The walls were made of concrete block, with not a single scrap of plaster or paint on the floor, ceiling or walls. There were two doors on opposite sides of the room. One was wooden and the other looked like it might have been forged out of a single block of iron. It was locked; probably the exit.

Hoping the wooden door led to a bathroom, he opened it and confirmed his guess. The sink had two drawers below, one filled with soap, shampoo and towels while the other held clean clothes. Pulling out a shirt and pants, he noticed they were just about his size.

He put the clothes back in the drawer, frowning. The bathroom was clean; in fact the whole place nearly screamed simplistic, utilitarian cleanliness. At least it seemed whoever had brought him here wasn't planning anything as crude as torture.

A table next to the bathroom door held a terra cotta jug of fresh water. He poured himself a drink and crossed the room to a desk covered with pencils and pieces of paper. Digging in the drawers yielded nothing but more pencils and paper. He sat on the bed to think.

As he drank the refreshingly cool water he set about trying to remember what had happened before he blacked out. He had set out to examine a secluded cove, he remembered that much. Concentrating, he thought back past the haze in his mind.

Another drink of water and his brain was sufficiently recovered to recall two men watching him from a small speedboat. He had ignored them, but they had circled close to him and he had felt something sharp in his shoulder. In hindsight he realized it had been a tranquilizer dart.

His next memory was waking up here.

His thoughts quickly turned to his wife and son. Did they know he was safe? Did they even know he was alive?

Minutes later Chauncy heard footsteps coming down a set of stairs, confirming his assumption that he was in a basement of some kind. A brief, muted conversation in Spanish took place outside the iron door, and Chauncy could hear the jingling of keys. His heart beat faster.

The iron door swung open and three men walked into the room. Two of them were obviously bodyguards; large muscular men with shoulder holsters prominently displayed. Chauncy was reminded of the two men in the boat that had been circling him.

The third man didn't appear to be armed but was obviously in charge. His expensive suit emphasized his protruding belly and small arms. His smile contrasted with his strange eyes, which opened and closed slowly, almost like a lizard's.

"Hello Mr. Rollock," he boomed in thickly accented English. "I apologize for the inconvenience that we have caused you. Rest assured that, as you may have already noticed, we have tried to supply you with the most modern amenities for your comfort."

"Who are you?" Chauncy asked as he stood from the bed. "And how do you know my name?"

"My name is Santo Domingo but you may call me Santo. We are honored to have you as our guest."

Though noticing Santo had ignored his question, Chauncy smiled inwardly. He wondered to himself why any mother would have named her son "Holy Sunday."

"So are you holding me for ransom? How much do you want? What am I worth, one hundred thousand dollars, two hundred thousand dollars? I suppose you know that I am a famous archaeologist."

Santo laughed from deep within his protruding belly. "No, Señor Rollock, we do not want any money from you."

"Then what do you want?"

Santo set a black briefcase on the desk. Opening it he removed a thick scroll.

"What we need, Señor Rollock, are your *talents*."

"My talents, what on earth do you want my talents for?" Chauncy asked as he nervously walked to the desk.

Santo unrolled the scroll and Chauncy immediately recognized the glyphs that were drawn on it.

"We want you to translate the Mayan Code for us, Mr. Rollock."

CHAPTER THREE

In the usual hustle and bustle of downtown Guadalajara, people went about their business despite yesterday's excitement. In an office high above downtown sat Captain De Leon, absorbed in one of the many reports scattered across his desk.

It was an in-depth, technical discussion of the helicopters used by the Mexican National Army, with details on everything from fuel consumption to how many times a month they needed maintenance. Also included was a listing of the flight schedules of every one of those helicopters for the surrounding area for the last two weeks. It was a longer list than he had anticipated. He struggled to wrap his brain around all the locations and times.

He was interrupted by an annoying buzz from the intercom on his desk.

"What is it, Laura?" he asked his secretary, trying not to sound as irritated as he was.

"A representative from the United States Embassy, a Mr. George Hawkins, is here to see you sir."

De Leon's irritation turned to exasperation. After the media, the thing he most despised were politicians, especially foreign politicians. They were always so condescending. Everything was always Mexico's fault. Everything. Always. The drug war was far from over; the illegal immigration issue was hot in the border areas—and who was the perfect whipping boy to get all the blame? Mexico, the Mexican military, the Federal Police and the Chief of Police—and now it would be even worse, what with the incident in

Guadalajara.

"Show him in, Laura," he said, strained resignation in his voice. *This is not going to be good,* he thought.

He stood up from his desk and moved toward the door just as Laura opened it and ushered in two men. One had a camera around his neck—a reporter—which made the other man George Hawkins. The embassy representative was young for his post, probably late thirties, and dangerously thin. The reporter asked them to shake hands for a photo. They faced the camera and offered their best phony smiles. Once finished, the reporter walked briskly from the office.

De Leon's smile promptly vanished. He motioned Mr. Hawkins to take a seat on the leather couch that De Leon reserved for special guests. The embassy rep put his briefcase on his knees, opened it, and took out a few documents.

"Well, Mr. Hawkins, first I must apologize for not being prepared for your visit. As you can see, it has not been a good week for Mexico and I am up to my neck in trouble trying to find Mr. Madrid."

Hawkins shuffled the papers from his briefcase and his right eyebrow rose slowly as he spoke. "Well, yes, I understand perfectly Mr. De Leon. No doubt the recent news has kept us all distracted, hasn't it? And that, Mr. De Leon, is the reason for my visit. I have spoken with the President of the United States and he is very disturbed by the incident."

De Leon fumed. "Why don't you go bother the chief of police? It's his job to enforce law and order in Mexico, not mine."

A smug smile came to Hawkins face. "I am aware of that fact, Mr. De Leon, but it was a Mexican military aircraft involved in the crime. That means this incident falls squarely under *your* jurisdiction." Hawkins paused to shuffle more papers. "What a pity. You had Mr. Madrid right where everyone wanted him, but because of your internal corruption he escaped right under your nose! Obviously we at the

Embassy want to know what you are doing to prevent such a thing from happening again."

De Leon took a deep breath in an effort to calm himself before speaking. "It seems to me, Mr. Hawkins, that all eyes are upon *me* as if I may have had something to do with this. I am investigating this matter very thoroughly."

"I trust your integrity, Mr. De Leon. At least from what I have heard about you. Rest assured that not once did it cross my mind that you were responsible for this fiasco. However, after what has transpired, we feel that the corruption in the Mexican military is sufficient to cause our government to lose confidence in your ability to control your own men, Mr. De Leon. Can you imagine the damage this has caused to our international relations? We just took a major step backwards in the drug war. Jose Padilla Madrid is a dangerous outlaw and now he is running around this country. It is only a matter of time before he reorganizes and the cocaine will flow across the border."

Another deep breath then De Leon's fingers found a pencil; he started twirling it to disperse the angry energy welling up inside him. "Mr. Hawkins, for the record, let it be known that corruption is not the exclusive property of the Mexican government. It runs everywhere, including *your* country."

"Yes of course, Mr. De Leon, I am aware of that. But look how blatant yours is; a military helicopter in broad daylight rescues the most powerful drug lord of Central and South America! Can it get any worse? The populace of both our nations has lost confidence in the law enforcement agencies and national defense organizations of Mexico. If the chief of police and the head of the Mexican military can't prevent these things from occurring, then fear will soon set in and tourism will drop considerably. This will spell a great economic loss for your country."

De Leon nodded his head. "I am aware of the consequences. But I suppose you didn't come here to give me a lesson in economics, right?"

Hawkins waved some important-looking papers. "As you can see, I have my most recent reports here. It sure would be a pity to have nothing positive to say about your performance when our presidents meet next month!"

"My performance?" De Leon said, his eyes squinting at Hawkins as he slowly stood up. "Are you threatening me? Was this the sole purpose of your meeting? To advise me of my *grades* like some elementary school teacher?"

Hawkins smiled and raised his eyebrow again. "No, no, my friend, of course not, I have no authority or desire to make changes in your government's assigned positions. I am simply a humble servant of the United States of America. Actually, I came as a friend; I am here to help you, to warn you, Mr. De Leon."

"Warn me?" De Leon retorted, his hands on his hips. "Warn me of what?"

"The bottom line is this: we would like to see a deeper investigation into the internal affairs of your military organization. Cut the corruption, cut it out like a cancer, Mr. De Leon! There is a rumor circulating that if you can't find the culprit, some people who are higher up than you or I may be looking for your replacement."

"As I have already stated, Mr. Hawkins, I am deeply interested in getting to the bottom of this issue. I will find who in my department was capable of taking a military craft and rescuing Mr. Madrid. Kindly keep in mind that the investigation has just begun and it is too premature to start pointing fingers at anyone. Finding Madrid is and will continue to be my number-one priority. As for the 'cocaine flowing across the border,' if your government would educate its people to stop *consuming* the drug, then perhaps the drug lords would look elsewhere to peddle their poison. Now if you'll excuse me Mr. Hawkins, I have much work to do. I do not have the luxury of time to sit here and take verbal abuses from you."

"Yes, of course, I understand," Mr. Hawkins said with a sardonic smile.

De Leon strode toward the door, signaling that the meeting was over. Hawkins put his papers away and walked to the door.

"Mr. De Leon, it was a pleasure talking with you. I will keep in touch. Good day."

"The pleasure was mine, Mr. Hawkins. Good day," De Leon said with a forced smile.

Once the door was firmly closed, De Leon snapped the pencil in two and glared at the couch Hawkins had vacated.

The next day De Leon picked up Arturo from his apartment and headed toward the prison. The traffic was heavy as always in Guadalajara; the trip was going to take a while. De Leon kept to himself, deep in thought.

"How are you today, Captain?" Arturo asked twenty minutes into the drive, more as a way to break the ice than a true bid for information.

De Leon sighed as he aggressively changed lanes in an effort to shave a few minutes off their travel time. "Not good. I need a solid break in this case, Arturo."

"Did you find the reports of the helicopter flight schedules to be informative?"

De Leon nodded. "Yes I did, however, there was nothing earth-shattering in the reports to speak of. I will talk to you about those points later. For now, we need to coax information out of the prison guards and see if they can help in solving this situation."

Up ahead the ancient towers of the prison jutted in sharp contrast to the modern buildings. As they drew closer, more and more details were visible: first the steel reinforcements built into the towers, then the old brickwork showing where the plaster had broken off, and finally even the vines clinging to the walls. De Leon parked in a reserved spot and got out, his mind focused and his steps brisk and sure.

After being cleared by the guards they walked up the stone steps to the building. As they moved, De Leon spoke quietly to his assistant.

"Let me do the talking, Arturo, this isn't going to be easy."

Mr. Verdugo had already been informed of De Leon's visit. In minutes they were on their way to an interrogation room down the hall, a guard leading the way. De Leon fell quickly in step behind him as Arturo struggled to keep up. He was used to De Leon's famous energy, but today it seemed overwhelming.

The floor had already been cleaned from what everyone was now calling "The Incident." The fires had been put out, but a heavy stench of smoke and wet rags still filled the air. Guards were everywhere in sight, their guns at the ready, making sure nothing was amiss. Loud voices echoed in the hallways.

Pulling a set of keys from his pocket, the guard opened a heavy metal door and showed De Leon and Arturo into the room. Several ancient wooden chairs were the only furniture in the bare-block room. Thick iron barred the cracked and dirty window. De Leon appeared not to notice the grimy light and smell of sweat embedded in the walls.

A door opened on the other side of the room and four men in handcuffs were led in. De Leon paced like a caged lion, a hard look of disgust in his eyes as he spoke to the seated men.

"I hope you all understand why you were put under arrest. You were assigned to guard this prison. The incident that occurred recently has shamed our nation. It has demonstrated to the world our weakness and corruption! This is intolerable! I want you to explain to me why you behaved the way you did that morning of the rescue. First you," De Leon kicked the chair of the first man seated on the left. "Tell me what happened!" he yelled.

The man did not raise his head as he spoke. "Captain ... when I saw the helicopter flying above our prison I immediately rang the alarm."

"So? Why didn't you shoot at the helicopter?"

"I—I panicked, Captain, but I did shoot a few rounds at the helicopter."

"Panicked?" De Leon barked. "It's your job to defend the prison. We don't pay you to panic."

The guard sat silently, staring at the floor.

"And what about you?" De Leon said as he turned his attention to the second guard.

"I ran, sir. I also panicked, but I did fire at the aircraft too."

"You did?" De Leon asked, his tone dripping with sarcasm. "You missed by two kilometers. Aren't you a trained sharpshooter?"

Without waiting for an answer, De Leon turned to look at the other two, his eyes fiery. "Is that the same story for the rest of you men? You panicked, you ran?"

They nodded, none looking at the Captain.

"That's your story?" De Leon asked, waiting in vain for a spoken answer.

De Leon shook his head, his disgust completely evident on his face. "Allow me to tell you what really happened. The truth is that you are all cowards, yes, but you are also liars! You should have defended the prison with your lives. The least, the very least you should have done is put up a good fight and fire at the helicopter. But your rifles were inspected, and not a single bullet had been fired from them! You want to know why? Because you sold yourselves out to Jose Madrid, that's why. His men paid you off to let the helicopter in! What did this betrayal gain you? I'll tell you. You will spend the rest of your days on the other side of the prison walls. I hope you all rot in there."

De Leon took a breath and turned toward the guard that had brought them into the room. "Get this scum out of my sight."

When the men had been hauled away, the guard returned, a perplexed look on his face. "How did you know they were bribed?" he asked.

"My assistant, here, Arturo, made some background checks on these men. About two months ago those four guards suddenly started to live 'the good life.' They bought fancy cars and trucks, parading them around their neighborhoods. Three of them moved into nicer homes. Now, you and I both know quite well that there is no way those guards could afford that, not on the wages they are paid here. With that knowledge it wasn't hard to put the pieces together."

De Leon and Arturo left the prison and headed back downtown through even heavier traffic. The trip to the laboratory was made in silence; De Leon was deep in thought and Arturo was disinclined to interrupt.

Once inside the modern glass and steel skyscraper, the two men took a secured elevator down to the basement. When the doors opened they proceeded briskly to their destination: a sprawling forensics and ballistics lab.

A man with thick glasses spotted them as they entered. "Ah, Captain De Leon, it is good to see you back."

"Doctor Ernesto Rubio," De Leon acknowledged, shaking the other's hand vigorously. "This is my assistant Arturo Benavidez."

The tall, thin doctor peered through his glasses at Arturo. "Ah, so this is the one I have heard good reports about—a pleasure to meet you, young man."

De Leon quickly got to the business at hand. "I'm aware that you are a busy man so I will make this brief. What do you have for me? Any results yet?"

"Yes, yes of course. Follow me."

The three men walked through a maze of humming,

clicking equipment. Along the walls dozens of men examined vials of chemicals. Everywhere, information flickered from computer screens or spewed from printers.

Dr. Rubio tore the printout from one. "Here are the results of the metallurgical tests, Captain."

As De Leon read the report, a smile came to his face, the trademark smile that meant one of his hunches had been confirmed. Folding the report up carefully, he placed it inside his coat pocket and turned back to Rubio. "The ballistics reports, Doctor? Do you have those?"

The doctor nodded and motioned them to follow as he moved to another room. Once there, he opened a folder and handed a report to De Leon. The captain searched the list until he found what he was looking for, and his telltale grin grew even larger.

"Ernesto, my *compadre*, you have done a wonderful job, as always. You have copies?"

"They are in a secure location, as per your instructions."

"Excellent, excellent, again, you have done a most glorious job, doctor!"

Ernesto bowed from the waist. "I am always at your service, my captain."

As they left the building, Arturo could tell that De Leon was in excellent spirits. It wasn't long before the captain spoke.

"Arturo, I'm buying lunch today. I have much to tell you!"

In the heart of downtown Guadalajara, the two men sat in a remote corner of a posh restaurant. De Leon waited until after the server had brought their food before speaking.

"This is what we know so far: According to the flight reports, there were no helicopters scheduled to fly in the state of Jalisco. There were, however, a couple north of us in Sinaloa transporting a platoon of soldiers who were burning marijuana fields. Also, south of here in Chiapas three helicopters were scouting the mountains for rebels, but again, there were none here in Guadalajara. So the question is: where did the helicopter that rescued Madrid come from?"

Arturo took a sip of his cola before venturing an answer. "Perhaps the report was incorrect, or had been modified."

De Leon nodded. "So you're saying that someone inside our military modified the reports?"

"Yes, that has to be it!" Arturo said, looking pleased.

"That's a possibility, but remember that some of the material is dated and your request included data several days prior to the incident."

"True, true—but let's say that someone changed the report once I went snooping around."

De Leon grinned widely with satisfaction. "Recall, though, that I have the results from the lab concerning the metallurgical tests."

"Oh yeah, what were the results?"

"Well, permit me to refresh your memory. When we first entered the prison, I saw some debris that caught my attention. The guards who had not been paid off had indeed fired at the helicopter, and pieces of its hull shrapnel were littered about the courtyard. When I picked up this shrapnel, however, I immediately realized that it was lighter than usual. I've been to several helicopter crash sites and have examined similar material, but this felt quite out of the ordinary. However, I needed the expert opinion of a metallurgist to confirm my hunch."

Arturo raised his eyebrow in an expression De Leon knew well. After taking a drink De Leon continued. "Enter Ernesto Rubio, the metallurgist. He is an expert at studying the internal structure of metal and alloys; we do not have too many of those types of scientists in Mexico. There are only two laboratories with the equipment needed, one being in Mexico City and the other, thankfully for us the one here in Guadalajara. Dr. Rubio extended his studies and became a forensic ballistics expert. Now allow me to demonstrate the results of his analyses."

De Leon held up a small and twisted piece of metal that had been in his jacket pocket.

"You'll recognize this as one of the samples I directed you to send to the lab. It turns out that my hunch was correct! According to Dr. Rubio's report, the metal debris that fell from the helicopter that rescued Madrid is not the same type of metal that our national helicopters are made of."

Arturo's eyes widened slightly. "What? How can that be? Hundreds of eyewitnesses claimed that it was most definitely our national aircraft that hovered above the prison!"

"I know, but the helicopters currently in use by the Mexican military are older models, and many of them can barely fly. Of course, there are exceptions to this rule, but it is only officials in the higher ranks, such as myself, that use newer helicopters. But all of them are accounted for. The helicopter in question, the one that invaded the prison, was supposedly an older model. It was, in fact, a very late model aircraft."

Arturo rubbed his chin. "So you're saying that the rescue helicopter was disguised as one of ours. Correct?"

De Leon nodded. "Indeed! The helicopter that came to the prison was manufactured in another country, but which one I am not sure. Somebody purchased it via the black market, smuggled it in somehow, and disguised it to look like one of ours. Clever, don't you think? A concerted effort was put forth to make it look like our military was responsible for the rescue mission."

De Leon leaned back, a look of satisfaction on his face.

"But are you absolutely certain of this? What about the ballistics reports?" Arturo asked.

"A qualified yes for the first question, as for the second question, the shells that were fired from the rescue copter's Mini-gun were also among the samples studied by Dr. Rubio.

He confirmed that they are not the type of bullet we use in the Mexican military, being of a larger caliber."

"Amazing!" Arturo responded, trying to absorb it all.

De Leon leaned forward and stared intensely at Arturo as he continued. "So, there are a lot of things we know, but we cannot afford to get overconfident, as there are many things we do not know. We know that four guards were bribed not to interfere with the rescue. We also know that Madrid had foreign help to make the operation successful. What we don't know, however, is what country the helicopter came from. It could have been Colombia, as they are heavily involved in the drug trade, or Honduras, which would be more likely to have a modern helicopter. But it could just as easily been the USA or even someplace in Europe. We also don't know where Madrid is now. But, my friend, I have a feeling that we will know soon."

De Leon picked up his fork and started to eat.

Arturo smiled. "I admire your abilities, Captain. Have you ever thought about becoming a private detective?"

De Leon paused with his fork halfway to his mouth. A mischievous smile crossed his face, but he continued eating without further comment.

CHAPTER FOUR

"The Mayan Code?" Chauncy tried his best to feign ignorance. "What're you talking about? Surely you must have the wrong man, Mr. Domingo. I'm a paleontologist; I study fossils and such."

The smile left Santo Domingo's face. He turned the wooden chair to face Chauncy and sat down. After a moment, he spoke, his voice deadly serious.

"Let's not play games, Mr. Rollock. I do not have time to waste; in fact, time is of the essence. We are very much aware of who you are and what you know. So you can stop playing dumb, it doesn't suit you. We were planning to entice you to come down here from the States but when we found out that you were coming for a vacation ... well, you cannot imagine how pleased we were.

"We know that approximately five years ago you were down here in Yucatan, working with Doctor Sova in Palenque making plans to exhume a Mayan king. We also know that you two invented a personal code based on the Mayan hieroglyphs, which you refer to as the Mayan Code. So please, do not insult us by lying."

Chauncy sat back against the wall very slowly. Suddenly it seemed the throbbing in his head was from his thoughts instead of the tranquilizer dart. *They know. They know all about Dr. Sova and me.*

Chauncy realized his face had given him away. There was no point in trying to bluff. "All right, who are you people? Why didn't you just hire me to translate the Mayan Code, instead of abducting me? Better yet, why didn't you just get

Dr. Sova to translate it for you?"

Santo smiled; his logic was getting results. He crossed his arms and spoke. "Well, let's start from the beginning, shall we? You would not have come voluntarily if you had known who we are, and you are not the type to take on a job when you don't know full details of who you're working for. So we had to use, shall we say, a little persuasion."

"I've already surmised that you are criminals," Chauncy said.

Santo's smile widened, causing his eyes to become mere slits in his face, and then he went somber again. "Dr. Sova was a good friend of yours, so you probably know all about his gambling habit. Let me inform you of more recent events. After you left Mexico, he completely lost control. His debts mounted until he was desperate.

"He met some members of our organization who saw his value. He had a good head for finances despite his gambling problem. My employer offered him an opportunity to work off his debts. For quite a while things went well. But it was only a matter of time before his habit came back to haunt him. After he used up his own money, he began using my employer's: first hundreds, then thousands.

"Of course we could never tolerate that. But somehow Dr. Sova found out about our plans to deal with him. He disappeared with one million."

"A million!" Chauncy said, completely amazed. "Pesos or dollars?"

"Dollars, Mr. Rollock, one million American greenbacks! He took the money and hid it somewhere in the jungle. We caught up with him as he was trying to leave the country, apparently planning to return when he thought it was safe. Those who tortured him were unskilled. He died without revealing the location of the money and they threw him into a *cenote* with a boulder tied to his neck."

Chauncy closed his eyes in grief. The Mayans had used

those large, circular, limestone sinkholes called *cenotes* as a repository for human sacrifices. The mental visuals of seeing Dr. Sova unceremoniously tossed into a watery grave pained him. Doctor Sova wasn't perfect, but he had been a friend and mentor to Chauncy. Perhaps he should have made a greater effort to talk to Dr. Sova about his habit, or tried harder to reach him during the five years since they had been together.

But now it was too late.

Santo continued. "What a symbolic way to die, at least if you are an archaeologist. Anyway, all we found was this."

He pulled a scroll-like paper from his briefcase and unrolled it. On it were a series of Mayan glyphs.

"As you can see, the good doctor wrote in his Mayan Code. In better times, Dr. Sova had mentioned that only two people on earth knew how to decipher the code. The first, of course, was him, and the second was *you*. All we are asking is that you decipher it. Once we find the money he took from us, we let you go. It's that simple."

Anger washed over Chauncy. "You killed Doctor Sova? How dare you!"

Santo stood up and the two bodyguards stepped forward, muscles tensed for action.

"He got what he deserved," Santo abruptly replied. "We want to know where the money is hidden! You will start on this project now. As you can see, we've done our best to accommodate you, and you have all the materials you will need. Food will be delivered twice a day, and we will be checking on your progress. I do hope the love you have for your family will motivate you to hurry." He turned on his heel and his bodyguards followed him out.

The reference to his family cut like a knife. I hope to God that they never find out there is another person who knows the Mayan Code, he thought.

There was a loud knock on Anita's hotel door. "Who is it?"

she asked, her voice quailed.

"It's us, Marlo and Gloria."

She quickly opened the door. They could tell she had been crying and gave her a hug after she let them in.

"I couldn't sleep at all last night. I have been so worried about poor Chauncy. I hope he's okay," she said in a shaky voice.

Marlo tried to sound calm. "Well, the note mentioned that as long as we do not contact the authorities, he'll be fine. Kidnappings and abductions are becoming common down here. Let's just sit tight and see what they want. Most likely a large sum of money will soon be requested of us."

"If it's money, they should have contacted us by now," Gloria said.

Anita walked toward the window, wiping away a tear. "Well, Chauncy always taught me to remain calm during difficult situations, to try and think things out and not act out of sheer emotion. 'Emotions and panic can kill you' he always says. I won't panic. I won't let my nerves get the best of me."

"Yeah," Marlo agreed. "He taught me the same thing when we were down in Chile. I nearly learned it the hard way. Take a deep breath and try to relax."

A knock at the door startled them. Marlo jumped up. Walking toward the door, fists clenched, he said, "Who is it?"

"Front desk sir, I have a message for the occupant of this room," a woman's voice answered.

Marlo glanced through the peephole at the uniformed clerk. Opening the door, he quickly took the envelope, thanked her brusquely and shut the door.

He handed the envelope to Anita, who sat down and nervously opened it.

"What does it say, Mom?" Troy asked.

She unfolded the letter inside and read it aloud:

"Mr. Rollock is in good health. When he is finished with his assignment, he will be released. If you want to see him alive again, do not contact the authorities."

Anita stared vacantly as she thought out loud. "They don't want any money? But then what could they want?"

Marlo scratched his head, his brow furrowed. "Well, there goes my abduction theory. Assignment? This is bizarre!"

Gloria sat down on the couch next to Anita. "I guess we'll just have to sit tight until things work out."

Troy sat down on the floor and crossed his arms. "I wish I could go rescue Dad."

Chauncy stared blankly at the scroll lying on the desk in front of him. After five years his memory of the code was rusty. He knew the translated code could be would be gibberish to anyone but the author. Death threats didn't make it easier.

So many things could go wrong. Suppose the translation was correct, but the money wasn't where the scroll said it would be? What if the writing was misleading? Would his captors accuse him of lying or deliberately stalling? Would he then be tortured and murdered just like Dr. Sova? Would they then turn on his wife and child?

He propped his elbows on the desk and lowered his head onto his hands, rubbing his face and eyes as he tried to calm himself. Emotion and panic would kill him. He heaved a sigh and returned his attention to the scroll and what Dr. Sova had taught him about the Mayan language.

Ancient manuscripts such as the *Popol Vuh,* or *Book of the Community,* had barely survived. The *Popol Vuh* had been a collection of ancient myths written by a young Mayan noble named Quiche Maya, and it was instrumental in helping archaeologists on the path to learning the written Mayan language. The most famous, and most helpful, book had been the *Madrid Codex.* That codex had been rescued from oblivion in the 19th century in Spain, and had proven to be invaluable in deciphering the Mayan script.

Chauncy smiled, recalling the words of his mentor. "They don't teach you these things in the universities or books, Chauncy! No, but you must always use your head, your brain, your thinking ability to its fullest potential if you want to become successful."

Chauncy's mind wandered back to the past when he met Dr. Sova. The initial testing, the slow work on the temple, the startling revelation at the hacienda in Merida, the long days and nights learning the Mayan language and practicing the Mayan Code with him, the many days of being the student of the greatest linguist in the world, the dangerous adventure with the rebels and their wannabe leader. Then there were the long months of learning before their paths had separated.

Chauncy snapped back to reality. They were separated permanently. Those 'good old days' were gone, as was Dr. Sova himself. Despite the doctor's own admonition to "always use your head," he had succumbed to his own vices and been killed for it. If a man so intelligent could fail, Chauncy knew he had his work cut out for him if he wanted to avoid the same fate.

Taking a deep breath, he once more focused on the scroll in front of him.

CHAPTER FIVE

Chauncy awoke with a start. His neck hurt terribly. After a few disoriented moments, he realized he had fallen asleep with his head on the desk. Sitting up, he rubbed his neck, grimacing. He hadn't fallen asleep at his work desk in ages.

He rubbed his eyes, trying to wake up. He couldn't remember how late he was up last night, scribbling away as he tried to translate the message, and trying to come up with a plan. He had an inkling of an idea. He knew from past experience that if he pushed the idea too hard he would lose it.

He opened his eyes and stared again at the scroll. Within the cryptic symbols was the location of one million dollars. *The filthy scoundrels,* he thought sullenly. *That ill-gotten money probably cost a whole lot of innocent blood.*

He heard the jingling of keys and turned toward the door as it swung open. Santo Domingo was accompanied by the same guards as yesterday. One carried steaming food on a plastic tray. After putting it on the table, he returned to Domingo's side.

"Your breakfast is here," Santo announced with a smile. "How is the project coming along?"

Chauncy stood up and made his way toward the table. "Well, keep in mind that this is only the second day that I have been here. If you don't count the time I was unconscious, this will be the first full day. This isn't going to be an easy project, Mr. Domingo, but I am positive that I will have the document translated for you in a week or so."

Santo's cheerfulness evaporated. "That is not acceptable!"

His tone left no room for argument. "It is too much time, Mr. Rollock. We need to find the money soon. Speed up the translation!"

"I will try my best, Mr. Domingo. Keep in mind that we are dealing with cryptic language, and that I must decipher, translate, and then somehow understand the meaning behind the translation. It's no easy task."

The three men headed for the door. Santo stopped for a moment before leaving and turned to look at Chauncy. "Work faster, Mr. Rollock. And do not try to bluff me."

The sound of the heavy metal door seemed to bounce around Chauncy's mind along with the warning. *These people are not going to play around.* Quickly finishing the plate of *papas con huevos*, a potato and egg mixture, he got back to work.

Santo returned twice, the second time with a plate of tacos. Both visits were brief; apparently Santo was satisfied with watching Chauncy work instead of interrogating him.

There was no clock in the room, but Chauncy figured it was close to ten o'clock at night by the time he called it quits. He stumbled over to the bed, pulled the light-switch cord, and flopped down.

Despite the strain of the day's work, his brain apparently wasn't done. In his mind's eye he saw the Mayan hieroglyphs over and over again. The cryptic message Dr. Sova had left wouldn't leave his mind.

It wasn't until the next morning that he realized what his brain had been trying to tell him.

He was already hard at work when Santo brought breakfast. This time, the other guard held a metal folding chair, and for a split second Chauncy feared that they had moved past threats and were going to beat him. But the guard simply set the chair a few feet away and Santo sat down.

"So," he said, with a grim smile. "Let's see your progress."

Once Chauncy's pulse returned to normal, he spoke, consulting his notes. "Well, I have managed to translate some of it. This is what I have so far:

"The mighty sacred triangle, where kings once ruled.

The three mighty cities, there is where you will begin."

Santo raised his eyebrows. "What does that mean?"

Chauncy stared at his notes, a perplexed look on his face. "It's too early into the translation to say for sure, Mr. Domingo. This may be indicating where the money is, or it may just be symbolic. The reference to 'where you will begin' implies to me that it is indeed referring to the money, so I ask you to please be patient with me. By tonight I should have finished the paragraph."

Santo's face lit up. "Excellent! At least some progress has been made."

Noting Santo's mood, Chauncy decided to risk the crazy idea he'd had the night before. He trembled. If he could pull this off, he would be free. Of course if he didn't, he would die.

"Mr. Domingo, I was wondering if I might ask a favor of you?"

Santo squinted. Peering at Chauncy, he asked, "What do you want?"

Chauncy took a quick breath and plunged in. "You see, Mr. Domingo, I have been thinking and worrying about a very important matter. It has to do with my wife, Anita. She suffers from a chronic case of nerves and panics easily. Once the panic takes hold, who knows what she will do. I fear that she might even go to the authorities, and that would jeopardize both my life and the translation of this document! I would like to send her a video of me. You can even write a script for me to read."

Chauncy held his breath as Santo stared at the ceiling, stroking his chin. "Well," he said slowly, "I guess if I write the script, I don't see any harm in this. Let me run this by the boss."

Evidently still thinking, Santo and the guards left, taking the folding chair with them.

Chauncy let his breath out slowly, a trickle of sweat winding its way down his forehead. So far, so good! He returned his attention to the scroll and tried to focus on the translation.

In the morning when the trio brought breakfast, Santo asked for a progress report. Chauncy paused his scribbling and read from his clipboard:

"The mighty sacred triangle, where kings once ruled.
The three mighty cities, there is where you will begin.
One of the three is where it will be. Three worlds there are
The heavens and the middle world and the underworld."

Santo stared at Chauncy, clearly awaiting an explanation. Chauncy looked over the symbols on his clipboard for a moment before turning to Santo and speaking.

"We are getting closer. Since the doctor used symbolic language, I'll need to analyze the complete translation to decipher it."

Santo looked nervous. "My boss is getting anxious, Mr. Rollock. You must hurry and get this deciphered. We have pressing matters to attend to."

"I am doing the best I can, Mr. Domingo."

"Good," Santo said. "The boss says you can make the video for your wife—after you finish deciphering the Mayan Code."

Chauncy nodded. "I understand."

The three took their leave to the familiar sounds of door and keys and ascending footsteps.

For the first time in days, Chauncy smiled.

At the following morning's breakfast report, Chauncy had excellent news. "I'm very excited, Mr. Domingo. I've finished the translation."

"The mighty sacred triangle, where kings once ruled.
The three mighty cities, there is where you will begin.
One of the three is where it will be. Three worlds there are
The heavens and the middle world and the under-
world. In them a king lies, under him it must be.
Where I once was."

He paused for a moment. "I believe this is what the doctor meant to write. The Mayan Code was designed to be phonetic, so some of the words may sound like what I just said, but have an entirely different meaning. Either way, you can tell your boss that I have finished the text. Now all I have to do is decipher the meaning behind the words."

Santo wiped his face with a handkerchief. Heaving a big sigh, he then smiled broadly. "Good, good! It has been almost a week now; my boss has been anxious. I will tell him how far you have come. Perhaps tomorrow you will meet him." Santo left.

The following morning Santo and the guards caught Chauncy's enthusiasm even before Chauncy announced:

"Mr. Domingo! Call your boss, for I believe I know where the money is!"

Santo barked an order to one of the guards who ran from the room. Santo turned to Chauncy, his expression a mixture of threat and joy. "I hope you are right, Mr. Rollock."

In moments, Chauncy heard footsteps on the stairs. A single voice spoke excitedly. As they entered the room Chauncy tried to place the familiar figure following.

He spoke with only the slightest trace of an accent. "Good morning, Mr. Rollock. Please allow me to introduce myself: I am Jose Padilla Madrid."

"Mr. Madrid … I … I didn't know that I was working for you!" Chauncy gasped.

Madrid smiled. "Ah, Mr. Rollock, does it matter if I am who I am or just a petty thief? Now let's get down to business, shall we? As Mr. Domingo has had occasion to tell you, I have some important matters to take care of before leaving the country. So the sooner we get to the bottom of this 'Mayan Code' the better."

Chauncy took a deep nervous breath, it took a few seconds for him to calm down, if such a thing were possible. He sat down to explain the mystery of the puzzling code. "Dr. Sova was a clever man. He disguised the answer not only in Mayan hieroglyphs, but in a riddle. One must understand a little about the Mayan culture to uncover the answer, or else the message would mean nothing. Let's start with the first sentence:

'The mighty sacred triangle, where kings once ruled'

"This refers to the geographical location of the extent of the Maya civilization. If you look at this map," Chauncy said, pointing to a map of the Yucatan peninsula, "You will see that the Maya empire spread through Mexico, Guatemala, Belize, Honduras and El Salvador. The next line:

"*The three mighty cities,*"

"This refers to Tikal or Copan, Palenque and Chichen Itza. If you connect these cities, it makes a triangle—like this."

Chauncy took out a pencil and drew a line between the three cities, which turned out to form a nearly perfect triangle.

"Now the rest of the second sentence:

"*is where you will begin.*"

"That tells us we need to look within this 'mighty sacred triangle.'"

Madrid shook his head, scowling. "That's too large an area to search."

"I know," Chauncy added. "Ah, that is what the next sentence is for!

"*One of the three is where it will be.*"

"We now narrow it down to one of the three cities. Chichen Itza, Palenque, or Copan. Which do you think it is? The answer is in the following verses, but first we have to understand something about their religious beliefs."

Chauncy was still very nervous; he paused to catch his breath. "Here is what the next part says:

Three worlds there are: the heavens and the middle world and the underworld."

"The Mayans were firm believers in the existence of three worlds. The 'heavens above' means the first world, the earth was the 'middle world' and the 'underworld' was the place of the dead."

Santo spoke up. "Well, the money must be in the middle world then."

"Sounds reasonable," Chauncy said. "Keep in mind, however, that Doctor Sova was using symbolic language. Consequently, the money is hidden underneath something. That's why he makes reference to the underworld. One would also presume that he is speaking about a cave, right? Not so, for the Mayan word for cave is *Xibalba*. However, Dr. Sova used the word *K'nich Yenal* for *underworld*."

"What does that mean?" Madrid asked in an exasperated tone.

Chauncy explained. "*K'nich Yenal* is another name for the underworld, except that it is also the name of a Mayan god. It can mean cave, or jaguar-god. The jaguar-god is one of the underworld gods and is the protector of royal kings. So the use of *K'nich Yenal* is used in reference to a king. This makes sense because the text continues:

"*In them a king lies, under him it must be*."

"This is where the translation became difficult. The word Dr. Sova used for king is 'Chak,' which also happens to be the name of the rain god. So I asked myself, is he making reference to the rain god Chak, or to the name of King Chac? After much thought I realized he was referring to a buried king! For many decades archaeologists had no idea that the Mayan pyramids were also used as tombs; it was believed that only the Egyptian pyramids were. However, in 1949 a

Mexican archaeologist by the name of Alberto Ruz discovered King Paca inside a pyramid. With that fact in mind, I realized that Dr. Sova was making reference to a tomb in the underworld, or inside of a Mayan pyramid. King Chac was found in Palenque by Dr. Sova, therefore he can rightfully say about himself:

"*Where I once was*."

"The money is in Palenque, deep inside Temple #22 where King Chac's remains were discovered. It makes perfect sense. Dr. Sova knew the area well."

Madrid was impressed. "Well, Mr. Rollock, I can see it was no mistake to have you brought here to help us decipher the Mayan Code. So Dr. Sova tried to outsmart me! What an idiot! Nobody outsmarts me."

Madrid's expression suddenly turned gloomy. "Now we make an expedition to Palenque and retrieve the money. How many men will we need, and how difficult will it be to get inside that tomb?"

Chauncy stood up and rubbed his chin. "It has been some time since I last visited the area. If we assume that no more excavations have been made since then, I don't think it will be very difficult to enter the tomb. Perhaps Dr. Sova didn't have had anyone help him, therefore the five of us will suffice."

Madrid nodded once, sharply, and spoke. "Tomorrow we go to Palenque. You may want to wash and shave now. As you requested, you'll be making a video."

Chauncy smiled.

CHAPTER SIX

When Marlo and Gloria answered Anita's rapid knocking at their hotel door, she seemed excited.

"Marlo, Gloria, look what someone brought me. It's a message from Chauncy! It was delivered to me from the front desk a few minutes ago."

Marlo raised an eyebrow. "A movie, are you saying you have a message from Chauncy and it's in a movie? That's crazy!"

"Apparently so," Anita replied as they walked to the DVD player.

She inserted the disc into the player and fiddled with the buttons. The blue screen of the TV instantly disappeared and the image of Chauncy Rollock came on the screen.

"Hey, it's Dad!" Troy shouted.

Anita stared at the screen. "Shhh!"

Chauncy was clean-shaven and was wearing a plain brown shirt and dark pants. Behind him was a wooden desk. Behind that was a map of Yucatan pinned to the wall. Next to the map was a large poster with handwritten Mayan glyphs.

Chauncy began to speak, his voice slow, deliberate and clear. It was obvious that he had been told to speak in an emotionless monotone and that he was reading a prearranged script. They all listened with interest.

"*My dear Anita, as you can see I am doing fine. They are treating me well. When my assignment is done I will then be free to see you again. Please do not attempt to call the authorities. Give my love to all, especially to our son Troy. I love you. Goodbye.*"

The recording stopped and the television screen went blank. No one spoke.

Gloria turned to Anita while Marlo stood up to turn off the DVD player. "That's it? At least he does look well. I mean, they aren't torturing him or anything like that." Gloria said.

Anita didn't even register the words. Instead, she sat mesmerized, staring at the blank screen. "Play it again, Marlo," she whispered, sounding preoccupied.

Marlo glanced at her quizzically, but shrugged and pressed the play button.

Anita's eyes widened. When it was over, she spoke again, her voice filled with excitement. "Run it again, Marlo. You are not going to believe what I saw! Stop! Pause it, right there!"

Marlo stared at the screen. It was exactly the same as it had been before. He turned to look at Anita. "What is it? What do you see that I don't? You're freaking me out."

Anita's breathing was heavy with fear or excitement, or maybe both. "Okay, I'll tell you," she said, her eyes glued to the TV screen. "But you're not going to believe me. Chauncy sent me a message, he's asking for help!"

Marlo looked at the screen for a moment then back at Anita. "Are you sure? It's obvious he's reading a script, and he's not moving at all."

"It's what he *wrote* in the background," she exclaimed, pointing to the TV screen.

In unison they all looked at the screen. Behind Chauncy was the map of Yucatan and the poster with the Mayan hieroglyphs.

"Okay, fair enough," Marlo stated. "But all I see are Mayan hieroglyphs and I can't understand them."

"Neither can I," Gloria chimed in.

Anita looked at each of them. "I know you can't, but I can. Chauncy taught me the Mayan Code!"

"You *know* the Mayan Code?" Marlo asked.

"Yes, I do," Anita said. "Well...sort of. There are only three people in the world that know it: Chauncy and I, and a French archaeologist, Doctor Sova. Chauncy worked with Dr. Sova some time ago. They even co-wrote a book."

"Yeah, yeah, I remember now," Marlo said as he snapped his fingers. "I remember Chauncy mentioned the Mayan Code while we were in Chile."

"Wait a minute, why couldn't they get this, this Dr. Soso to decode the hieroglyphs?" Gloria said.

"Dr. Sova," Anita corrected her. "I don't know why they couldn't get him. Maybe he's in France and these kidnappers knew Chauncy was coming to Yucatan. Of course, Dr. Sova doesn't know that Chauncy taught me basic Mayan words. It's hard to keep secrets when you're married. Besides it was a fun way to communicate with Chauncy when he was away."

"Then I wonder what they are looking for?" Marlo said, looking at the television.

"I don't know. But if you look at the scene, it's obvious they have him doing some kind of Mayan translation. Otherwise the presence of the hieroglyphs would have clued them in to his message. The point is that Chauncy has this message for me and he's definitely trying to communicate with me."

"What is Dad trying to tell you, Mom?" Troy asked.

"Well, I haven't used the code in a long time, but the opening is code for *'Anita, my love.'* Chauncy always started his code messages to me with those glyphs. I can't tell what the rest says yet. I need to study it for a while. Can you both do me a favor? Take Troy with you for the rest of the day and bring me some dinner later on. I need to be alone for a while."

Gloria took Troy's hand. "Sure, Anita, don't worry. We'll find some fun ways to entertain him."

Anita gave Troy a reassuring hug. Once the three were gone, she closed the door after them. A great sense of doom enveloped her. *God, I don't think I can go through with this!*

She paced around the room, her mind and emotions running wild. Somehow she would have to properly translate the cryptic Mayan Code, something she hadn't done for years.

She thought of Troy. How would he fare if he were suddenly deprived of his father? How would he react if he ever found out that it was his mother who had failed them?

Tears streamed down her face as she gazed out the window. Down on the beach, tourists were throwing beach balls, swimming and running, oblivious to the danger to her family. She had a sudden urge to run and tell the whole world about her plight.

But the warning not to notify the authorities was branded into her memory. No amount of emotion could override that.

She wiped her tears away and took a deep, shuddering breath in an effort to calm herself. No amount of crying, no amount of wishing was going to save her husband. Whether she liked it or not, the fate of her family was in *her* hands. Only logic would get them all out of this. She sat down in front of the TV and copied the code. Four hours later she finally came to a translation:

ANTMLVHLPFRMAYOAFARMERTELLIONTHATSPANISHBIRDYUCATAN

The first part was easy as she had already translated it: ANTMLV came out to 'Anita, my love.' Chauncy had taught her to isolate the words that were easily recognizable. After highlighting them, she came to this:

HLPFRMAYOA-FARMER-TELL-LION-THT-SPANISH-BIRD-YUCATAN

She stared at the letters, her mind whirling with possibilities. HLP was phonetic for "Help." FRM became "From"—but what was AYOA? Remembering what Chauncy had taught her, she spoke out loud. "Aye oh ahh ... aye-oh-ahh ... that's it! Iowa!"

She had something! "Anita, my love, help from Iowa farmer ..."

Within a few moments she had the rest of the message. She stared at the message, her hope fading.

Anita-my-love-help-from-Iowa-farmer-tell-lion-Spanish-bird-Yucatan

It made no sense. The first part was easy enough to understand, but what "lion" was she supposed to tell? And what was she supposed to tell him/her/it? What was the Spanish bird?

She ran her hands through her hair, frustration and hopelessness tugging at her. She felt like crying again; the stress of knowing that if she was improperly translating the message, it would mean her husband's life.

She gritted her teeth and remembered Chauncy's words: Emotions can kill you. They had never been truer. Be strong, Anita, you can do it. You've already come this far.

The others returned at dinnertime. Troy carried a covered plate.

"I brought your favorite, Mom, two chicken enchiladas, with rice and beans of course."

Smiling, Anita invited them in, took the plate from Troy and gave him a hug. "I have some good news and some bad news," she announced. "I've decoded and translated the message!"

"That's very good news, I think." Marlo was visibly relieved.

"What's the bad news?" Gloria asked with fear in her voice.

Anita's smile faded. "Chauncy is in a lot of trouble and in bad company. I mean really bad company."

"What do you mean?" Marlo warily asked. "You're talking in circles again."

Anita put her dinner on the table and they all sat down.

"These are the words that I put together from Chauncy's message. "'Anita my love, get help from the Iowan farmer and tell the lion that his Spanish bird is in Yucatan.'"

Marlo and Gloria traded glances.

"Huh? What does that mean?" Gloria asked.

Marlo scratched his head. "Great! We're right back where we started: clueless."

Anita continued with her explanation. "Let's start from the beginning. First of all, Chauncy is requesting that I get help from an Iowan farmer. I know who he is talking about: Kelly Sorenson."

"Kelly who? Who is she?" A perplexed Gloria asked.

"No, not a she, it's a he. Kelly Sorenson is a good friend of ours who lives in Iowa. Chauncy saved his life many years ago, and Kelly swore that if Chauncy was ever in trouble, he would do all he could to help. Well, it's time to collect."

Marlo nodded. "Okay, what about the lion and the Spanish bird?"

Anita smiled. "How do you say "lion" in Spanish?"

"Leon," Gloria answered.

"Exactly, and what is the name of the military captain in Guadalajara?"

Troy beat them all to the punch. "Captain De Leon!"

"Very good Troy," Anita said, smiling. "Now, what is the capital of Spain?"

Marlo was getting irritated. "That's easy, it's Madrid. Come on, Anita, you're freaking me out again. We're not playing *Trivial Pursuit* now are we? What's your point?"

"Don't you see the message? Here, let me translate it into clear English:

Anita my love, go get help from Kelly Sorenson and tell Gustavo De Leon that Jose Padilla Madrid, the escaped jailbird, is in Yucatan."

Marlo stood up. "Anita, that's brilliant! Chauncy didn't marry no fool, that's for sure. Now let's get moving!"

Gloria spoke up. "Uh, hello, is anybody home? You guys are missing one very important factor—we're not supposed to contact the authorities."

Anita turned to Gloria. "Apparently Chauncy trusts De Leon. I have a plan, but leave that to me. I just need a small favor from you, Marlo."

Marlo raised his hand to stop her. "Let me guess—it involves a trip to Iowa."

"How perceptive of you!"

"And I suppose you have Mr. Sorenson's address in your head?" Marlo said with a smile.

"1843 N. 140th Lane," Anita replied with a larger smile. "I always used to send letters for Chauncy. It's in a rural area of southwest Iowa. I'll call the airport and make reservations for you."

CHAPTER SEVEN

The plane flew toward Des Moines, Iowa, with the northern hemisphere in deep winter. It was such a different world from where Marlo had come, but he had been in similar weather only a couple of weeks ago. Relaxing in his airline seat, his mind wandered back to the day when this recent adventure had started, when he had sat in Chauncy's spacious ranch house, warming himself in front of a roaring fire. He could still smell the pinewood, a scent that had permeated the entire house and had gone a long way to fostering a contented feeling. He had reminisced with Chauncy, noticing how little his friend had changed in three years; his short frame still powerfully built, but his blond hair more gray. Then Chauncy had revealed the plane tickets, and Marlo had looked forward to the trip down to Cancun. But life was funny in a strange way. Marlo's vacation was cut short by the sudden change of events.

The bumpy landing jarred him out of his musings. The long walkway that connected the plane to the airport was a welcome relief, but he could still feel the chill. After a few confusing minutes he found the car rental place, provided his information, and was directed to the parking lot. Once outside, he buttoned his large overcoat and shivered as he walked rapidly to his car.

Within an hour he had made it out of the bustling metropolis of Des Moines and was driving toward the farmlands of the great Midwest. Marlo found it hard to believe that somewhere in Iowa, on some rural farm, was a man who would be able to help Chauncy out of his predicament. Marlo couldn't even begin to fathom the connection; he had left too quickly to ask Anita any questions or details. He had his orders: find Kelly Sorenson and bring him to Yucatan.

He took a sip of his hot coffee and glanced at the map again. He wondered how a simple vacation had turned into this. He hoped that this trip would prove successful. What would he do if he returned empty-handed?

An hour later Marlo left the freeway and turned north. He passed rolling hills so unlike the mountains he was used to. The barren brown soil with patches of melting snow was unappealing, but Marlo knew that in a few months the empty fields would be brimming with corn and soybeans.

He pulled onto a gravel road and drove east, passing several white two-story farmhouses. When he finally found the address, his heart sank after he got a good look at the house through the trees. He glanced at the address on the piece of paper in his hand, then back again at the house. This was indeed the place.

The dilapidated house looked abandoned. Marlo surveyed the area and then exited the car and walked across the property.

Rusting farm equipment was everywhere. Tall brown weeds grew where they wanted. Engine parts were scattered around four abandoned cars. Marlo heard a sound from the barn. He went over to investigate and was overwhelmed by the smell. *Hogs!*

He could only imagine what the place smelled like in the summer when the heat and humidity were at their zenith! He returned to the house, a bit more confident that someone did indeed live here. The beasts had to be fed and he doubted that someone would travel snow-filled roads just to feed some hogs in an abandoned barn.

He walked up a few steps to the front door. With no doorbell in sight, he knocked loudly. He heard nothing. After a few moments he knocked again, even louder.

No answer.

Marlo had almost given up when he heard the sound of shuffling feet within. *Ah, someone is here.*

The front door took a while to unlock. Finally the door opened and a medium-built older man stuck his face out into the cold. He appeared to be in his late fifties. Marlo's gaze brushed passed the wrinkled face, the large nose, the bald head, and focused on the man's bloodshot eyes.

In a gruff voice he demanded, "Are you one of Jehovah's Witnesses?"

"Uh, no sir, I …."

"Are you a stinkin' salesman? Because if you are, then I'm gonna blow yer legs off if you don't git off my property!"

"No, no!" Marlo blurted. "Chauncy needs your help!"

The man's belligerent expression abruptly disappeared. "Chauncy, you mean my buddy, Chauncy Rollock?"

Marlo nodded and the old man opened the door. "Well, why didn't you say so in the first place, son? Come on in. Whatcha doing out in the cold?"

The inside of the house was warmer but didn't look any better than the outside. The furniture looked as old as the house and there was a musty smell. A handful of cats glared at Marlo and he glared back. He was then startled by a friendly dog licking his hand.

"Here, sit here," the old man said, motioning Marlo to sit on an old sofa. He removed a pile of old newspapers, which, like everything else, seemed to have been accumulating since the house was built.

"My name is Kelly, Kelly Sorenson. What did you say your name was, boy?"

"Oh, I'm sorry, I didn't introduce myself. My name is Marlo Gund. Chauncy and I work together. But we're also good friends."

Kelly walked over to his stove. "Want some coffee, Mr.

Gund?"

"Uh, no thank you; I just had some," Marlo said quickly. He was dying for another cup, but not from that kitchen.

Kelly ignored the negative response and placed a full cup in front of Marlo before taking a seat in an ancient armchair. "So tell me, son, what kind of trouble is Chauncy in?"

"Well, I'll tell you the edited version. I had been involved with Chauncy about three years ago on an archaeological expedition to Chile. Life got in the way afterwards and we hadn't seen each other in a while, so last week Chauncy invited my wife and me to his house and surprised us with tickets to Cancun for a vacation with his family. While we were in Cancun, Chauncy was kidnapped, apparently by Jose Padilla Madrid, the drug lord. Long story short, we received a cryptic message from Chauncy that instructed us to get your help, Mr. Sorenson. He specifically asked for you! That's why I'm here today. We need your help."

Kelly rubbed his chin, staring out the window. "That man sure has a knack for getting into the strangest types of trouble."

"Amen to that!" Marlo exclaimed.

"And where in Mexico did you say this happened?"

"This happened in Cancun, the Yucatan peninsula."

A pained expression came over Kelly's face as he closed his eyes. "Oh no," he muttered, almost shaking. Kelly opened his eyes. "I hate the jungle, Mr. Gund. I hate it with a passion! I have promised myself that I would never ever set foot again in a jungle. I'm sorry. I wish I could help poor Chauncy."

"But—but Mr. Sorenson," he pleaded. "Chauncy really needs your help. He specifically asked for you!"

Kelly stood and walked to the window. He stared outside at the patchy snow-filled landscape, rubbed his face and took a deep breath.

"I was born here in Iowa, I was raised here on this farm, and so was my dad and my dad's dad. But the war came and soon I found myself flying choppers in 'Nam. It was a dreadful, dreadful war, son, most likely before you were born. It was my job to do search-and-rescue missions. I had to airlift wounded men from the battlefield, in the jungle."

He paused for a moment, swallowing. "Do you know what it's like to pull injured men from the jungle?" he asked, his eyes gazing off into the past. "They's all screamin' and yellin' in pain, you know. Most o' the time they were missing limbs; blood all over the place. I knew that with some of these boys, if they survived, they'd be livin' the rest o' their lives in wheelchairs. It was a sad thing to experience, son."

He took another breath, closed his eyes, and shuddered. "It was only a matter of time before I got hit." Kelly pulled up his long-sleeved shirt. A horrible scar twisted its way up his left arm.

"I was hurt bad and I was bleeding all over the place. I had to pull the chopper away from the firing line. I had to leave the wounded behind—it was a terrible, horrible thing, boy. I left around twenty wounded men in the jungle 'cause I could barely fly the chopper, know what I mean? I heard their voices on my radio. I can still hear their voices to this day.

"What was I to do? We would have all died, me and the men I'd already pulled from an earlier job! That experience, it left me crazy in the head. Post-trauma something or other the doctors said, know what I mean"? Kelly ran a nervous hand over his head. The memories were too traumatizing.

"After the war I started having terrible nightmares! I would see these men in my dreams, hear them screaming at me, and I'd see 'em with their limbs all blown off, and asking me why I left 'em, why I abandoned them; you don't know how terrible it was, boy, no idea what the mind can do to you. I dreamt about their mothers spitting on me, screaming at me and cursing me …."

He wiped his face with his shirtsleeve. After taking a few shallow breaths he continued. "It wasn't fair—I was just a young man. I wouldn't wish this on anyone, not even my worst enemy. I had just been trying my best to serve my country and get through the war! I couldn't stand the nightmares anymore, so I took to drink and drugs to forget the pain. It wasn't long before I was living on the streets.

"Chauncy found me on a street in Wyoming. He must o' felt sorry for me. He took me to a restaurant and fed me. We was talkin' for a while and he found out about my past. 'So you know how to fly helicopters?' he asked. Well, o' course I did, and I said so. One thing lead to another and before I knew it, he'd cleaned me up and given me a job flying choppers for him, airliftin' giant pieces of granite from some excavation site in the canyons of the Dakota Badlands. I worked for Chauncy on and off for years. Then my dad died and I decided to come back to the farm. I've been farmin' and raisin' hogs for the last ten years or so. But all thanks to Chauncy. He saved my life. I woulda been dead long 'fore now, the way I was going."

Marlo had a pained expression. "I'm really sorry for what you went through, Mr. Sorenson. No doubt it was a very horrible experience. And I understand if you feel you can't go down to Cancun and help Chauncy. I guess I'll have to tell Anita why I came back empty-handed."

Marlo stood up, sighed, and pulled on his gloves and jacket. "It won't be easy to tell her. I'm not sure how she'll react to more bad news."

Kelly stared at the floor, then looked up and saw Marlo slowly heading for the door. "Anita, eh?" he asked.

"Yes, Anita. This is breaking her heart."

Kelly winced. "She was good to me too. She fed me well when I worked for Chauncy."

"She is going through a horrible ordeal," Marlo said.

Kelly clenched his teeth. "She was such a sweetheart. I will never forget her kindness."

"There is only one way to show your appreciation." Marlo

pleaded .

Kelly's face was downcast. "I know."

There was a moment of silence. Marlo sensed he was done. He figured the old man wasn't going to budge, so he slowly made his way out the door. He turned to see him still sitting there all forlorn. Marlo silently berated himself. Had he come all this way just to fail in his mission? It was too much for him to bear. Standing out in the cold he spread his arms out in a pleading gesture. "Come on! You gotta come with me! There's no way can go back empty handed! I can help you, man. I'm serious. I can walk you through this. Just don't let Anita down!"

Kelly peered pensively at Marlo.

Marlo sensed Kelly was going to capitulate. "Anita was crying when I left her!"

Kelly finally broke. "Ah! You drive a hard bargain, son. Anita has always been very good to me. I suppose I can't break her heart, can I?"

Marlo grinned as he turned to face Kelly. "Got any plans?"

Kelly scratched his chin as he went into deep thought. "Well, I got a buddy down in Belize, he was my gunner back in 'Nam. He's different from me—he loves the jungle! But he don't like the States, he says there is too much racism you know, 'cause he's black. So he decided to move to Belize, 'cause they speak English there. Anyhow, he's a chopper mechanic and I know he can set us up with a good bird."

"So you'll really do it, Mr. Sorenson?"

A smile crept across the older man's face. "Call me Kelly, and I suppose so! But I don't suppose you got a plane ticket for me?"

"Actually, Anita insisted. I don't know if she knew or just hoped. You'd best grab anything you want to take with you."

Kelly walked to a dresser in the hallway. He opened the top drawer and pulled out a passport and a dirty white envelope. Glancing inside the envelope, he smiled and shoved it in his shirt pocket.

Kelly returned to the living room. "Chauncy ain't no dummy, son," he said as he patted the pocket that contained the envelope. "He knew I was the best one to help him outta this mess. Now if you'll be so kind as to stop by my neighbor's on our way to the airport, I can tell him to look after my hogs, dogs, and cats."

As the two drove down the gravel road, dark storm clouds filled the sky. But for Marlo, the future looked just a little brighter.

CHAPTER EIGHT

Blindfolded and handcuffed, Chauncy tried to stay calm. He kept in mind that they needed him alive to find the money. At the top of the stairs their footsteps echoed, as if in a large empty warehouse. A moment later he heard the telltale squeaking of a large door sliding open.

His senses were assaulted by the hot humid jungle air and the sounds of nature. Both were so different from the cool quiet of his basement prison. Even through his blindfold he could see the sunlight as they stepped from the warehouse. A guard held his head down and pushed him into a vehicle as its engine roared to life.

After quite a while, the vehicle they were in stopped and they transferred to another. To Chauncy's horror, this time it was a small plane. As much as he hated flying, flying blindfolded was even worse.

After Chauncy survived the flight and the landing there was the careening down a bumpy road in yet another vehicle. His captors finally removed the blindfold. He blinked against the harsh sunlight. He was in a Humvee with Domingo, Madrid and the two bodyguards. Thick vegetation surrounded the dirt road they drove on.

"We will be in Palenque in twenty minutes," Madrid announced. "From that point onward you will direct us to the pyramid."

"What about military roadblocks? Or tourists?" Chauncy asked.

Santo smiled. "Not to worry; that has all been dealt with."

"Temporarily," Madrid said, glaring at him in the mirror.

"I hope we are not delayed."

Chauncy looked out the window. "I hope so too."

Twenty minutes later, the Humvee stopped in a clearing in the jungle. Though it had been a long time, Chauncy recognized the area immediately. The guard and the driver were the first out, their weapons sweeping the area. They motioned all-clear and the others got out of the vehicle. The guards motioned Chauncy to the back of the Humvee, where they removed two large suitcases—and a set of ankle chains. The driver removed the handcuffs while the other guard shackled Chauncy's legs, then handed him the suitcases to carry.

"Quickly!" Madrid snapped. "Where to?"

Chauncy took a quick look at their map. "Temple #22 is straight ahead of us down this path."

As the group made their way through the jungle, the howling of monkeys and screeching of birds mixed with the unceasing whirring and clicking of millions of insects.

They passed smaller ruins covered with vegetation, where the jungle choked out man's incursions. The giant roots of ancient trees had long since tumbled these glorious buildings into disjointed masses of bricks. Like a mighty hand, the vegetation was slowly dismantling all traces of a once-powerful civilization.

"Do you know why the Maya disappeared?" Chauncy asked no one in particular as they continued their trek.

"No, why?" gasped Santo between breaths.

"It was due to deforestation, ecological disasters, hunger, war, overpopulation, mass migration to cities, less farmers in the rural areas, less production of food. They trusted in their gods to save them, and so they built more temples. The elite class was so isolated from the common worker that soon their society collapsed, the mighty empire vanished. There are many similarities with our generation, the same things are occurring today on a global scale. The only difference is that the gods have changed. The god that people worship today is money."

Santo simply grunted.

Stopping abruptly, Chauncy pointed and said, "There it is; Temple #22!"

He stared at the temple that had made such an impact on his life five years earlier, rising high above the jungle canopy, defying Nature's death grip on the lesser ruins. Centuries of wear and tear from the elements had removed any sharp features of the structure, but not its regal splendor.

After trudging through the heat of the jungle the climb up the steep stairs was excruciating. They stopped to rest more than once. Reaching the final step they passed under a stone canopy. Chauncy mentioned that this was probably where the priests performed their rituals.

Madrid wasn’t interested in a history class. He walked back and forth under the canopy looking down. "Where's the entrance?" he demanded.

Chauncy pointed to the floor. "Right here; see these flagstones?"

Madrid snapped his fingers and pointed to the flagstones. The guards swung their guns onto their backs and began pulling on the stones.

Headlamps strapped in place, four of them descended the triangular shaped tunnel. One guard remained outside while the other led the way down, his weapon at the ready. Despite the darkness and humidity of the tunnel Chauncy smiled, remembering the excitement of the first time he had come down this tunnel with Dr. Sova.

"What do we find at the bottom?" Santo asked. "Are the remains of the Mayan King still down there?"

"Of course not, King Chac's remains have been in a museum in Mexico City for the past five years, along with the sarcophagus, stone cover, and all the jewelry and other artifacts that had been found. All that is left down here are these steps and perhaps, one million dollars."

After what seemed like ages, the stairs ended and they entered the stifling darkness of the crypt. It was larger than the cramped stairs they had just descended, about twelve feet across.

Chauncy dropped the suitcases and crawled along the floor, peering closely at every crack. "It said 'under him it must be,' so I think it must be under the crypt. Ahh, I think I found a loose stone—come here!"

The guard helped him wipe away the sand covering the flagstones. One of them was indeed loose, and the guard ordered Chauncy to move out of the way as he lifted it up.

“How did Dr. Sova accomplish this task by himself?” Santo mused.

“He knew a lot of people who worked in this area. He could have bribed them to keep silent. Knowing him, he could have opened the temple in a sequential order, not disclosing the reason to his workers and then placed the money in the temple by himself.” Chauncy answered.

Santo grunted with approval at Chauncy’s explanation. “Makes sense.”

Underneath the stone was a square niche, and within this niche were two large wooden crates, their lids strapped shut. Even Chauncy was excited as the guard heaved one of the boxes from its niche and pried open the top.

Madrid was the first to react. "Ha! It's the money! We found the money!"

Chauncy let out a sigh of relief as he stepped back and watched. The men yelled and whooped with excitement as they clenched the money in their fists.

As the initial excitement passed, Madrid barked an order, "Quickly, get out the other box and fill the suitcases with the money. We have to get out of here!"

It was late at night when the crew finally arrived back at

the basement where Chauncy had been for that past week. Santo led him down to his room and told him that they would be leaving in two days; there were now many things to prepare. Santo also promised that they would release him at that time, but for now he should rest.

Chauncy hit the bed in sheer exhaustion. They had made him walk all the way back to the vehicle carrying two heavy suitcases full of money with his legs bound in chains. On top of that, his body was covered with insect bites, his arms and face were sunburned, and he had not eaten well.

He was miserable, physically and emotionally. He had no way of knowing if his wife had actually figured out his encrypted message. What if she hadn't? What if his plan wasn't working? What if they decided to kill him?

The next day Santo and his guards came into the room. He was holding a letter and a book. "Your wife is a very smart lady, Mr. Rollock."

"What do you mean, Mr. Domingo?" Chauncy's heart pounded. Do they know? Did they find out about the message?

Santo walked up to Chauncy and then turned to the desk. "She's a smart lady and also religiously inclined, wouldn't you say?"

Careful what you say! Chauncy thought. His heart pounded so hard that he imagined that Santo could hear it. He offered a half-hearted smile. "Yeah, I suppose; depends on the week. Why do you say that?"

"She left a Bible and a letter for you at the front desk of her hotel. She assumed, correctly, that our courier would pick them up and deliver them to us."

Chauncy licked suddenly dry lips, fearful of how to answer.

Santo continued. "We took the liberty, Mr. Rollock, of reading the letter and also examined the Bible, but we have found nothing wrong with them. You are now welcome to these two items. Early tomorrow morning, around three, we are leaving for good."

When Chauncy was alone again, he leaned against the wall, his heart pounding so fiercely it was difficult to breathe. When he had calmed down enough to walk to the desk, he picked up the letter with a trembling hand and read it:

Dear Chauncy,

I hope that all is well with you. We have been praying for your safe return. I hope the following scriptures will bring you relief. You will see from them how God's message comes together for your comfort.

Matthew 10:8

Proverbs 30:1

Exodus 2:23

Exodus 16:1

And the second set of scriptures will be of great spiritual comfort too.

Joshua 10:9

Genesis 8:9

Exodus 8:6

Please keep safe. I love you and hope to see you soon.

Your loving wife,

Anita

Chauncy found himself grinning as he read the letter. I used to play this with her when we were away from each other. If it wasn't the Mayan Code, it was the Bible Code!

He quickly started to look up the scriptures. In each, one word was underlined softly in pencil.

Matthew 10:8 "...you ***received*** *free, give free."*

Proverbs 30:1 " ... the weighty ***message*** *... "*

Exodus 2:23 " ... their cry for ***help*** *kept ... "*

Exodus 16:1 " ... ***coming*** *out of the land of Egypt."*

Joshua 10:9 " ... against them by ***surprise****."*

Genesis 8:9 " ... brought it ***inside*** *the ark."*

Exodus 8:6 "... frogs began to come up and ***cover*** *the land of Egypt."*

Chauncy smiled and read the underlined words:

"***Received-message-help-coming-surprise-inside-cover***."

She translated my message! She did it! But what was this 'surprise-inside-cover'?

Opening the Bible he carefully ran his fingers up and down inside the front cover. He felt a slight bump. Something was glued inside the cover! Glancing around nervously, he took the Bible and the note with him into the bathroom. Working carefully, he managed to slice open the binding with the razor from his shaver.

A wafer-thin microchip about one inch-square fell out onto the sink.

A large grin spread across Chauncy's face as his eyes widened. *Of course, a micro-transmitter! How brilliant. This has to belong to Kelly—that's how he's going to track me down! He most likely will be using a helicopter to rescue me!*

Chauncy pulled off one of his shoes. Using the razor he cut a small opening in the shoe's leather for the transmitter and hid it inside. He ripped the paper containing the decoded scriptures into tiny pieces and flushed them down the toilet.

That night he slept soundly.

CHAPTER NINE

Fuming, Captain Gustavo De Leon glared at the newspaper stand.

Is "The Incorruptible" Blameless?

or

Is "The Incorruptible" Corrupt?

When it wasn't the media, it was the government pressuring him to apprehend Jose Padilla Madrid. And then there was the American Embassy. It seemed that George Hawkins had a personal vendetta. De Leon had heard that Hawkins was trying to get "The Incorruptible" removed from office, charging De Leon with incompetence and fraud. It was only a matter of time before the bubble burst. He had some evidence that the Mexican military had not been involved. But he needed the complete picture to prove his case, and for the moment, he did not have it.

Arturo kept hitting dead ends as he investigated every possible lead. He knew that some members of his unit had turned their back on their captain. They had been paid off handsomely, De Leon was sure, in order to remain quiet or destroy evidence regarding Madrid's whereabouts. The captain was furious.

Scowling, he walked into the office lobby. He picked up a newspaper and saw a picture of Mr. Hawkins in a front-page article. He glanced over the article, which read:

Take the Corrupt Ones out of office!

George Hawkins, a representative of the United States Embassy says: "How can our government have trust in your government if corruption continues unabated? Where are the leaders of the military? Why should....

De Leon didn't bother to finish reading. He threw the newspaper into the trash. *Idiot.*

As he crossed to his office, Laura greeted him cheerfully. "Good morning, Captain."

"What's so good about it?" he grumbled as he walked into his office and slammed the door behind him.

He dropped wearily into his chair. Surrounded by plaques, awards, and photographs of him shaking hands with visiting dignitaries, he thought about all of the years he had served so well.

And for what? he asked himself. It's all going down the drain anyway.

He logged onto his computer and checked his voice mail while he waited.

"You have twenty messages," the recorded voice announced.

Probably all complaints. He thought. Unfortunately he was right. Now he had to check his e-mail, equally certain there would be nothing but complaints. Sipping his coffee, he waded through the first four messages with grim determination. The fifth message, though, was different. It was written in English, and his interest grew rapidly as he read it:

Dear Mr. De Leon,

My name is Anita Rollock. My husband, Chauncy Rollock, is the well-known archaeologist who co-wrote a book entitled "The Mayan Mystery, Solved!" five years ago.

We're vacationing in Cancun my husband was kidnapped. I received a note from the abductors warning us not to contact the authorities. Just a few days ago I received a DVD that had a recording of Chauncy telling me that he was safe, which included an encoded message for me. He indicated that I should get help from a friend in the United States, but that I should also inform you that the person who abducted him was Jose Padilla Madrid. He is somewhere in Yucatan.

We were able to smuggle a small tracking device to my husband. We've organized a mission to follow it and rescue him.

Please assist us in any way you can, I fear for my husband's life. Do not try to contact me in Cancun; I have a hunch that someone here at El Mirador may be working for Madrid.

Desperately needing your help,

Anita Rollock

He closed his eyes, rubbed them, and then opened them again and stared at the message on his screen. He printed out the message and read it again. *What if this is a prank?*

He looked up the number for the El Mirador in Cancun. Using his untraceable private number, he called.

"Good morning and thank you for calling the El Mirador Hotel. How may I help you?" a cheerful female voice asked.

"Yes, good morning," De Leon said, in what he hoped was a disguised voice. He figured his voice was well known due to the interviews on television. "Can you tell me if a Mr. Rollock has checked into your hotel?"

"Hold on a moment, sir," the voice replied. After a moment of mariachi music, the clerk returned. "Yes, sir, we do have a Mr. Rollock here, would you like me to transfer you?"

"Excellent!" De Leon exclaimed. "What an interview! The great Rollock returning to Cancun! Yes, please connect me."

He waited for the telltale click of the call being transferred, then hung up.

After a few minutes searching on the Internet he reached for his phone and dialed another number.

A recorded message came on:

"*Hi! Thank you for calling the Rollocks. We're not here*

right now because we're on vacation in Cancun! Sorry you couldn't come with us. Please leave a message and we will get back to you once we return."

He hung up and quickly dialed Arturo's cell phone.

"What is it, Captain?"

"Get over to my office as fast as you can!"

He walked out of his office and headed toward the restroom, a large smile on his face.

"Good morning, Laura! What a wonderful day! Tell Arturo to wait in my office."

She stared after him. For the first time in a week, De Leon chuckled.

"Come on in you guys, I'm almost finished," Anita said as she continued packing.

Kelly, Marlo and Gloria came in.

Kelly smiled at Troy. "Hey young man, how ya doing today?"

"Real cool, Kelly, but I miss my dad."

"Well you just sit tight my boy 'cause we're gonna find him."

The phone rang, and Anita paused her packing to answer it. "Hello? Yes, that's me. Right now? I'd rather—well, okay."

Irritated, she hung up the phone. "It's the newspaper; they found out that my husband is in town. They want to interview the 'famous archaeologist.' I can't believe this; I really don't have time for this nonsense."

She ran a brush through her hair, double-checked her makeup, and then headed for the door. "I'll be right back."

Downstairs in the lobby she spotted a young Mexican man wearing garish clothes and thick black sunglasses.

"Ahhh, you must be Mrs. Rollock?" he called out in thickly accented English. "My name is Rolando. I am a reporter from *The Mexican Daily.* Let's sit here, no?" he said. He pointed to a sofa and led the way. Anita rolled her eyes and followed him.

"Where is the famous Mr. Rollock?" he asked as he sat down.

Anita smiled politely. "Mr. Rollock left for a couple days. I'm sorry you missed him."

"Oh yes, yes; I see. I'm so sorry to hear that. We really wanted to interview such a famous person. I guess the paper will be none the worse for an interview with his wife."

At the end of what seemed a short interview Rolando suggested a photo next to the veranda.

Just a few more minutes of this nonsense, Anita thought as the two left the lobby.

Rolando took out his camera and pointed it at her. "This is a good place for a photo, no?"

As he adjusted the lens, he said quietly: "Mrs. Rollock, my real name is Arturo and I work for Captain Gustavo De Leon."

"You got my message?" she asked in restrained excitement.

"Yes, but we needed to verify it and get the transmitter frequency. You did not provide it in your e-mail."

Anita wanted to slap herself. "I can't believe it. How stupid can I be?" She took Arturo's writing pad and scribbled the frequency. "There. Now go get him!"

Arturo snapped a picture of her and walked back to the lobby, calling over his shoulder, "Well, Mrs. Rollock, thank you for the photo and the autograph! So sorry I missed your husband. Maybe next time I can see him, goodbye."

Bursting into the hotel room, she announced, "The Lion is going after his Spanish jailbird!"

Five minutes later they were on their way.

As the plane banked to the left, Belize City appeared through the plane window. Anita was far too preoccupied to enjoy the tropical scenery below. It did not matter to her that the barrier reef below was the second largest in the world. She had no interest in sightseeing or exploring the emerald islands that hugged the coast. All she cared about was Chauncy.

She did have two reasons to be interested in Belize though. The first was that Kelly claimed there was a man there who owned a helicopter they could use. The second was that from Belize it would be easy to fly below the radar into Yucatan.

Driving north toward the township of Orange Walk, Kelly directed Anita to turn down a dirt road. A bumpy half-hour later they arrived at a large clearing.

A junked helicopter and small airplane were surrounded by mechanical bits and pieces. In the middle of the lot was a large old trailer; a tethered dog near the trailer barked incessantly.

A tall, wiry black man watched suspiciously from the door. Wiping his greasy hands with a greasy rag, he shouted, "Watcha want?"

Kelly stepped forward. "Hey man, don't ya recognize me? It's me, Kelly Sorenson."

"Kelly? Kelly? The dude that use to fly with me in 'Nam?"

"Yeah man, it's me. We found your place and name by searching the Internet."

"Well I'll be a monkey's hairy tail! Is that you, you old man?"

"Stop it, Charlie, you ain't gotten any younger either."

Anita cleared her throat loudly.

"Oh, I'm sorry," Kelly stammered. "I forgot to introduce these two. Charlie; this is Marlo Gund and Anita Rollock."

"Pleased to meet ya." Charlie led them under a large awning made from a camouflage parachute. "What brings ya to my palace?"

"Well, we need two things, Charlie." Anita was in a hurry. "We need to rent a chopper and we need *you* to come with us."

"Hmmm." Charlie sat down on a rickety chair. He stared, rubbing his chin. "Watch you need it for?"

Kelly answered. "We need to go into Mexico."

"Mexico? What for? Ain't they got choppers for tourists?"

"Not with guns on 'em, Charlie. It's a rescue mission. Anita's husband is in trouble." Kelly said.

"What kinda trouble—trouble with the law?" Charlie asked with a suspicious glance as he raised his eyebrows.

"No, we need to rescue him from Jose Padilla Madrid and we need you as the side gunner."

Charlie sprang from his chair in a burst of energy that surprised everyone. "You're all plumb crazy! What's the matter with you? You all want me to go gunning down Jose Padilla with a Mini-gun on a chopper in Mexico? Ha, ha, ha, you're all crazy, man!"

He started to walk toward his trailer, but Anita stood up and followed him. "Now wait just a minute, Charlie, you can't just walk away from someone that needs your help."

Charlie spun around and glared at her. "I can and I will, lady. I ain't gonna risk my life in that jungle shootin' at no drug lords!"

Anita took her checkbook out of her purse. "What's your last name, Charlie?"

"Watson, Charlie Watson. Why?"

She wrote on the check, ripped it from the book and gave it to Charlie. After he'd counted the zeros after the one, he looked Anita in the eye. She said, "And there's another check for the same amount with your name on it waiting for you when we get back from Mexico. I trust the rescue will be quick and easy."

Charlie looked at the check, then back at Anita. "You don't realize what you're taking about. You ever done this before?"

"Of course not." Anita responded. "But don't get all self righteous on me. I'm sure you've had offers. After all you live here on the border."

"So? What makes ya think I can be bought?"

Anita gave him a wry smile. "I took acting lessons in school. It's one of those 'it takes one to know one' things. In other words, false indignation doesn't befit you. You were holding out for more zeros on the check. Am I right?"

Charlie smiled.

Anita took another checkout and shoved it into his greedy hands. "Here!"

"Follow me, ma'am."

They rounded the corner of the trailer house, where several helicopters in various states of disrepair came into view. One was under a large black parachute. It was to this one that Charlie led them.

"This one here is for special operations," he said with a twinkle in his eye. As he spoke, he pulled back the parachute to reveal an old U.S. military helicopter.

Kelly stared in surprise. "Wow man...that looks like the one I flew in 'Nam!"

"Yep, it's an old Huey; bought it at an auction a long time ago. Brings back memories, eh?"

Kelly walked around the aircraft, the surprise fading from his face. "It still has the guns; do they work?"

"I hope so, hadn't a reason to use them, ya know. Not too many tourists come asking for helicopter rides that have working guns on 'em." Charlie said, grinning from ear to ear. "Mighty proud of this one."

Marlo, noticing the change in Kelly's expression, walked over to the veteran and put a hand on his shoulder. "You okay?" he asked quietly.

He could feel Kelly shaking. "It's rough ... there's too many memories you know? This chopper is an exact model of the one I flew in 'Nam…and here we are…in the jungle."

Marlo squeezed Kelly's shoulder, but there was nothing to say.

Anita turned to Charlie. "My husband has a radio transmitter on him. Can you set us up with a locator?"

Charlie scratched his head as he surveyed the junkyard. "Yeah, yeah, the newer planes have them. I think one of those Cessnas has one."

"How soon can you have it working?"

"Coupla hours."

"Good." Anita looked at her watch. "Call us when you are done."

It was painfully early in the morning when Chauncy heard the rattling of keys in the door. Santo and his bodyguard stepped into the room to find Chauncy already dressed in khaki shorts, a short sleeve shirt, and hiking boots—one of which now hid the transmitter.

"Well, I see that you are ready to leave," Santo remarked.

"Any time we leave will never be too soon."

Santo ordered the guard to handcuff and blindfold Chauncy. Leg irons were placed around his ankles once again. In a repeat of yesterday's activities, minus the oppressive heat, they loaded Chauncy into a vehicle. For about an hour he rode in darkness. When the blindfold was removed, he realized it didn't really matter. He couldn't see anything but the dirt road illuminated by the headlights. It was the same black Humvee and the same seating arrangement.

Madrid's expression seemed cheerful, but his voice was nervous. "I won't be happy until we leave Mexico," he stated. "But first we have to take care of some important business."

They traveled for a while longer down the bumpy dirt road. Madrid turned to talk to Chauncy again. "We are close to the pyramids of Chichen Itza. We should be there in ten minutes."

Soon their headlights shone on an old building, an aircraft hangar. They all got out of the vehicle and entered the hangar through a small side door. One of the guards walked over to some equipment in the corner. The building lit up as a generator came to life, but there wasn't much to illuminate. The large sliding doors that permitted planes to enter or depart were locked shut.

Madrid looked at his watch and spoke to Santo. "Five more minutes!"

They tied Chauncy to a beam at the rear of the hangar with a rope, his hands lifted above his head. He heard the distant thumping of an approaching helicopter and began to worry. Who was coming? Why had they not let him go free? Why were they letting him see all of this?

The sound of the helicopter was deafening as it landed in front of the building. He could see the glow of the lights from the aircraft through the fiberglass panels in the doors. Madrid and Santo stood next to Chauncy as the guards left to greet the mysterious visitor.

Santo opened up a folding table and put it next to Chauncy. Chauncy heard voices outside. As two guards entered, a third man followed with a large suitcase in his hand.

In the dim lights Chauncy couldn't see the man's face. As he got closer he looked up and Chauncy could clearly see his face. He was dumbfounded for a moment, because he knew he had seen the face somewhere but couldn't place it.

His memory clicked: the CNN interview that Chauncy saw in the hotel. "What are *you* doing here?" Chauncy asked.

CHAPTER TEN

George Hawkins smiled. "I'm honored that you would recognize a humble American Embassy representative." He walked closer. "Come now, you shouldn't be so surprised. I love the good life, just like anyone else." He opened a large suitcase and set it on the table as he addressed the other men. "Fill 'er up, all one million dollars of it, my friends."

Three men with automatic weapons walked through the small hangar door. Chauncy knew that Hawkins was well aware the power of greed and he wasn't going to give Madrid a chance to try anything.

Chauncy was suddenly overwhelmed, he felt like an animal waiting for the slaughter. "You lied to me," he glared at Madrid. "You wouldn't be letting me see all this if you planned to release me."

Madrid kept his eyes on the money as Santo counted it and placed it in Hawkins' suitcase. "As the pirates of old used to say, 'Dead men tell no tales,' Mr. Rollock. It's business, not love." He laughed and looked around to see if anyone had heard him. "Isn't that original?"

Chauncy shifted his glare to Hawkins. "And you, betraying your country. These drug dealers are going to walk out of here to continue their drug-dealing."

"Lecture somewhere else, Mr. Rollock. And shut up while we're counting."

As the final stack of dollar bills went into the suitcase, Hawkins closed and locked the bulging piece of luggage. "Good, good! You have all done a wonderful job, including you, Mr. Rollock. Thank you for your assistance in locating the money. Tell me something, Mr. Rollock, do you recall how the Mayans sacrificed their victims to their gods, here in Chichen Itza?"

Chauncy made a face. "So you're going to dump me into a *cenote* like Dr. Sova?"

"You'll be in good company," he answered with a sneer. "The doctor is waiting for you."

One of Hawkins' men shouted from the hangar door. "*Señor* Hawkins, a helicopter is approaching!"

There was silence as everybody listened. Barely audible but growing louder was the sound of a helicopter.

Hawkins whirled to face Madrid. "What is this?" he demanded. "I swear to God I'll shoot you down right now if—"

"I don't know what this is about!" Madrid yelled as he ordered his guards to go outside.

As Madrid and his guards ran, so did Hawkins. He struggled to keep up carrying the heavy suitcase.

With everybody's attention elsewhere, Chauncy struggled to escape. He tugged as hard as he could, but all he did was lift himself off the ground, his arms straining from the exertion.

Santo spotted him and swung viciously. As he raised his hand to strike again the sound of the helicopter rotors was joined by the noise of gunfire. Glass shattered everywhere in the hangar. Men shouted as the gunfire continued unabated.

Realizing that he had forgotten his briefcase during the melee, Madrid quickly turned and ran back into the hangar. He tried his best to ignore Santo and Chauncy as he approached them to pick up his belongings.

"He's trying to escape!" Santo complained to Madrid.

"Finish him off!" Madrid hissed. "We have bigger problems to deal with."

Seated in the helicopter, De Leon noticed stacked fuel barrels on the side of the hangar. He instinctively squeezed the trigger in his control stick and a barrage of bullets hit the target. The fuel barrels exploded in a rolling fireball. Chauncy was flung bodily on top of Madrid and Santo.

Then there was only blackness.

Captain Gustavo De Leon and his soldiers leapt from the helicopter. Arturo and two soldiers ran to the other helicopter where a certain familiar American Embassy representative was attempting to escape. Suddenly, Hawkins was face-to-face with three gun barrels pointing at his head.

"Good morning, Mr. Hawkins." De Leon boomed. "Have you been sightseeing in our beautiful country?"

"Ah, Captain De Leon, these men were attempting to kidnap me!" Hawkins said.

Arturo pulled Hawkins' suitcase off the helicopter and unceremoniously opened it for all to see the cash.

"Really?" De Leon said, a humorless smile on his face. "Since when do the abductors pay a ransom to the abducted?"

Hawkins kept his head high. "There's one million dollars in that suitcase. Half of it is yours if you just walk away. If you turn it over to your superiors, you won't see a penny of it."

The Captain slowly shook his head. "You're pathetic. That's why you were trying so hard to get me out of the way. You knew I couldn't be bribed, and yet here you still try. I'll be paid in full knowing you're rotting in a Mexican prison for the rest of your life."

The sounds and smells of the fire slowly brought Chauncy to consciousness. Coughing and sputtering, he shook his head and looked around. Debris was scattered everywhere; some of it on top of him. He realized with a start that he was lying on top of someone's legs. Moving a bit of the debris he recognized Santo, who was lying very still. Was he dead? Well, good riddance.

Madrid lay motionless on his back nearby. Had the blast killed them both but left Chauncy alive? If he could just shuffle over to Madrid he could find the keys and get himself out of these infernal leg chains. Instead he found himself looking down the barrel of Madrid's pistol.

"Don't shoot! You don't know this, but I am responsible for this rescue!"

Madrid looked shocked. "What? *You*, you did this?"

"Yes, I communicated with my wife."

Madrid was dumbfounded. "How did you do that?"

"Do you remember the video you took of me? I simply wrote a message in the Mayan code."

Madrid shook his head in disgust. He muttered obscenities as he raised his gun to kill Chauncy.

"Wait! I can get us out of here, I swear."

As they handcuffed Hawkins, De Leon's attention suddenly shifted to people in the burning hangar. He motioned to one of his men. "We need to find a way to get in there!"

One of the soldiers protested. "But captain…the building is burning!"

"Find a way!" De Leon barked.

"And you expect me to trust you?" Madrid yelled. "Explain why I should not shoot you right here and now?"

"I specifically instructed her to notify De Leon that you were here in Yucatan. That is most likely him out there right now. If you stay he will arrest you. If you unlock the chains from my legs and untie the ropes from my hands I'll take you with me."

"And exactly *who* is going to rescue *us*?"

"I also instructed my wife to get another person to rescue me. I have a friend who flies helicopters. Hurry! Make your choice!"

Seeing no other viable option at hand, Madrid took the keys from his pocket and unlocked Chauncy's legs and proceeded to untie his hands.

As flaming debris fell around them they scrambled through the door and into the Humvee. Madrid handed Chauncy the keys and in seconds they were tearing down the dirt path. With headlights off, the early morning light was just enough to show Chauncy the road. Slamming through ruts and potholes Chauncy could feel bruises and scrapes and trickles of blood all over his body.

"Where to?" Madrid growled over the roar of the engine.

Chauncy glanced at the GPS unit built into the dashboard. "If we are to be rescued it is going to be on high ground. We should go towards the pyramids of Chichen Itza!"

Madrid frantically typed the information into the GPS system.

"Captain! Madrid is gone!" Arturo yelled.

"Call for backup, Arturo, and stay with Hawkins until it arrives," De Leon pointed to three of his soldiers. "You three, come with me!"

He ran to his helicopter as the rotors started moving. De Leon noticed a blip on his screen indicating that there was a transmitter on board the Humvee from Chauncy.

Charlie's helicopter sputtered but didn't start. Kelly turned to look at Charlie, who shrugged. Shrugging also, Kelly tried again. This time the engine caught and the rotors started spinning.

"Aaaalllright!" Kelly yelled over the loud engine noise.

"Gonna hafta fly low to avoid radar, Kelly," Charlie reminded him.

Kelly shot a look behind him at his comrade. "I fly, you gun, right?"

After another thumbs-up from his new co-pilot, Marlo,

they lifted off. Anita, seated near the winch, watched the tracking monitor for Chauncy's signal.

Skimming the treetops, they crossed the border into Mexico.

De Leon sat uncomfortably, despite his ultramodern helicopter. They had lost track of Chauncy's transmitter, so De Leon had spent the last few minutes fiddling with the equipment.

The blip came on the screen again. "There he is!" De Leon shouted as he pointed to the device. "East!"

As they turned toward the pyramids of Chichen Itza, a small plume of dust the Hummer was making in its trail was visible.

De Leon pointed. "And there they are!"

Kelly looked down at the jungle and shuddered. He could hear the screams, "*Come back, come back.*"

He shook his head trying to dislodge the phantoms of the past.

He felt Marlo's comforting hand on his shoulder. "It's okay, buddy, relax, relax."

He squeezed his eyes shut for a second, forcing back the voices, the memories. He smiled weakly at his co-pilot. "Yeah."

Anita had her eyes glued to the screen. "I see something! It's definitely a blip, but it keeps disappearing! It's Chauncy, but he needs to get to higher ground, but where can he go? This area of Yucatan is all flat topography."

"He's catching up with us!" Madrid exclaimed as he spied De Leon's helicopter. With grim determination, he put his pistol down and reached into the rear of the Humvee. A moment later he retrieved a green metal box and pulled out a shoulder rocket launcher.

Chauncy glanced in the rear view mirror and saw De Leon's helicopter swoop down like an eagle after its prey. Two Mini-Guns from the sides of his helicopter opened fire in perfect unison, spitting a barrage of bullets. The slugs slammed into the dirt, kicking up a considerable amount of dust.

A nearly deafening roar caught Chauncy off guard as Madrid fired a rocket from the sunroof of the vehicle. The aircraft veered off course and barely avoided the deadly missile.

De Leon looked at his gunner. "Can you stop them without killing the passengers in the vehicle?"

"The target's path is erratic, sir. I can't guarantee it!"

Mentally, De Leon flipped a coin. He turned to his gunner. "Do your best."

"Yes, Captain."

Slamming into the dirt just in front of the Humvee, the rocket sent the vehicle flying in a cloud of dirt. It seemed to hang in the air before crunching to the ground on its side, coming to a stop completely upside down.

Chauncy was surprised at how difficult it was to unbuckle the seatbelt while hanging upside down. He scrambled through the broken windshield, coughing and wheezing in the cloud of dust. Madrid must have done the same, but Chauncy's attention was on the pyramid right in front of them.

"We have to get up there!" he shouted to Madrid who was rummaging through the debris inside the Hummer. "We need to get to higher ground if our rescuers are going to spot us."]

"Not yet we don't!" Madrid shouted back.

To Chauncy's horror, the drug lord leaned against the wrecked vehicle with the rocket launcher on his shoulder. The missile screamed toward the helicopter, found its target, and caused the tail rotor to disappear in a ball of flame.

"Tail rotor's gone!" the pilot shouted over the sirens and alarms.

De Leon didn't need the pilot's warning. Without the tail rotor, the helicopter yielded to the laws of physics and began spinning toward the ground.

Squinting his eyes against the nauseating blur of the outside world, De Leon noticed that the pilot was wrestling the aircraft toward the jungle. The vegetation would absorb the impact—or so the theory went. Within seconds the theory was tested as the helicopter hit the treetops.

With is heart beating fast with excitement, Chauncy watched in amazement as the helicopter ripped through the vegetation. Dirt flew as the rotors hit the ground, cutting deep furrows into the jungle floor. Another half spin and it stopped. He shook his head, hoping that no one had been killed. Turning his mind away from the unpleasant possibilities, he started toward the pyramid.

"Not so fast Mr. Rollock!" Madrid's pistol was pointed straight at Chauncy's head. "For your sake, I hope you don't have any tricks up your sleeve."

Chauncy frantically pointed to the pyramid. "I already told you we have to climb to higher ground so they can locate us. The park isn't open to the tourists yet. Let's go before the place gets crowded!"

Running through the brush they entered the fairground and ran toward the pyramid. Chauncy pushed the metal guard railing out of the way and motioned for Madrid to begin climbing. The climb was arduous since the steps were steep, Chauncy could hear Madrid gasping for breath, his face covered in sweat.

Anita's eyes widened in surprise as the blip blinked on her

screen again. "I see the signal. It's much stronger now," she shouted over the engine noise. "Go west Kelly, go west!"

Kelly adjusted course. Charlie pointed at the pyramid. "That's Chichen Itza."

De Leon coughed and blinked his eyes against the stinging smoke. The helicopter was lying on its side. Grabbing his seat firmly with one hand, he unbuckled his seatbelt and slowly lowered himself to what had once been the side of his personal helicopter.

Smoke began to fill the cockpit. The pilot was unconscious or dead. De Leon made his way through the wreckage to the cabin. He checked for a pulse and was relieved to find one. Cutting loose the pilot's seatbelt, he heaved him onto his shoulder and carried him out of the burning aircraft.

The gunner was lying in a pool of fuel, but he was alive as well. De Leon moved the man out and laid him on the grass next to the pilot. Wiping his brow, De Leon glanced at the pyramid. Chauncy and Madrid were starting to climb it. He turned toward the helicopter, but the third soldier was staggering out on his own. De Leon instructed him to care for the others while he ran back into the helicopter.

He rummaged through cases of weapons, all the time aware of the approaching flames. Coughing and near blind, he grabbed a sniper rifle and a round of ammunition.

As he stepped from the wreck, the first fuel tank exploded. De Leon went hurling into the air and landed on his back. Regaining consciousness seconds later he looked up at the third soldier.

"There is another helicopter approaching, sir! It is still far away, but I can hear its rotors!" the soldier said.

De Leon struggled to stand.

"Your leg, sir. That doesn't look good. Let me help."

"No!" De Leon snapped. "Look after the others. That's an order, soldier!"

Using the rifle as a crutch, De Leon shuffled toward the pyramid. Moments later, the second fuel tank exploded in a ball of fire and black smoke. De Leon didn't even spare a backward glance. He was focused. His target was ahead of him.

Kelly was the first to notice the fireball. "Uh, oh—something is a happening over there and I don't think it's a barbecue," he said, pointing toward the smoke.

Anita's eyes widened. "That's where Chauncy is!"

Kelly dipped the helicopter's nose and they picked up speed.

Madrid dropped to his knees. "I can't go any further. Stop. Stop," he said, his face pale and sickly as he waved his gun.

"We can't stop. Look!" Chauncy said as he pointed down the pyramid.

Madrid looked down at the jungle floor. That could only be Gustavo De Leon. The sun glinted off the weapon he held.

Madrid's breaths were rasping and harsh. His clothes were drenched. But the thought of getting shot by De Leon was enough to put him back on his feet. The stress, the heat, the humidity, the exertion—it was more than he could bear. His legs were numb. His heart hammered.

Shielding his eyes from the sun, Chauncy scanned the horizon for the helicopter. "Here they come!" he shouted.

Madrid felt a sharp pain in his chest.

De Leon gasped in pain as his leg gave out. Climbing the pyramid was impossible. Crouching on his good knee, he lifted the rifle and aimed.

The helicopter approached Chichen Itza. The strange assortment of buildings that had once been the hallmark of a powerful civilization were now little more than tourist attractions. Testimony to that were the multiple hotels that were nearby.

"There!" Marlo shouted, pointing at the pyramid. "See? Looks like two people climbing, and I'll bet one of them is Chauncy!"

The helicopter reached the top of the pyramid at the same time as the climbers did. It was too narrow to land. In its center was a *stele,* a tall platform rising toward the heavens.

"I'm going to have to lower the cable!" Anita shouted. "And bring both of them up."

"Both? I thought we were only bringin' one guy up!" Charlie shouted.

"We have an extra 'guest'—that other guy is Jose Padilla Madrid," Anita said.

"No way Jose, he ain't coming aboard my chopper!" Charlie shouted. He slapped Kelly on the shoulder. "Turn this chopper around and head back to Belize!"

"No!" Anita said. "We came to get Chauncy!"

Charlie gave Anita an evil glare. "Look, lady! It's bad enough I crossed the Mexican border with guns on my airship. Now you want me to board a drug lord? That was never part of my agreement! Do you understand? I ain't going to no Mexican prison, ya hear?"

Anita glared at Charlie. "That's my husband! You get him right now!"

"Well guess what? This is *my* chopper!" Charlie retorted.

"I just ordered you to get Chauncy!" Anita yelled back.

Charlie simply sneered at her and turned his attention back to Kelly. "I said take this chopper back to Belize, Kelly."

Anita grabbed Charlie's shirtsleeve. She changed her demeanor and softened her voice. "Look, we came this far to get Chauncy; we can't turn back now. You are in too deep anyway. I have enough money to bail all of us out of prison. I will plead our case to the consulate if we get arrested. If you don't take Madrid, he will kill him. Please, Charlie, please!"

"She's right, Charlie," Marlo said. "Madrid's pointing a gun at Chauncy. We better cooperate or he may kill him."

Charlie looked down at the pyramid, then he snarled. Making a motion with his hand he instructed Anita to lower the cable.

The winch's motor growled as it slowly unraveled the cable down toward the two desperate men. Then, without warning the winch stopped.

Anita had a horrified expression. "Charlie! The winch isn't working!"

For a quick second Charlie seemed motionless as he stared at the winch.

Madrid motioned Chauncy away from the cable. As he reached for the cable, a shot echoed across the pyramids. Madrid dropped his gun, grabbed his arm and cried out in pain.

He swayed about like a drunken man. The pain from the bullet wound was drowned out by the roaring pain in his chest. His heart seemed to beat in time with the helicopter rotors above him: *thump ... thump ... thump ....* He grabbed again for the cable. He missed, crumpling to his knees.

Chauncy tried to grab the wind-whipped cable as it flayed around, it seeming to toy with him as he attempted to grasp at it. After a few attempts he finally caught it.

Madrid raised his head to look up at Chauncy. "Well, it looks like you outsmarted me, in the end."

Chauncy made fist at Madrid. "No, Dr. Sova did, I was only a disciple of his."

Madrid nodded in agreement, then closed his eyes and toppled backward down the steep stairs of the pyramid.

Charlie quickly rummaged through an old toolbox and pulled out a rusty wrench. "Get back!" he yelled as he swung the wrench with all his might at the winch motor. A loud clanging sound reverberated in the cabin as the winch came back to life. Chauncy wrapped the cable around his wrists, then with much concentration, he snaked the cable around his ankles too. The cable commenced to pull Chauncy upwards to the helicopter.

"Let's go Kelly!" Marlo shouted.

But Kelly was back in Vietnam, voices screaming from the jungle. He could feel the bullet wound; feel the blood running down his arm. *Come back! Come back*! the voices cried in his mind. *I can't leave them here in the jungle to die....*

A hard slap on his shoulder brought him back to reality. "Let's move it soldier!" Marlo shouted. "Move-move-move, we have the man we came for!"

Nodding weakly, Kelly pushed the throttle forward and turned the helicopter toward Belize.

As the jeep slid to a halt, Arturo jumped out and ran to where De Leon lay. "Are you all right? What happened?"

De Leon waved his hand to where Madrid's broken body lay. Hotel personnel were running to the fairground to see what the commotion was all about. They had horrified expressions when they saw a corpse on the grass surrounded by officials.

De Leon ignored the excited voices in the background as he addressed Arturo. "Today, we killed a big *cucaracha*. But soon another *cucaracha* will take his place and the game will start all over again." He sighed. "You know what, Arturo? I hope to God that I am not here when that happens."

CHAPTER ELEVEN

Two days later the atmosphere was festive at the outdoor bar of a hotel in Belize. Loud conversations were punctuated by laughter. Up in the corner a TV broadcast a 24-hour sports channel. A warm breeze blew puffy clouds across the sky and brought with it the exotic scents of the jungle. Of all the guests that were enjoying themselves, seven had particular reason to celebrate. Chauncy, Anita, Troy, Marlo, Gloria, Kelly and Charlie were near the bar, laughing and talking.

Chauncy was seated in a large, comfortable chair. An oversized sombrero and thick sunglasses would have been comical if it hadn't been for the bandages that were visible wherever his shirt and shorts did not cover. There wasn't a single muscle in his body that didn't hurt, despite loads of painkillers. The doctors had forbidden alcohol; so he sipped an enormous iced tea.

Anita was at his right side, clinging to a small spot on his arm where there were no bandages. Troy was on his left. Chauncy could smell something delicious sizzling on the outdoor barbecue. All in all, life was good.

He gave his wife a tender kiss. He had been in too much pain during the helicopter ride to be coherent, and after that he had been the exclusive property of the doctors, so this was the first time in twenty-four hours that he was able to truly talk to his family and friends.

"Thank you, my love. It was a shot in the dark, but I had hoped you'd figure out the message in the video I sent you."

She smiled. "You taught me everything dear; I simply followed your lead."

Marlo came over, a large smile on his face. "Good to see

you again Chauncy—especially good to see you all in *one* piece!"

"You think so?" Chauncy chided.

Marlo's smile grew larger as he gripped his friend's hand. "You know what, I've been thinking about something. Every time we travel together, it seems we always get into some kind of trouble. Next time, Gloria and I are going on vacation without you."

A hearty laugh broke out amongst the group. Kelly grabbed Marlo's shoulder and grinned at him. "Hey man, thank you so much. I think I'm cured man, ya know what I mean? I can handle the jungle now! And you, Chauncy, do me a favor would ya? Stop getting in so much trouble."

Chauncy shrugged. "I'll do what I can, but no promises."

"Here you go, Charlie" Anita said, as she fluttered a check at him.

Charlie grinned from ear to ear.

"Well, rich man, what are you going to spend this on?" Anita asked.

"Well I've got some helicopters to repair. And I'll have to spruce the place up a little if I'm going to convince Kelly to come hang out now that he's okay with the jungle again," he said, putting his arm around Kelly. "Come on, we've got some plans to make." Charlie and Kelly walked toward the pool.

Anita and Gloria took Troy to refill his drink, leaving Chauncy and Marlo alone.

Chauncy motioned his friend closer. "Marlo, let me tell you a secret!"

Marlo furrowed his brow and leaned toward Chauncy.

"You should study the Mayan language, Marlo, forget geology."

"Oh yeah? What on earth for?"

Chauncy lowered his voice even further. "Dr. Sova was right. There is a treasure hidden out there in Palenque. No one else has figured it out. You're still young; I'm telling you

Marlo, there is a great archaeological treasure out there! It’s a pity I can’t pursue it. Anita and I are already overdue for that project in Jerusalem. The riddle on the steps of Temple #22 is still exposed—sometime, somehow, someone is going to read that riddle and figure out that it is a guide to the hidden treasure! I want it to be you."

Marlo wasn't looking at Chauncy anymore. He was watching Gloria as she stood by the bar. "I don’t know, Chauncy. Gloria and I want a family. I don’t think she’ll want me to spend my time searching for treasures in a Mexican jungle. Besides, the food here is tearing my guts up."

Disappointment flashed across Chauncy’s face but it changed into a smile. "Well, I guess you have to do what you have to do."

The bartender suddenly turned off the music and shouted, "Hey everyone, listen up. It's about Jose Padilla Madrid."

The whole crowd quieted as they all turned to stare at the large-screen TV mounted on the wall. After a moment, Captain Gustavo De Leon appeared.

"Ladies and gentlemen, yesterday morning our troops intercepted Jose Padilla Madrid at Chichen Itza, where he was preparing to leave the country. Madrid was killed and his men captured.

"I am pleased to announce that we also captured the person responsible for Madrid’s liberation from the federal maximum security prison. A representative of the American Embassy, George Hawkins, was also planning to leave the country with one million American dollars. He has confessed to arranging the charade that framed the Mexican military for Madrid's escape.

"I would personally like to thank the members of the Mexican Military forces for helping me capture these men. I have always had confidence in their integrity."

Gustavo De Leon looked straight at the camera, with a small grin and a glint in his eye. "I would also like to express deep gratitude to the non-military foreigners that assisted in the capture of Mr. Madrid."

Despite his pain, Chauncy stood up and raised his glass of iced tea toward the television.

"You are welcome, Captain Gustavo De Leon," he murmured. "You are very welcome."

Book Three
The Mayan Treasure

CHAPTER ONE

Gustavo De Leon surveyed his new office with a satisfied smile. Workers were scurrying about, putting the finishing touches on the remodeling. Technicians worked on whatever it is they did with computers. Decorators nudged furniture into position. Electricians completed their work on the upgraded electrical system.

The sun was slipping below the horizon, casting long shadows in the room. De Leon spared a glance at the darkening hills. Twilight always held a certain fascination for him since it represented the disappearance of earth's primary celestial light, the nexus of two worlds: the world of the day, where most people were now preparing for sleep and the world of the night, where the criminal element prepared for something else.

And that was what he was preparing for.

He looked down at the bustling intersection below. His new office was on the top floor of a two-story building that had stood on this corner in downtown Cuernavaca for over a hundred years. Retail shops filled the lower level, but his floor had been abandoned for decades.

Rubbing his eyes, De Leon pondered for a moment the sequence of events that had brought him here.

I can retire early, collect a pension and start a business of my own! I have the talent to be an excellent private investigator. Less hassle and stress to deal with, and I can set my own hours and dictate my own income.

Although barely in his fifties, he could tell that being a captain in the Mexican military was destroying his health. Six months ago he had injured his leg in the pursuit of Jose Padilla Madrid. The doctors said he was fully recovered—at least physically.

Despite the many awards and accolades for a job well done, he had more personal concerns. He had always maintained a spotless reputation, but it seemed like he was always looking over his shoulder at those who worked around him. He knew the inevitable day was coming when he was going to call it quits.

That day had finally arrived.

His many years of service in the Mexican military had allowed him to build up a very large network of people he could turn to for information. And as a retired government employee, he had access to facilities that the average citizen did not. He was a natural at ferreting out information and following a trail. He was confident that he would succeed in his new business venture.

It was his wife, Miranda, who had found this building and approached the owner with an offer he couldn't refuse. Cuernavaca was the perfect compromise between Guadalajara and Mexico City, places where De Leon had many resources. De Leon and his wife had sunk their entire savings into this office and in a modest house close by, confident that everything would work out.

He stepped carefully over electrical cords and drop cloths, his slight limp reminding him of the troubles he had left behind. The computer technician approached the ex-captain with an expectant look on his face.

"All finished?" De Leon asked.

"Si, Señor."

De Leon pulled his wallet out of his back pocket and carefully counted out a few bills. "Here you go, with a little extra. Buy the guys some *cervezas*."

The technician smiled appreciatively. "*Gracias, Señor*!" He whistled to his workers, and they disappeared from the building.

The other contractors had already left. He had power in the front office and reception area but would have to wait until tomorrow to get any in the back rooms. The computer technicians had wired everything to be ready for that. Gustavo walked into the empty back portion of his office and looked at the line of computers. Everything was in order.

His cell phone rang; it was Miranda. "Almost finished?"

"Just locking up to come home my dear."

He hung up and heaved a sigh as he looked at the chaotic mess that would soon be the smoothly functioning office of a private investigator. He flipped on the only working light in the front waiting room and grabbed a flashlight. Methodically he checked all the windows, making sure they were locked secure for the night. All was quiet in the rooms except for the din of the evening traffic as cars passed by.

As he crossed the waiting room, he heard the clanging of footsteps on the metal staircase.

What did you forget this time, Paco? He thought.

He looked around, trying to see what the forgetful electrician had left behind. His search was interrupted by a frantic knocking on his door.

"Hold on," Gustavo yelled as he picked his way through the construction mess by flashlight. The knocking became louder and more frantic. "I said hold on!" he shouted.

Reaching the door, he turned on the outside light and glanced through the peephole. It wasn't Paco. It was someone he didn't recognize. Opening the door slightly, he spoke to a short, heavy man who had knocked so frantically.

"And who are you sir?" De Leon asked.

"Please, *Señor*, you must help me!" the man wailed in a high-pitched voice.

"What seems to be the matter? Was there an accident?"

"No, no," the man replied. "I need your professional help! I have come to seek your services. Mr. De Leon, please, I beg of you, it is very important."

"You are looking for my services?" De Leon asked with a surprised look on his face. "I won't be open for business until next week."

The man held his hands cupped together as he pleaded. "Please, something horrible has occurred. Please, Mr. De Leon, please! I need your help now! This is a matter of great urgency!"

"Can't it wait for a couple of days? My office isn't even fully functional."

"What I have to tell you cannot wait! No, not for one second more! If we do not do something quick, there will be national consequences for Mexico."

Despite the fact that the stranger was sounding more and more like a madman, Gustavo could tell that nothing short of physical violence would get him off the doorstep.

"Fine, come on in."

The stranger smiled with relief as he quickly walked in. "Thank you sir," he gushed. "Thank you very much. May God bless you for your kindness."

Gustavo pulled off the protective sheets from the waiting room furniture and directed the stranger to sit on a couch. Rummaging through a box, he removed a small voice recorder and placed it on the table next to the couch. He then moved his office chair in order to face the stranger.

After speaking a quick introduction into the recorder, De Leon turned again to the stranger. "Please, tell me what's wrong."

The stranger wrung his hands nervously as he attempted to talk. "Oh, Mr. De Leon, I don't know where to begin! You see, a great theft has occurred! Oh my, just to think of it I tremble. Mexico is in trouble!"

Gustavo held up his hand, stopped the recording, and rummaged around in a nearby box for a bottle of tequila and a shot glass. After carefully filling the shot glass, he handed it to his client. "Drink this, you need it."

The stranger downed the fiery liquid in one gulp. He coughed and sputtered, but some color returned to his face. Gustavo poured another round, which the stranger swallowed as quickly as the first.

"Okay, now relax, just relax and tell me your story. How could Mexico be in more trouble than it already is? First let's start with your name."

The stranger closed his eyes and took a few deep breaths. "Okay, I will start from the beginning."

"No better place to start," Gustavo joked.

"My name is Octavio Mendoza. I am a pharmacist by trade. I owned a few pharmacies in Mexico City, so needless to say, I became rather wealthy. Unfortunately my marriage was not as successful and I divorced a couple of years ago. I then faced two choices: to increase my pharmaceutical business or do something completely different in life. Once free of marital obligations, I decided to take a different course, something more challenging than operating a chain of stores.

"I chose to become a real estate broker. I hoped that occupation would open up wonderful opportunities not only to make money and travel, but to perhaps meet someone new, a woman with whom I could share my life.

"A few months later, I was wheeling and dealing in high-end real estate. I specialize in the purchase and resale of mansions for the rich and famous. One day I was informed that there was going to be a gala festival, a place where all the successful real estate agents in Mexico were going to meet. I figured this would be a great opportunity to network and make more business contacts.

"Little did I know that this meeting would drastically change my life and set in motion the series of events that would have dire consequences for Mexico!"

CHAPTER TWO

"It was there that I met a man named Antonio Barrios. Mr. Barrios seemed to have a good head for business. He specialized in distress sales and auctions. One thing led to another and we started doing business together. He would advise me when an excellent piece of property was to become available, offering me the advantage of pre-bidding the property before it went on the market.

"I asked him if he knew of any real estate for my personal use, preferably in Merida. He had just come into possession of a beautiful estate which had been owned by Marie Sova."

De Leon arched an eyebrow. "You mean the wife of the famous Mayanist, Dr. Rene Sova?"

Octavio nodded. "Indeed, she was. Her husband was missing, presumed dead, and she wanted out of Mexico. Arrangements were made for me to see it. I fell in love with it instantly. It is a large estate; exquisitely beautiful.

"Even better was that she had sold everything to Mr. Barrios—the furniture, the wine cellar, everything! Her only stipulation in the contract was that the three helpers, Jose, Lucio, and an older gentleman by the name of Miguelito, would stay and look after the house as long as it stood. I had to have that house. After agreeing to a fair price, I bought it from my business partner, and we opened a fantastic bottle of French wine to celebrate the occasion.

"You may find it unbelievable, but I hadn't even thoroughly inspected the house. One room, in fact, was still locked. Fortunately, the key was on the ring Mrs. Sova had given Barrios. It was the study of Dr. Sova himself! I don't know how much you know about the man, Mr. De Leon, but I had read his book about the Mayan mystery and it was evident by all the books, computers, and drawings that this was the room where he had deciphered the meaning of the Mayan hieroglyphs, leading to the discovery of King Chac's remains!"

Octavio abruptly ended his narrative and sat silently, staring at his hands. De Leon waited patiently. After a few moments, Octavio took a deep breath and continued. "Then I saw a familiar-looking desk at one corner of the study."

"Familiar? How?" Gustavo inquired.

Octavio shook his head and clenched his fists. "I should never have mentioned it in Antonio's presence. It was just like a desk that my grandmother had, one with a secret drawer. Sure enough, after hitting the side of the desk a wooden handle came down, and after pulling that a drawer came out. And in the drawer was a scroll.

"At first I couldn't figure out what it was. In one corner was the plan of a courtyard of Mayan pyramids. The rest of the scroll contained a large group of Mayan hieroglyphs. At the bottom, however, was a phrase written in Spanish, *El Tesoro del Rey Maya!* The Treasure of the Mayan King. It was a treasure map, Mr. De Leon! Mrs. Sova must not have known about it, otherwise she would never have let it remain in the house when she sold it. If I could see what it was, so could Barrios. He smiled at me and asked, 'What are we going to do about this?' 'We? There is no 'we,' this scroll is mine, it came as part of the house!' But he would have none of that.

"He made a good argument: I would need help to translate the document. 'If we find this we will be millionaires, we will be rich beyond our wildest dreams!' I told him we couldn't plunder the national property of Mexico. He said 'We don't have to take all of it Octavio, just a small finder's fee.' I knew then that I wouldn't be able to leave him out. Well, the next day he introduced me to an archaeological appraiser named Raul Martinez. Martinez had an extensive knowledge of indigenous antiquities and a working knowledge of the Mayan language. The two of them, Barrios and Martinez, came daily to study and examine the scroll. You can be sure that I watched them like a hawk! I never left them alone with the scroll, not even for a moment.

"He was a devious person, this Martinez. He hacked into Dr. Sova's computers, looking for hints or clues in the doctor's personal files. If his excitement was any indication, he was progressing rapidly. But as each day passed I got more and more nervous. I knew that these two men were not to be trusted."

Octavio paused. "Speaking of it drives me mad, but you must know all the facts. I had already begun living in the hacienda. One Saturday while I was in the local town, I decided I needed a break from all the stress over the map. I stayed at a hotel that night. The next day I returned to my house very late. As always when returning home, I checked on the map. When I went into the study to check on it—my God, the map was gone!"

"Go on," Gustavo said with more interest.

"Of course I tried calling those two, but they did not return my calls. That's why I'm here at your office. Don't you see the consequences of this? Those two dogs are going to loot the national treasures of Mexico. They won't leave anything for our country, not one *peso*!" Wringing his hands nervously, he continued, "As we speak they are making plans to go to Palenque, if they haven't already. You must stop them!"

De Leon nodded. "Certainly. We must act quickly."

"Does that mean you will take the case?" Octavio asked eagerly.

"Yes."

For the first time Octavio's face relaxed. "Good, good. I

will pay you well." Octavio took a checkbook from his pocket. He scribbled an amount onto a check, signed it, and handed it to Gustavo.

"This check is your first installment, Mr. De Leon. For every scoundrel you apprehend, you will receive a check for the same amount. Bring them to justice! If you bring me the map, however, I will give you a check, for *three* times the amount!"

Octavio pulled a few more documents from his envelope. "Here is the address of the hotel where I am staying in Cuernavaca, and here is my cell phone number. Also, here is the pertinent information regarding the other two individuals: photographs, business cards, a few other odds and ends. Please, please keep me informed of any new developments."

De Leon carefully filed away the papers that his client had given him. "Rest assured, Mr. Mendoza. Soon I will have them in custody, and I promise you that they will squeal like pigs once they are in jail. We'll have the map."

Octavio let out a long sigh of relief. "I hope so. I really hope so."

It was extremely late when Gustavo entered his house. He quietly crept into his bedroom. Miranda was in bed reading. She looked up as he attempted to sneak into the room.

"It's about time. What happened?"

"I thought you were sleeping," Gustavo said with raised eyebrows. He sat on the bed, smiling at his wife as he told her all about his evening.

Miranda nodded her head. "The case seems challenging enough. And the money, well, that's good too."

"This is going to be a very simple case," he said. Miranda could hear the self-assured tone in his voice; she knew it well. "It is not as complicated as it appears. All I really have to do is apprehend Mr. Barrios tomorrow, and bang, he produces the map of the treasure of the Mayan king. Can you watch the office for me tomorrow? All the contractors are coming to finish."

"I guess I should get used to it since I'm going to be your secretary until I hire one. Yes, *I* will make that choice since I certainly don't want some cute young thing running around the office flirting with you."

"Miranda! Shame on you, you should know me by now."

Miranda glared at Gustavo. "I do."

Though it was late, Gustavo looked once more through the documents his client had given him. He put the hotel business card with Octavio's cell phone number in his wallet.

Next was a business card for Raul Martinez, proclaiming him to be an "Appraiser of Antiquities and Archaeological Artifacts." Gustavo jotted down the address, phone number and e-mail address on the card. The next business card was for "Antonio Barrios, Realty, Sales & Auctions."

The final item was a photograph of Octavio with two other men. The tall thin man with a hawk-like nose and beady eyes had to be Antonio Barrios. The third man, by far the youngest, was quite a bit darker than the others, revealing a life spent outdoors in the tropical sun. This, then, was Raul Martinez.

Gustavo stared at Raul's face. There was something familiar.

The picture was a pleasant one, set against the backdrop of a large hacienda. The three men had their arms across each other's shoulders like the best of friends.

Gustavo grunted. If only Octavio knew what they had been planning when this photo was taken.

The long shadows cast by the rising sun found Gustavo hard at work on his computer.

Miranda walked in to announce that his breakfast was ready. Seeing that he was furiously typing an e-mail, she asked instead, "Who are you writing to, Gustavo?"

"Chauncy Rollock."

“Who?”

Gustavo stopped typing, deep in thought, and stared at the monitor for a few seconds before answering her. "This case I'm working on has a strange connection to Chauncy Rollock, remember him? He was the American kidnapped by Jose Padilla Madrid."

Forgetting the breakfast, Miranda slowly sat down on a chair next to Gustavo. "Oh, yes! Now I remember, the archaeologist, the one who helped capture Mr. Hawkins. How is he connected to this?"

Gustavo slowly swiveled his chair around to face her, and leaned back. "Chauncy Rollock and Dr. Sova collaborated on a book about the Mayan king whose treasure map was stolen by Octavio’s associates. Since Dr. Sova is presumed dead, Chauncy Rollock is the only one alive who can shed light on it. He knows Yucatan; he knows where Martinez and Barrios are headed."

Miranda looked doubtful. "That sounds like a shot in the dark."

Gustavo nodded. "I know, I know. But my gut tells me that I shouldn't leave him out of the equation."

After sending the e-mail and eating breakfast, Gustavo set off for Mexico City to locate Mr. Barrios and retrieve the map. Miranda spent the rest of the day in the office directing the contractors.

It was late again when Gustavo returned home. Miranda heard his slow footsteps and could tell that there was trouble.

"What’s the problem?" she asked.

He walked into the bedroom and threw his keys on the bed.

"Mr. Barrios," he said in a grim tone, "has left his place of residence, closed up his office and shut down phone service. None of his acquaintances knows where he's gone. Mr. Barrios has vanished into thin air."

CHAPTER THREE

A cool wind whipped up a considerable amount of dust on the embankment overlooking Jerusalem's old city, where Chancy Rollock was standing. He and a fellow archaeologist were engaged in a recent excavation of an ancient fortification that dated back to 3000 B.C. The company that hired the men wanted them to prove as fact the Bible narrative about King Solomon. Apparently there was debate among scholars and historians about the king's ability to build large-scale fortifications so long ago. Some had even argued that the monarchy of Solomon's father, King David, was mythical.

To help set the record straight, Chauncy and his colleague were studying a recently excavated wall that dated to the time of Solomon. The dig had revealed a seventy-seven yard section of the wall and a monumental portion of a gatehouse, thus proving the Biblical account of the buildings to be true. The ruin also revealed that both King David and King Solomon had the resources and manpower required to build such massive structures. Jerusalem had been home to a strong central government.

Chauncy wiped the dust from his clothes and smiled at his companion. "It's getting late. I suppose we had better shut things down for the day."

"I agree Chauncy. Let's do the digital imagery tomorrow."

"Sounds like a plan," Chauncy replied as his cell phone began to buzz. He looked at the caller ID display and exclaimed, "It's my wife!"

Anita and Troy were visiting Chauncy in Jerusalem. They

were staying in a hotel in Tel Aviv.

Chauncy answered the phone. “Hello sweetheart.”

Anita sounded excited. “Chauncy, I was checking our e-mail and you received something from Gustavo De Leon!”

Chauncy’s eyebrows shot up. “You mean *the* Gustavo De Leon from Mexico?”

“I can’t think of any other,” Anita sarcastically remarked.

“What does he want?”

“I don’t know. The e-mail is addressed to you. Do you want me to open and read it?”

“Yes, please do,” Chauncy said.

While cradling the telephone on her shoulder, Anita used both hands to bring up the e-mail on her laptop. She then read aloud:

To: Chauncy Rollock
From: Gustavo De Leon
Greetings amigo! I hope that all is going well with you.
I shall be brief in explaining the purpose of this email.
As you know I have just started my new business as a private investigator. I received my first case and what a strange one it is! Apparently my client bought the late Dr. Sova's hacienda and purportedly found a treasure map that leads to a Mayan treasure. Anyway, I figured you, of all people, would have knowledge about these matters. My client says that two of his former associates have run off with the map. This not only poses a financial loss for my client but it also means Mexico's national treasures are at risk of being plundered. Any assistance that you can provide will be greatly appreciated. I will see to it that my government will compensate you. I respectfully await your kind reply.

“What do you think of it?” Anita asked. There was a moment of silence. “Chauncy, can you hear me?”

Chauncy was stunned. “Sorry love, wow, that sure was

rather shocking news! I thought all this Mexico stuff was behind me."

"So did I."

Chauncy swallowed hard. "I suppose this is a big problem and not one I can ignore."

"What do you want to do?"

With his free hand he ran his fingers over his head. "Let's discuss this over dinner."

The waves of the Mediterranean Sea lazily broke on the Tel Aviv beach as Chauncy and Anita dined at the restaurant adjacent to their hotel. A fine feast lay before them that included roast lamb, stuffed grape leaves and a large bowl of hummus. But Chauncy was not as interested in the meal as he was in the e-mail from De Leon.

He pushed the hummus around with his spoon and remarked, "This is crazy. The thieves who stole the treasure map are probably going to destroy the site once they find where the treasure is hidden and loot it, just as De Leon surmised," he said.

"What's your gut feeling, Chauncy?"

He drew in a deep breath. "I am an archaeologist, so my first concern is with the possible destruction of the antiquities."

"And what is your second concern?"

"De Leon saved my life. I do owe him something."

Anita looked away. "Why don't you just e-mail him the information he needs?"

Chauncy slowly shook his head. "I can't. The information I have cannot be e-mailed, it has to be delivered in person."

Anita's eyes misted. "Oh Chauncy, after all we went through, with you sequestered and everything."

"I know, I know. But this time no drug lords are involved. I should be dealing exclusively with De Leon. Once I give him the information I can quietly take my leave."

"With you nothing is ever quiet, Chauncy!"

Chauncy grinned sheepishly. "I know."

"So, I suppose you *will* be going to Mexico?"

Chauncy didn't verbally answer; he simply nodded.

Anita knew better than to argue. "You must promise me that you will not go on any jungle expeditions!"

He chuckled. "Why would I? I simply need to deliver some information."

CHAPTER FOUR

The sleek silver Jaguar fought its way through the congested traffic of downtown Mexico City. The powerful vehicle entered the business district, skyscrapers reflected in its immaculate finish. A few turns later the car eased into an exclusive parking garage.

After turning off the car, Luisa Morales took out a makeup case and applied a few final touches. Satisfied, she stepped out of the car and took one last look at her reflection in the shiny surface of the Jaguar before activating the alarm.

The clicking of her heels echoed through the parking structure as she walked toward a large multi-storied luxury hotel. A short ride in an elevator brought her to the main lobby, and she made her way gracefully across the marble floor toward the elegant restaurant.

"Good morning, *Señora*. How may I help you?"

She took a business card from a jewel-encrusted holder and handed it to the attendant. "My name is Luisa Morales. I'm here to see Mr. Barrios."

The attendant glanced at the card in his hand, then back at her. He nodded once, sharply. "I will page him. Please wait here."

Minutes later he reappeared, smiling. "Follow me, please."

He led her past private booths until they came to one where a man sat alone.

"Mr. Barrios, Ms. Luisa Morales has arrived," the attendant stated with a gracious bow before leaving the two alone.

Mr. Barrios stood, smiling broadly. *Pretty and rich,* he

thought to himself. "Oh, Ms. Morales, it is a pleasure to meet you." He gently guided her to the chair he had pulled out for her.

She sat down and waited for him to do the same before speaking. "Mr. Barrios, do you realize how difficult it has been to locate you?"

"Yes, yes," he said, after taking a sip of coffee. "Let's just say that I am making some bold new strategic business moves that I have not yet revealed to the public."

"Interesting. My sources tell me you are the best in the business and that you are, shall we say, discreet."

"Really?" Barrios asked, staring. This was getting better and better. "And who are your sources?"

"Oh, they don't like to be named. Isn't it enough that I moved heaven and earth just to find you?"

Barrios smiled. "Well, how can I assist you, Ms. Morales?"

"Please, call me Luisa."

"Splendid! I hope you will call me Antonio."

"Certainly. Permit me then, Antonio, to tell you my story. Ten years ago I met a man in Acapulco. His name was Ricardo Morales. We lived in Miami where he operated a very successful import/export business until his death three months ago."

"I am very sorry."

Luisa waved it away. "Don't be. It was a marriage of convenience: he desired me, and I, his money. We both got what we wanted."

"Ah, I see. Please, continue."

"My part of the inheritance, including life insurance, amounted to—" she paused, pulled a leather case from her large purse. From within the case she extracted a bank statement that she placed on the table, pointing to a figure on it, "three million dollars."

Barrios' eyes widened. "Well, that is a very generous

inheritance, indeed!"

"But there is more," she said. "You see, after he died, I discovered that he had a hidden bank account. The scoundrel was holding out on me! My lawyer helped me retrieve the money and close the account. The employees filed a lawsuit claiming that their retirement funds had been stolen. Apparently, he had indeed been embezzling from his own company. The truth is, I don't care. I had to put up with that idiotic man and his foul temper for ten years. As far as I'm concerned, that money is mine."

"And how much was there, Luisa?" he asked, trying to sound disinterested.

Luisa pulled two more bank statements out of the leather case and presented them. "I put the money in two separate accounts," she said as she directed Barrios' eyes to a line on the statements. "Add them up and you have ..."

"Six million dollars!" he blurted almost snorting the coffee in his nostrils.

Luisa glanced around nervously and lowered her voice. "Add that to my existing account and the total comes to nine million."

Barrios took a deep breath and another sip from his coffee. "And how exactly do I fit into this picture, Luisa? Why are you telling me this?"

"The employees in my late husband's company have already started a class-action suit against me. My lawyer advised me that in three days a court order will be issued to freeze my bank accounts. But I am not going to hang around that long, I plan to leave the United States for good. I have three days to take my money and sink it into Mexican real estate. Hah! They will never find the money. I trust that you can help me."

Mr. Barrios cleared his throat. "Luisa, Luisa, of course I can help you. It will be a pleasure."

"I'm not offering you pleasure, Antonio." She paused,

smiling. "I'm offering you one million dollars if you can invest five million in three days."

Barrios' eyes twitched. Then he smiled. "I don't think that should be a problem."

"Ah! But there is a problem Antonio."

His face clouded. "What is it?"

Luisa lowered her voice again. "I think I'm being followed. Six million dollars is a lot of money and there are two hundred angry employees after it. I know I can't go back to the States. But I'd prefer that no one knew where I was, even here in Mexico, so I don't want anymore public meetings. Although, of course, I trust you implicitly, you'll forgive me if I don't invite you to my hotel room. What do you suggest, Antonio?"

He thought for a few moments, his black eyes darting around. "My home would be perfectly safe for you. No one knows I live there and the guards at the gate are extremely discreet."

He wrote his address and gave it to Luisa. "My address. Trust me. I am as interested in confidentiality as you are."

She slipped the address into her leather case and stood. "Your guards can watch for a silver Jaguar—and you can watch for me," she said. She walked away, leaving him smiling smugly.

'What a lovely meal ticket. Tonight we will have dinner, a little bit of wine, and she will melt into my arms. Then I invest her five million dollars in bogus real estate and take her for all she has!'

He walked from the restaurant, chuckling to himself. With the Mayan business, and now this, he could barely believe his ingenuity. Whistling softly, he began arranging his plans.

"Marcelo? How is dinner coming along?" Mr. Barrios asked as he entered the dining room, adjusting his collar.

His butler was busy setting the dinner table in Mr. Barrio's lavish home. A wrought-iron chandelier cast soft shadows over the thick wooden table and beautifully carved chairs.

"Oh, *Señor,* the meal will be perfect!"

"Ah, excellent. Here Marcelo," Barrios said, taking out his wallet and then handing the butler a wad of bills. "Take Graciela out to dinner. Take the evening off," he said patting Marcelo on the shoulder.

"Oh *gracias*, *Señor*. Goodnight!" Marcelo answered with a knowing smile, and then he was gone.

Moments later the intercom buzzed, and the voice of the security guard crackled through the speaker:

"Mr. Barrios, the silver Jaguar has entered the grounds."

"Excellent," replied Barrios. He walked over to a mirror and double-checked his reflection. *Ah Antonio, you handsome devil.*

The doorbell rang. "Coming my dear!" Antonio said as he walked over to the door, humming a romantic melody. Opening the door, he stopped cold. "What the—? Who are you?" he demanded.

"Good evening, Mr. Barrios," the man at the door said with a smile as he flashed his badge. "I am Gustavo De Leon, private investigator."

"What?" Antonio raged. "Who let you in?"

"Why, your guard did of course. I came in the silver Jaguar."

"But ... but ... !"

"Luisa Morales will not be joining you for dinner, I'm afraid, since her real name is Miranda De Leon; she is my wife."

Antonio was momentarily stunned, then he regained his posture. "Ah, sheesh! I was fooled by an old trick."

"Yes—you were."

"Then, I have nothing to say to you!" Antonio snarled.

"Ah, but I'm sure you'd rather discuss a certain Mayan treasure map with me than with the police."

Barrios took a step backward, stunned. His brain was working rapidly, examining his options. The very idea of having the police snooping around was enough to make him sick. "Very well, come in. But when I tell you my story, you will see that I have nothing to hide, absolutely nothing!"

CHAPTER FIVE

Gustavo sat down on a comfortable sofa, his smile fixed on his face. It had taken him longer than he had anticipated, but he had managed to locate his prime suspect. Gustavo was confident that soon the whole case would be resolved and that Mr. Barrios would produce the map.

Barrios sat down on a large chair across from Gustavo. De Leon could tell that he was suffering from the idea that he had just lost a wonderful financial opportunity.

Barrios shook his head. "I should have taken the time to do a background check on her, but she seemed in such a hurry, and those dollar bills were dancing around in my head. Well done, Mr. De Leon. Well done."

"Let's hear your story, shall we?" Gustavo put his recorder on the table and adjusted his notebook.

"I don't really have a choice, do I? But first, tell me something. How did you find out about me?"

"My client, Octavio Mendoza, hired me to find the thief of the treasure map."

Barrios sneered. "That stupid wimp, of course he went crying to you. I am sure he claims I was the thief, eh? I tell you, that whiner didn't deserve that map in the first place! Minutes after we signed the deal, and bang, he finds this incredible treasure map! It should have been mine! I admit it's my fault for not searching the house thoroughly before selling it, but still ... "

He paused, taking a calming breath. "Anyway, as you probably already know, I am an auctioneer and I specialize in distress sales. Ninety percent of the time my clients are in a very big hurry to sell their properties due to many misfortunes. You know how life is full of surprises, don't you? One moment you're in the lap of luxury, and the next you're scrambling for your meals. I have seen my share of troubles as a result of bad deals with customers." Barrios shifted in his chair.

"Take Mrs. Sova for example. I received a call from her a few months ago. She said she needed to sell her house as soon as possible since her husband was presumed dead. The next day I was at her hacienda in Yucatan. Now, in all my years of buying and selling property, I have met all kinds of people and personalities and I must say that I have rarely seen a person such as Mrs. Sova."

"What do you mean?" Gustavo asked.

"She was such as spiteful person, you know? She really hated her husband. She said all she wanted to do was to sell the estate and hightail it to France. As we toured the house, all I got out of her was a hate speech about Dr. Sova and an account of his terrible antics. When we got to the hallway where the study was, she emphatically stated that she did not want to go in there because it reminded her of him. By then I had had enough of her and figured I could check it out later.

"I endured an hour or so of this torture until we came to an agreement on the price. Once the papers were signed, she sighed with great relief, as did I, I can tell you. She then looked at me and said:

'I curse the day I married that man! All I want are my clothes and some personal documents. As far as I am concerned the rest of this house can burn to the ground'

"A week later, I received a call from Mr. Mendoza. He was looking for a home to buy for himself."

"Hmmm," Gustavo said. "Wait a minute, back up a bit. Did Mrs. Sova mention anything about the map in the study?"

"No, not at all. As I said before, she did not even want to go in the study."

"Very well," Gustavo said, satisfied. "Continue with your story."

"Octavio has obviously told you about how we found the map. We were unable to translate the document, so we had to find somebody that could, but who? I didn't want the entire scientific community involved.

"I finally remembered Raul Martinez, an archaeological appraiser I had met through a client. Martinez confided in me that many of his appraisals were for sales requiring a certain amount of discretion, if you know what I mean. I called him and soon the three of us were deeply involved in the translation, working on it every day. Octavio's greed and distrust were obvious from the start. He wouldn't let the scroll out of his sight even when he went to the bathroom! Whenever he would leave the room, he would lock it up. Can you imagine that?"

"I think I can," Gustavo answered, trying not to smile.

Oblivious to the sarcasm, Barrios continued. "Raul was constantly trying to convince Octavio to let him copy some portions of the scroll. It seemed the more progress he made on the translation, the more frustrated he became with Octavio's distrust. He told us that he was beginning to understand some of the writing and its meaning, but that there was still much to learn from the scroll. We asked him what he could understand, and he said something about 'winged serpents,' strange shadows and the 'sun god being eaten up.'"

"What does that mean?" Gustavo interrupted.

Barrios stared off into space and stroked his chin. "I, I don't remember the details. It seemed like so much nonsense to me and I said so. He said that the riddle was written in metaphors, and once we found out what they meant we would find the treasure of the Mayan king.

"As the days passed I was beginning to have second thoughts about continuing with the project. I was losing my trust in Raul. He did not seem as capable or educated as he had presented himself to be. There was a good deal of the charlatan in him. Most of the answers he gave came from Dr. Sova's computer files."

Antonio paused to collect his thoughts. "Of course, if he did actually figure out the riddle that meant a trek into the jungle. I hate the jungle, Mr. De Leon. Then, we'd have to find a hiding place for the treasure until we found the right clientele. It would take considerable time to find somebody willing to purchase our goods. I'm a businessman, not an adventurer. There was just too much work and risk. I decided that it would simply be best if I stole the map and sold it myself. However, one day when I was driving Raul to the hacienda, he suggested exactly the same thing!

"I panicked. He was going to ruin my plan! I told him that it sounded like a great idea, but we needed a little more time and patience. I knew, however, that it was time to act. That weekend I closed my office and moved here. The following week I returned to work at the hacienda. During a lunch break, Raul excused himself to the bathroom and Octavio walked outside onto the patio. While he was out there, I overheard him mention to a caretaker that he was going to be gone for the weekend." Barrios talked with demonstrative gestures.

"Saturday afternoon I drove up to the hacienda. I told Lucio that I was retrieving some documents for Octavio, showing him and Jose the spare keys I had made. They let me pass and other than the demented old man, there was no one else around. But when I got to the office—"

He closed his eyes and clenched his fists.

"Yes?" prompted Gustavo.

"The treasure map was *gone*, Mr. De Leon, the secret drawer was open! Raul had beaten me to the punch, that little ...."

"Of course he had." Gustavo sarcastically intoned.

Antonio sprang to his feet, his face flushed red with anger.

"I am not lying! I have told you nothing but God's own truth, I swear it!"

Gustavo stood as well. "Come now, Mr. Barrios. You admit to having a key to the house, and you admit to being in the place when it disappeared. Who else could have stolen the map?"

"Raul could have broken in!" Antonio shouted.

"Mr. Mendoza said that there was no evidence of forced entry. I don't want to play games, Barrios."

"I am not playing games!"

Gustavo sneered. "You will be hearing from me again. Don't try anything foolish like running away."

De Leon shut the door leaving Barrios, fists clenched, glaring after him.

Gustavo tried to focus on the hazy figure standing at the foot of his bed.

"Wake up sleepy head," the familiar voice said. "I brought you breakfast in bed."

"Wha ... ?" Gustavo said groggily as he propped himself up in bed. He was still half-asleep, but the smell of *huevos rancheros* was making its way past his wooziness. "Thank you, Miranda," he finally managed to say. "That was very nice of you. What do you want?"

Ignoring the question, Miranda put the breakfast tray in front of him. It was perfectly prepared, as always: two eggs sunny side up, stacked on a bed of lightly fried corn tortillas smothered with hot sauce and melted cheese. A healthy portion of refried beans on the side completed the meal.

Miranda sat on the bed next to her husband and waited a few moments before speaking. "Too bad things didn't work out with Barrios. Still empty-handed after all the work locating that dog!" she said.

Gustavo shoveled another forkful of eggs into his mouth and chewed thoughtfully before putting his fork down. He held his thumb and index finger barely apart. "I was this close; this close! But once I find Martinez, I'll have it all wrapped up."

"Well, let's hope. The good news is that we found Mr. Barrios. Mr. Mendoza now owes us a check." Miranda replied with an optimistic smile. "I need to go shopping."

Gustavo brightened. "Yes, yes that is good. I forgot all about that. Remind me to give him a call today so we can get our second payment."

"Have you heard from Mr. Rollock?" Miranda asked.

Gustavo wiped his mouth with his napkin as he quickly put the tray aside and jumped off the bed. "Let's find out."

They entered Gustavo's study and he sat at the computer.

"There is his answer!" They both leaned forward to read it.

To: Gustavo De Leon, Private Investigator
From: Chauncy Rollock
Dear Mr. De Leon,
First, I would like to convey my heartfelt congratulations on your new endeavor as a private investigator! I wish you success.
I am currently working on a project near Jerusalem where I am assisting another Bible archeologist. We are unearthing an ancient wall from the time of King Solomon. Now in reference to the Mayan case, I have kept silent concerning the treasure of the Mayan king for a long time. Like you, I feel that the treasure of King Chac should either be left untouched or be transferred to the Mexican authorities, not plundered for personal gain.
I have information which I believe will help you. Experience has shown that the only safe course is to give it to you in person, face-to-face. Just give the word and I will book a flight out of Jerusalem."

Gustavo took a deep breath as he finished reading. "Well, well. It looks like we'll be having a guest." He proceeded to type the following:

To: Chauncy Rollock
From: Gustavo De Leon
Thank you for your prompt response! We would be highly honored to have you come visit and assist us in solving this case. I would have preferred your visit to be under more pleasant circumstances. I am confident that whatever information you have will expedite justice. Please let me know when you will arrive at the International Airport in Mexico City so I can meet you.
Thank you so very much!

Gustavo smiled contentedly as he clicked the 'Send' button.

"Excellent! We'll have this wrapped up in no—" He was interrupted by his cell phone ringing.

Miranda handed it to him.

"Hello? Yes, I'm De Leon. What? You're joking, right? Are you sure? What happened? Yes, yes I'll be there as soon as possible."

Gustavo ended the call and stared at the wall.

"What's wrong?" Miranda asked as she saw the look on her husband's face.

Gustavo slowly turned to her, a look of disbelief on his face. "Antonio Barrios is dead."

CHAPTER SIX

"What? How?" Miranda asked in shock.

"From a heart attack of all things. The two undercover officers that I had trailing him said that this morning he had driven to a restaurant for breakfast. When he got out of his car, he grabbed his chest and fell to the ground. By the time they got to him, he was dead."

Miranda shook her head. "How sad. Something is very strange about this."

"I know. It's not a good sign when your primary suspect dies right in the middle of the investigation. I'm going over to the morgue to talk to the police and look at the body. And *you* are going to find Raul Martinez for me, since that seems to be your specialty."

The morgue, a nondescript white building with few windows, lay hidden among many other government buildings in Mexico City. Ironically it teemed with life. Police officers, private investigators, reporters, medical students, doctors, lawyers, government workers and surviving family members filled the lobbies, hallways and offices.

As a military captain, Gustavo De Leon had been no stranger to the morgue. Now, as a private investigator, he knew he would visit just as frequently. He walked briskly up a series of stone steps, passing the street vendors and newspaper sellers. The throng waiting to identify their dead loved ones spilled out onto the street. Despite his years of experience, De Leon had never fully come to terms with the sadness of the place.

Inside he performed the ritual of showing his identification to a guard who knew him well but knew procedure just as well. Passing through the security doors, Gustavo entered a large room that contained only a table, a few chairs, three of them occupied.

"Good morning gentlemen," he greeted the three police officers. Nothing ever changes ... the same furniture and the same echoes for the last twenty years, he thought.

"Thank you for joining me; I realize that you're busy and that I have no official status." He opened a file that was sitting on the table and perused it. "According to this police report, and the report I received earlier, Antonio Barrios left his house at three minutes after seven this morning. He was then followed to a restaurant. As he got out of the vehicle he grabbed his chest, cried out something about being shot, and collapsed to the sidewalk. He was dead by the time anybody got to him." He looked up at the policemen. "Does that sound right?"

The three nodded in unison.

Gustavo rubbed his forehead. "Well, gentlemen, which is it? The report says that he died of a heart attack, but he thought he'd been shot."

The officer who had been directing traffic at the scene spoke up. "The report is correct. There were no bullet wounds, no evidence of his being shot. Perhaps the pain was so severe he only thought he'd been shot."

"Perhaps, perhaps. Tell me anything you can remember that's not in the report."

"Other than a cyclist in a big hurry, it was just business as usual."

Gustavo raised an eyebrow. "What cyclist?"

"Just a man riding really fast on a bicycle—he came pretty close to Barrios. With his jacket fluttering, it's hard to say anything about his size. But he was obviously athletic. I was startled by how fast he was moving."

"Did he interact in any way with Barrios?"

"No, he did not."

“Is there anything else you men would like to add?” Gustavo asked.

The response was a series of shrugs.

Gustavo sighed and stood, as did the others. He raised his voice over the echoes of the sliding chairs. "Thank you. I’ll let you get back to work now."

Gustavo tucked his files under his arm and instead of following the officers to the exit, he went the other direction. He walked down a long flight of stairs. At the bottom, he opened a steel door and was greeted by a blast of cold air. Gustavo shivered and wrinkled his nose at the smell of formaldehyde.

Starting down the long hallway he shouted, "Hey, Hernandez!" to a stout figure in a white smock sitting at a table.

Dr. Emilio Hernandez answered without turning. "My, my, it’s Captain, I mean *Investigator* De Leon!"

He finished the notes he was writing, stood up and turned and embraced De Leon heartily. "How are you doing, Gustavo? It’s been a while."

“Busier than I'd like. How have you been?”

"I can’t complain," he said, adjusting his glasses. "Business is good. Everybody is just dying to get in here."

Gustavo groaned theatrically. "At least, when your time is up, you won’t have far to go; you’ll already be here."

They both laughed. As they walked down the corridor toward the "crypt" as Hernandez called it, Gustavo couldn’t help but marvel at his friend. Throughout the years, Dr. Hernandez had maintained a cheerful attitude even though he was surrounded by so much death. Gustavo knew that the constant joking was how he coped.

"So how is business, Gustavo?"

"Well, it was going all right until my prime suspect checked into your hotel."

"Yes, yes, that's what I heard. I suppose you came to visit him? I can assure you that he is getting proper rest." They stopped in front of another door. "You know the procedure; gloves and mask."

When both were ready, the doctor opened the door and they entered an even colder room.

"So how is Miranda?"

"She's well. She's helping me with my business, actually."

"Ah! So she is your partner in crime, then?"

"If it wasn't for crime, I would be working as a street performer."

"Thank God for crime, then."

Dr. Hernandez stopped and turned to study the names on the metal doors that were built into the walls of the large room. "Let's see—B, B, Barrios, Antonio Barrios, here he is."

Pulling the drawer out, the two men saw that Antonio's body was encased in a white bag. Hernandez unzipped the bag down to the navel.

Gustavo came close and stared at the frozen and contorted face. Despite thirty years in the military, the sight of a corpse always gave Gustavo the same strange feeling. He remembered how full of life and vibrant the victims had once been, and now there was a body, so lifeless, so still.

Dr. Hernandez adjusted his glasses again and pulled out a small file from the foot of the drawer. "Here is my initial report. 'Cause of death: cardiac arrest.' I see this every day, nothing out of the ordinary." He returned the file to its plastic holder and turned nonchalantly to De Leon.

"What are the scratch marks on his chest?" De Leon asked.

The doctor casually took a glance. "Those, my friend, are the marks of his fingernails as he clutched his chest. The pain must have been intense."

"So there were no knife marks, no bullet holes, no other wounds?"

"None whatsoever. I'll bet his life the autopsy shows just

another heart attack. It might take a few days before we get to him. If I discover anything unusual in the preliminary tests, I will inform you. However, if you find anything in your investigation, let me know. I can expedite the process for the autopsy—just call and say the word."

Gustavo nodded. "Thank you. Witnesses said that they heard him shout that he had been shot; any ideas?"

"You have no idea of the pain. It is not the first time someone who has experienced a heart attack thought they had been shot."

De Leon nodded as the doctor rolled the drawer back into its niche. They left the room and disposed of their latex gloves and masks.

Before Gustavo left the basement, however, he turned to his friend. "I need a special favor from you."

"For you Gustavo, I have one hundred. What do you need?"

"Was Mr. Barrios carrying any keys?"

Doctor Hernandez smiled. "Of course, follow me."

The security booth at Barrio's hacienda was empty but the gate wasn't locked. He got out of his car, pushed it open and drove through.

Five hours later Gustavo collapsed on the sofa. He shook his head in disgust—at himself, at Barrios, at the house, at the case. There was no map here.

The cell phone rang, Octavio answered it. "Hello?"

"Yes, Mr. Mendoza, this is Mr. De Leon. Did you hear about Mr. Barrios?"

"Yes, yes, I was delivering the second check to your office and your wife told me. Well, that is too bad for him. I would rather have seen him rot in prison! But the good news is that one scoundrel is out of the way. But what about the scroll, did you find it?"

"Unfortunately not. If it's in Barrios' house, I can't find it."

"What? How can that be?"

"I'm sorry Mr. Mendoza, I looked everywhere."

"Raul must have it! You must find him, I know he has it!"

"Yes, of course, but he's going to be hard to find."

"Oh, I am so frustrated! Martinez was so close to deciphering the Mayan inscriptions. He must know how to find the treasure by now. He must be making preparations to locate it. You must stop him—Mexico will suffer because of this!"

"Calm down, Mr. Mendoza. I didn't say it would be impossible to find him."

"Let me tell you something, if you find that map, I will give you a check for five times the amount of the others!"

"Thank you. I will call when I have any more news."

"God bless you, Mr. De Leon. Thank you. Good-bye."

It was late once again when Gustavo arrived home. Miranda was up in bed reading.

She closed her book and got up. "Well?"

Gustavo took off his jacket before throwing his keys on the nightstand. "I went over to Barrios' place and found nothing, absolutely nothing. There is no trace of the map. It just disappeared into thin air." He looked at her with tired eyes. "It's not as easy as I thought it would be."

Miranda had a concerned expression. "And it's not getting any easier; the scroll isn't the only thing that has disappeared. Raul Martinez is gone too. No trace at all. Nothing! What are we going to do now?"

CHAPTER SEVEN

The wind was blowing softly on another warm day in Cozumel, Quintana Roo. The traffic sped past pedestrians, beggars, street vendors, taxis, and donkeys. The city was abuzz with activity.

Dressed like every other tourist, and reading a copy of *Archaeology Today,* he was essentially invisible to everyone but the attractive woman seated next to him.

Her long hair fluttered in the wind as she giggled.

"What's so funny?" Raul asked, without taking his eyes off his magazine.

"Oh Rooly, the comics are really funny today."

"I told you to stop calling me that, Claudia."

"How much longer are we staying in Cozumel? I love it here!"

"Not long," he snapped. "It's expensive." Shuffling his magazine a bit as he adjusted his position, he continued reading.

"What are we going to do Rooly? Can we ask your daddy for money?"

Plopping his magazine down on the table, he looked at Claudia with an angry expression. "I don't know yet, but we are not asking my father for money."

As he picked up the magazine, an advertisement on the back cover caught his eye. "Hello, what's this?" he asked no one in particular as he straightened up.

"What is it?" Claudia asked eagerly.

"Shhh!" He waved his hand at her as he read:

ESTATE SALE
Large estate in Mexico City.
Everything must go. Seeking
certified appraisers knowledgeable
in ancient artifacts. Please call
for an appointment.

Raul began dialing the number.

The following day found Raul prowling the streets of a posh neighborhood in Mexico City. He cruised slowly in low gear, one hand on the steering wheel and his other hand holding a piece of paper upon which was written the address of his potential client. He glanced at the clock; he was right on time.

He came to a stop in front of a large house, fairly typical of the neighborhood. Red Spanish-tile roof, white plastered walls and large windows with wrought-iron bars. A well maintained, yet simple, yard was contained by a low, white-plastered wall topped by black wrought iron that matched the house.

He turned off the engine and looked in the mirror, combing his jet-black hair. His outfit was quite different than what he had been wearing just the day before. In place of sandals he wore brown snake-skin cowboy boots, and his shorts and Hawaiian shirt were exchanged for long slacks and a short-sleeve brown shirt with a Bolo tie.

Attaché in hand, he walked briskly through a small gate past the low wall and up a few steps. He adjusted his Bolo tie and smoothed his shirt before ringing the doorbell.

A weak voice came faintly through the thick wooden door. "Wait a minute, I'm coming ..."

It seemed twice that minute before the ornately carved door swung open to reveal a grizzled old man. White scraggly hair stuck out comically from underneath a black beret. His hands trembled as he clung to his hand-crafted wooden cane.

He peered at Raul through thick glasses. "Mr. Martinez?" His accent was so thick Martinez had to think for a moment to recognize his own name.

"Yes, we have an appointment, Mr. Allende."

"May I see your credentials, young man?"

"Certainly," Raul said, smiling as he propped his attaché on his knee and pulled out his business card and other papers.

Mr. Allende peered at the documents, his long white beard almost touching them. Raul wondered how the old man was able to read the small print, the way his hands trembled.

Mr. Allende seemed satisfied. "Yes, yes. Come right in please." He handed back the paperwork.

Raul stepped inside and let his eyes adjust to the darkened interior. He nodded. Glancing around with keen eyes, Raul guessed the man was single, probably a widower. The rooms were graced by expensive furniture imported from Spain. Artwork ranging from beautiful, photo-realistic paintings to simple abstract watercolors adorned nearly every square inch of wall. Wooden statues stood like sentinels in the living room. What immediately grabbed Raul's attention, however, was an alcove filled with Mayan artifacts.

"Now listen to me young man," Mr. Allende said, his voice becoming a bit stronger and easier to understand. "I'm a very old man. Let me explain why I asked you to come over. Many years ago I was a professor at the National Autonomous University of Mexico. I taught history and archaeology, but that was a long, long time ago, before you were born." Mr. Allende chuckled softly at the thought. "Anyway, as you can clearly see, throughout the years I have collected many Mayan artifacts. However, I plan to sell everything. My wife passed away recently, and the memories are too much for an old man, and I can't keep up the maintenance of this place all by myself. I am going to move, therefore I want top dollar for my possessions. That's why I need your services, Mr. Martinez."

The old man shuffled closer. He waved a trembling hand at the alcove displaying the ancient artifacts. "Those artifacts up on that shelf, Mr. Martinez, I want to fetch the best price for them. Yes, yes, the very best price. Once these items are sold, you will be properly compensated."

Raul walked over to the alcove and admired the items that were placed within. With a self-assured tone in his voice he said, "You have a fine collection here."

"Yes, yes, as I said, I have collected them through travels in Yucatan, Guatemala, and Belize. Some of these artifacts were obtained through—well, you know what I mean," he said with a wink, and then he nudged Raul with his elbow.

Raul smiled. "Yes, I understand. I can assure you of my policy of strict confidentiality."

"Good! I was hoping you would say that. Now, it is time for the test."

"A test?" Raul asked as he raised his eyebrows.

"Yes, yes the test. Tell me where each of these comes from. I already know, but I need to know if you do."

Raul swallowed hard. This was going to be a challenge.

Mr. Allende hobbled over to the first artifact. "Here, take this one down for me, will you? And tell me its origin. Careful, careful now, don't break it!"

Raul took down a shard of pottery and turned it over and over in his hands.

"Hmm. Chichen Itza ... pre-Colombian."

"Excellent, excellent, yes that is true. Now, how much is it worth?"

"On the black market, you'd fetch around three thousand dollars, sir."

"Oh, good, good, write that down will you? My hands tremble too much."

Raul sighed quietly with relief. He carefully replaced the pottery before pulling a notebook from his attaché and scribbling some notes.

"And this one?" Mr. Allende asked, pointing a shaking finger at another object.

Raul carefully picked up a small black dagger. "Obsidian. This is Aztec."

"But I found this in Bonampak, in Mayan territory," the old man said. "How is it possible that the Mayans possessed it if it belonged to the Aztecs?"

"Perhaps the Maya accepted this as a gift from an Aztec dignitary, a peace offering of some sort. Recent archaeological discoveries have revealed that the Mayas and the Aztecs may have had a friendly relationship for a time."

"Oh, you are correct, you are correct," Mr. Allende said, smiling.

Raul exhaled; he hadn't realized he was holding his breath. "I would put the price at five thousand dollars."

"Good, good. Write that down too, now, what about this one?" Mr. Allende pointed to the next item, which was a large jade necklace. "This is my prize. Tell me, where did it come from?"

Raul's hands trembled slightly as he turned the necklace over, his brain racing. "Why, this is the necklace of a king. Jade was prized, even more than gold. Only a king would have worn this!" he answered emphatically.

Mr. Allende squinted at Raul. "Yes, you are correct on that assumption. But the question is, Mr. Martinez, which king? And where is it from?"

"If you observe the markings, and particularly the way the necklace is constructed, the markings of the jade ornament, you will notice that these correspond to ... to ... the post-classic era of the Mayas. This necklace belonged to King Paca."

"King Paca? No, Mr. Martinez, you are wrong!" Mr. Allende barked.

"Really? And how do you know that?"

The look on Allende's face made Raul feel like a schoolboy. "That necklace does not belong to King Paca!" the old man shouted. "You are mistaken. Perhaps I should inspect your credentials again."

Raul folded his arms across his chest. "Well then, old man, you tell me. Who does it belong to?"

"This came from the military plunder of King Chac."

"What? King Chac?"

"Yes, yes—this was taken from a hidden treasure in Palenque; the treasure of a Mayan king. It belongs to King Chac."

Raul laughed out loud. "Ha, ha, that's impossible!"

"Why? Why is it impossible?" the old man shouted, banging his cane on the floor.

"Because the treasure of King Chac has yet to be discovered, that's why!" Raul finally managed to blurt out.

Mr. Allende stood, leaning on his cane, glaring at Raul. After a few seconds his anger dissolved in a warm smile. He chuckled. "Very, very, very good, congratulations. You are right. That necklace belongs to King Paca."

Raul once again let out a breath. Returning the old man's smile, he told him, "You will get two hundred thousand dollars for this necklace."

Mr. Allende was ecstatic. "I knew it was worth a lot, but not that much! Good, good. Now, Mr. Martinez, I have only one final question and I know that you will have the answer."

"Yes?"

"Why do you think that the treasure of King Chac has not been discovered?"

Raul shrugged. "How should I know?"

"Well, I know, and I'll tell you."

Mr. Allende shuffled over to a small desk and pulled open a drawer. "The reason that the treasure has not been found, Mr. Martinez, is ..."

Allende straightened and turned with a gun in his hand—

which no longer shook. He continued, the weak quivering replied by a rich baritone, " ... that the map to the Mayan treasure was stolen, Mr. Martinez—by you!"

CHAPTER EIGHT

"What!" Raul demanded. "Who are you?"

Allende pulled off his fake beard and removed his hat and glasses.

"De Leon!" Raul shouted as the image clicked in his memory. "Captain Gustavo De Leon!"

De Leon shook his head. "Wrong again. I am now Private Investigator Gustavo De Leon. Don't you read the news, boy?"

"A setup! A stinking setup!" Raul angrily shot back as his eyes quickly darted around the room.

"The house is surrounded. Don't do anything rash Martinez—or should I say, *Comandante* Solis?" He smiled at Raul's surprise. "You haven't changed so much that I didn't recognize the photograph Mendoza showed me. There's a bounty on your head either way. I want the map, Martinez, the map of the Mayan treasure that *you* stole from Octavio Mendoza."

"Nonsense!"

"Really, why?"

Raul threw his hands in the air and shouted, "Do you really think I'd be wasting my time on antique appraisals if I had the map?"

He seemed genuinely frustrated. Gustavo began wondering if perhaps it were true. "I'm listening."

Raul pulled a chair closer and sat down. His eyes were closed for a few seconds then he let out a sigh of exasperation as he commenced his narrative. "Well, you'll have to listen to my sad story, the sad story of how I almost had the map and how it slipped out of my hands. When I failed my archaeological studies in Texas, I ran away to Yucatan to escape my father's wrath. I'd learned enough to recognize the value of the antiquities I was stealing. My father may have been rich, but I planned to be even richer.

"That dog Sova, he destroyed my plan. I went home to my father with my tail between my legs. Lucky for me, my father just sent me away to another college—right here in Mexico. That's how I got the certification I showed you. Believe it or not, it's legitimate."

"And that's how you met Barrios?" De Leon asked.

Raul slowly raised his eyes at De Leon. "Yes, yes, imagine how I felt when he told me what I would be translating! What ironic revenge on Dr. Sova."

"And did you finish the translation?"

"The words but not the meanings."

"What does the shadow mean?"

Raul's eyes narrowed. "What do you mean?"

"Barrios told me about it. He knew it was important. He just didn't know what it was."

"It's something about the equinoxes; certain temples and the way the light falls on them. I've never seen it myself, but I just saw a TV documentary about it. I needed more time to study the scroll, but those idiots Octavio and Antonio were always in the way. One day while we were taking a break I overheard Octavio mention that he was going to be away for the weekend. I decided that was my opportunity to steal the scroll. That Sunday I drove myself to Octavio's house and—"

"Wait, did you say you went on Sunday?"

"Yes, why?"

"Never mind, continue."

"Anyway, first thing I did was search around the house to see if a window or door was open. But no, everything was shut tight and locked. I crept over to the window outside the doctor's study and looked in. One set of blinds was open, and the secret door of the desk was open—and empty! I must have checked it from fifty angles: tilting my head, jumping up and down. But the scroll was gone.

"There was no point breaking in for something that wasn't there. When I turned to go, I nearly jumped out of my skin. Miguelito was sitting in his rocking chair under a tree, staring at me with that stupid grin of his. I was almost positive no one had been there. I don't know how I missed him."

Gustavo stood up, scowling.

"Why do you have that angry expression?" Raul asked.

"You don't know that Mr. Barrios told me that the map was gone when he went a day before you, on Saturday. So, if both of your stories are correct, that means someone else stole the map before either of you went there. But nobody else had a motive or opportunity."

Gustavo took his cell phone out. He pressed the two-way button and barked an order. Two officers burst into the room. "Arrest this man!" He shook his head in disappointment. "You're a fool. You prefer to go to prison than turn in the map?"

Raul had a terrified expression. "Are you crazy? I told you nothing but the truth!"

Gustavo nodded to the officers. "Take this idiot away."

De Leon shut the door behind the officers and began pacing the living room. Once again he had turned up empty-handed. He had a second suspect but still no scroll. He ran both his hands through his hair, frustration gnawing at him.

He paused next to the front window and watched as the officers escorted Raul down the steps and past the gate. Gustavo pulled out his cell phone and dialed his wife. "Hello, Miranda?"

"Yes, Gustavo, how did it go?"

"Well, both good and bad. I have Raul in custody, but no map. He claims he doesn't have it."

"Now what?" his wife asked.

"Raul is a spoiled rich kid. Once he spends a few nights in one of our wonderful Mexican jails, he will start talking. Meanwhile I'm going to have to go to the hacienda and interview the caretakers to see if the stories told by Martinez and Barrios are true. You see I—"

"Gustavo? Gustavo? What's wrong?"

"I have to go, Raul Martinez is sprawled on the sidewalk! I'll call you back!"

He sprinted down the steps and ran to the sidewalk.

"What happened?"

"Mr. Martinez said he is having a heart attack!" a police officer informed him.

"A what?" Gustavo asked, his eyes widening. He quickly bent down to look closer at Raul. "Mr. Martinez? Raul? What's wrong? Can you hear me? Talk to me!"

Raul writhed in agony, whispered something to Gustavo and then was still.

Gustavo stood slowly. "He's dead."

"What did he say to you, Mr. De Leon?"

Gustavo stared blankly at the sky for a moment. "He said 'I've been shot!'"

"What about the man on the bicycle?" one of the officers asked.

Gustavo snapped out of his trance. "What? What man?"

"The man on the bicycle," the officer replied. "He sped past us just before Martinez fell."

"What did he look like?"

"Well, he had a baseball cap on, but all I could see of his face was the black beard and the big sunglasses."

"Was he fat, was he thin, dark, light?"

"I, I couldn't tell if he was thin or fat, his shirt was puffed out by the wind. He was dark though, I think."

"Did he have a gun?"

"No, both hands were on the handlebars."

"Anything else?"

"Well, I think he was smoking a cigarette."

"A cigarette? That's it?" Gustavo asked.

"I'm sorry Mr. De Leon, that's all I saw. He was riding really fast, I mean *really* fast."

"Which direction did he go?"

The officer pointed, and Gustavo took off running. Ignoring the pain that shot through his leg, he ran faster as he approached the corner where the residential neighborhood changed into a commercial district. He turned the corner and stopped abruptly. The street was packed: pedestrians and cars.

He bent over and rested his arms against his thighs, gasping. As soon as he thought he could speak, he approached one of the pedestrians.

"Excuse me sir, did you see a bearded man on a bicycle pass through here?"

"I didn't see anybody."

Gustavo grimaced and hobbled down the sidewalk. His old leg wound was throbbing something terrible. At the next corner he came to a taco vendor.

"Excuse me sir, did you happen to see a bearded man pass by here on a bicycle?"

The man looked at him with a suspicious expression. "Who wants to know?"

Gustavo flashed his PI badge. "I do."

The vendor scratched his neck. "I might have seen someone like that." He paused expectantly.

Gustavo threw a wad of pesos on the chopping block. "Where did he go?"

The pesos disappeared instantly into the man's shirt. "He seemed to be in a hurry."

"What did he look like?"

"Loose clothes, big sunglasses, big beard, I'll throw this in: I think the beard was fake. He threw his bike into the back of an old red truck and shot out of here like a bullet."

"Yeah," Gustavo grunted. "Thanks for the 'tacos.'"

He slipped into an alley and leaned against the wall, rubbing his injured leg. He closed his eyes and tried to think.

There was just too much going on, and Gustavo felt lost. What did all of this mean? Why were his suspects dying, one by one? Why were they saying that they had been shot? Who was the mysterious man on the bicycle that seemed to show up in both cases? If he was the murderer, if indeed murder had been committed, then where was his weapon? What did Raul see in a documentary that made him understand the Mayan riddle? And where in the world was the map? None of this was making any sense to Gustavo.

He pulled out his cell phone and dialed. "Hello, doc?"

"Gustavo! What's up?" Dr. Hernandez asked.

Gustavo grimaced as he rubbed his neck. "My new prime suspect just died, exactly like the first one."

"I assume we no longer think it was a heart attack."

"I don't. But you're the expert. I need you to expedite both autopsies. Martinez's body is on its way to the morgue as we speak."

"You just became my top priority, Gustavo."

"Thanks, doc. Please call me as soon as you find anything. Bye."

Gustavo arrived home, and performed what was now becoming his custom, to throw the keys on the bed and lay himself down in what seemed an air of defeat.

"Miranda, my love?" he asked as he rubbed his tired eyes.

"Yes, Gustavo?"

"Will you tell me why I wanted to become a private investigator?"

"Let me see ... your position in the military was too stressful, you wanted to make your own working hours so you could get enough rest, you knew you could solve most crimes in no time at all and you wanted to set your own prices and make a better living."

"Ha...well, one out of four isn't bad. If I ever do solve this tangled nightmare, Octavio promised a big fat check."

Miranda bent over and kissed his forehead. "Well, I have some news that might help. Three days from now you're picking up Chauncy Rollock at the airport."

CHAPTER NINE

Gustavo spent the morning, even during breakfast, re-reading every single note and reviewing every recording. On a large sheet of paper he drew a chart of everyone and everything related to the case and found every possible connection. Hanging it on the wall, he sat, staring, while he drank his coffee.

He drained his cup with a silent prayer that caffeine would accomplish what the many days of footwork and thinking hadn't.

It was early afternoon when it finally came to him.

He walked into the kitchen where Miranda was preparing his lunch. She knew by the expression on his face that he had something. "What is it?"

Gustavo dropped the thick case folder onto the table and pointed at it. "I know who has the map. I know who's had it all along!"

"Well?"

"Patience; let's see if you can follow my reasoning. I want to make sure there's no flaw in it."

Gustavo walked around the table, holding up a finger as he made each point. "First, Antonio Barrios went to the hacienda on Saturday afternoon and got in with his key. The map was already gone."

"Yes, that's *his* story."

Gustavo smiled. "Exactly, but I'm convinced he was telling the truth. So then we have Raul Martinez coming Sunday morning. From outside the house he saw that the map was gone."

"Right."

"Then Octavio Mendoza came back Sunday evening. And, of course, he went to the study and found that the scroll was gone. Miranda, the map was taken by someone else before Antonio Barrios came to the hacienda.

"Who could it possibly be?"

Who else had keys to the house?" Gustavo asked.

"Are you saying that Mrs. Sova took the map?" Miranda replied.

"Exactly! Mrs. Sova took the map! She had the original keys!"

"But why didn't she take it before she sold the house?"

Gustavo sat down and opened the folder. He flipped partway through the stack of papers.

"Let me read to you what she told Barrios: '*I curse the day I married that man! All I want are my clothes and some personal documents. As far as I am concerned, the rest of this house can burn to the ground.*' Did you notice that she confessed her financial situation and only wanted her clothes and some personal documents? Think, Miranda, what if she arrived in France and remembered the map? She is in debt, and she knows that the scroll can make her rich. So she returns to the hacienda, uses her keys, and takes it. She was back in France before they knew it was gone."

"Brilliant deduction, but I have a question. How did she get past the groundskeepers? Wouldn't they have told Octavio that Mrs. Sova was snooping around?"

"Those men worked loyally for Mrs. Sova for years and they had no reason to be suspicious."

"Okay, but what about the two deaths?"

"If I don't move quickly, there will be three. Octavio Mendoza is the next victim in line."

"What do you mean?"

"Consider: Mrs. Sova has the map but the other three have knowledge of the treasure. She knows that if they get to it before she does, the map is useless."

Miranda looked troubled. "That's terrible. Mrs. Sova, a murderer? I don't know. It doesn't seem right."

"Greed can have a powerful grip on people. I have seen what the love of money can do, trust me."

"Shouldn't we warn Octavio?"

"Once the autopsies are completed, I don't want Octavio running around like a chicken with its head cut off. I'm leaving for Yucatan today to talk to the caretakers and check the hacienda myself. By the way—"

"Yes, yes, yes, I know. You want me to find Mrs. Sova in France, right?"

"I love you, Miranda," Gustavo said with a sheepish grin, as he closed the door behind him and left the house.

Miranda was sitting at the table, idly picking at her food. Her forehead creased as a morbid thought came to her. *Octavio may be in danger, but so are we. Gustavo and I know about the treasure, and so does Chauncy Rollock. We may be next in line to die.*

It was another beautiful day in Yucatan. Gustavo chartered a plane to Merida. There he rented a truck for the long drive through the jungle. Mendoza had given him keys to the hacienda and precise driving directions.

The bumpy road did nothing to shake De Leon from his thoughts as his truck burst out of the jungle. There was the hacienda. He whistled softly. All three had mentioned the beauty of the place but now he knew why.

He came to a stop as two men approached the wooden gate.

"Good afternoon, *Señores*. My name is Gustavo De Leon, and I am a private investigator."

"*Buenos dias, Señor*; welcome. I'm Lucio and this is Jose."

After stepping from the truck, Gustavo looked around. "Is Miguelito here?"

Jose pointed. "Yes, he is over there *Señor*, under the tree."

"Excellent. I'm investigating the theft of an important document from Mr. Mendoza's office. After I look around the office, I'll want to speak with all three of you."

"*Si, Señor*, of course."

De Leon left the men and walked slowly around the yard. A careful inspection of every window and door showed no evidence of forced entry, just as he expected. He returned to the window of the study and looked in. The scene was exactly as Martinez had described it.

Satisfied that there was nothing else to learn outside, he entered the house and went into the study. Everything was larger than he had imagined: the room, the collection of books, the Mayan wall hangings and artifacts.

He visualized Dr. Sova bent over his desk, analyzing a glyph inscribed on a piece of stone. He imagined the master linguist digging through references, writing paper upon paper on the meaning of the glyph and how it fit into the Mayan language as a whole. It saddened him to think that, if greed hadn't interfered, the world would have benefited from the work that had gone on in this room.

Locking the front door of the hacienda he stepped across the porch. The two caretakers had joined Miguelito under the large tree.

Jose and Lucio were visibly nervous. De Leon didn't take that as a sign of guilt. Living in the middle of nowhere they weren't used to dealing with people from *La Capital*, Mexico City, let alone a private investigator.

Miguelito, on the other hand, just sat in a dilapidated rocking chair, with a fixed smile and a stare, as he was holding on to his cane.

Gustavo smiled at them. "*Hola Muchachos*. You've kept this place looking beautiful."

"Gracias, Señor."

"Mr. Mendoza has asked me to find a very important

document which may have been stolen. Did any of you see Antonio Barrios visit the hacienda a few Saturdays ago?"

Lucio nodded. "*Si Señor*, we saw him come on a Saturday. He said that he needed to get something for Mr. Mendoza. He showed us the keys and entered the house."

"How long did he stay inside?"

Jose answered, "Just a few minutes; four or five, *Señor*."

"And when he came out was he carrying anything?"

"No, no, *Señor*. His hands were empty."

"Yes," Lucio said. "He was very angry, shouting and swearing. He got in his car and left in a hurry."

Gustavo nodded. It was what he had expected. "What about Sunday?"

"We go home on Saturday night. We're never here on Sunday."

"You all leave?"

"No, *Señor*, Miguelito is always here," Jose said. "He watches over the property. There is a little hut behind the horse stalls where he lives."

De Leon knelt down next to the old man. "Miguelito, did you see anyone here that Sunday?"

Miguelito answered, but not in Spanish. Lucio turned to De Leon. "I have to translate, *Señor*, he only speaks the Mayan language."

Lucio spoke to Miguelito, who answered slowly. "He said: ‘yes I did.’"

"Who was it?"

"’It was Martinez,’" Lucio translated.

"What was he doing?"

"‘Walking around ... around the house.’"

"Did he go in the house?"

"‘No, he never entered.’"

All of a sudden the older man broke out into a long speech. Gustavo could tell that the old man was repeating something over and over again in the Mayan language:

"K' inich Aha, Quetzalcoatl, K' inich Aha, Xibalba."

"What's he saying?" Gustavo asked.

Lucio laughed. "It's just nonsense."

"What kind of nonsense?"

"Something about 'Flying serpents will show the way and the sun god will be swallowed up.'" Lucio said.

Gustavo stared at the old man. "What? Wait a minute, where did he learn that phrase? Ask him."

"Miguelito said 'that is what the other men always talked about. It was funny.'"

The poor old Mayan sat rocking back and forth, smiling as he repeated the phrase over and over again. "*K' inich Aha, Quetzalcoatl, K' inich Aha, Xibalba.*"

Gustavo nodded. "Of course, it makes sense. One last question; did Mrs. Sova ever come back to the house to visit or take anything?"

The two men seemed perplexed. They looked at each other and then at Gustavo. "Mrs. Sova? No, she never came back, never." Jose said.

"Really? Are you sure? Ask Miguelito."

"We are sure. Miguelito also says that Mrs. Sova never returned." Jose answered.

Gustavo's temper was starting to rise. "You'd better not be lying to me! Do you realize how horrible jails are in Mexico City?"

Both men visibly twitched. "Please believe us. We never saw her after she sold the house and left!" Lucio chimed in.

The conversation was interrupted by the ringing of De Leon's cell phone. "Excuse me for a moment. Hello?"

"It's me, Miranda. I have information on Mrs. Sova."

"Talk about perfect timing. What have you got?"

"I found her. But it won't do you any good."

"Why not?"

"She's in a cemetery. She died in a car accident as soon as she arrived in France. I have a copy of the newspaper obituary online."

Gustavo let out a long sigh of frustration.

After a moment Miranda spoke again. "Gustavo, are you there? Did you hear me?"

"Yes, yes I did. I'm finished here. I'll just come home."

Crestfallen, Gustavo closed his cell phone and turned to address the men. "Gentlemen, thank you for your cooperation. *Adios*."

He got into his truck, put the key in the ignition, and sat back, without starting it. He had been so sure about Mrs. Sova. *Now what*? he asked himself. *What am I going to do? I've exhausted all my leads. All my suspects are dead. I'm back where I started. What a complete failure*! He rubbed his face with both hands. *What am I going to tell Octavio?*

He started up his truck and drove slowly down the jungle road. His cell phone rang again. In a foul mood, he didn't wish to speak to anyone unless it was an important person.

He checked his phone and it was someone important. "Hello, Dr. Hernandez?"

"Hello Gustavo. I have some bad news."

"So what else is new?" Gustavo smirked.

"Those two men: Mr. Martinez and Mr. Barrios? We have confirmed that they didn't die of natural causes. They were both murdered."

"Murdered? How?"

"I can't say over the phone. Come to the morgue, I have something to show you."

Gustavo's thoughts were spinning. "Uh, yeah, I'm in Yucatan, I have to fly back to Mexico City."

CHAPTER TEN

The airliner Chauncy was flying in descended into the smoggy blanket that covered Mexico City. As usual, Chauncy gripped the armrest with apprehension. It was the same old feeling again: an unknown, inexplicable fear of descending in an airplane. This time though, Chauncy had to chuckle to himself. He realized how unfounded the whole phobia really was. After all the life-and-death situations he had been through, this was the least of his worries.

His mind came back to the reason he was again visiting Mexico.

He pulled out an envelope from his pocket and twirled it in his hands. *It's time*. He thought. *It's time for the truth to be told.*

It was dark when De Leon arrived at the morgue. He passed through security and walked down the corridor to Hernandez's office.

"Come in, come in," Hernandez said, glancing up.

"This better be good," De Leon said.

"Oh, I think you'll find this very interesting" Dr. Hernandez answered, as he handed Gustavo a pair of thick gloves. "Put these on, and be very careful how you handle this!" He opened a drawer and slowly pulled out a small plastic bag. "Exhibit A," Hernandez said as he passed the bag over to De Leon.

De Leon held the bag up to the light. "It looks like a small thorn—from a cactus, maybe."

"Correct, it's a cactus thorn. But most cactus thorns haven't been dipped in poison! We found this thorn in Barrios' neck and another just like it in Martinez's. Same poison, same type of thorn, same method."

"A blow pipe, the bearded man on the bicycle wasn't smoking a cigarette. It was a blow pipe!" Gustavo blurted out.

Dr. Hernandez nodded in agreement. "They really had been shot. The poison acted so quickly they just didn't have time to explain how."

"What kind of poison?"

The doctor shrugged his shoulders. "We don't know. It's some manufactured concoction. But whoever created it knew more about pharmaceuticals than the guys in our lab, and that's saying something."

"So we're looking for an expert pharmacist?" Gustavo asked. Suddenly a thundering revelation came to him.

"Apparently so." Dr. Hernandez added.

De Leon looked stunned. Octavio had mentioned that he had been a pharmacist.

"What's the matter, Gustavo?"

"May I borrow your phone? The battery on my cell phone is low."

"Certainly."

Gustavo grabbed the phone on Hernandez's desk. After dialing a number, a female voice came over the speaker. "Hello and thank you for calling the Hotel Feliz. How may I help you?"

"Yes, I'm looking for a friend of mine named Mr. Octavio Mendoza. Is he there?"

"I'm sorry sir, he checked out a few hours ago."

"He did? Did he mention where he was going?"

"No, but from the stuff I helped load in his van it looked like he was going to do some serious digging."

De Leon slammed the phone down; he was breathing hard.

Dr. Hernandez had a perplexed expression. "Care to tell me what is going on?"

De Leon stood up and clenched his teeth. “It will have to wait for another time,” he hissed and without any further explanation he ran from the office before Hernandez could say a word.

Gustavo sat at the table with his face in his hands. He didn't even smell the coffee Miranda set in front of him. "I'm a fool and a failure."

"Explain it to me again. Now you said the map was *never* stolen?"

Gustavo leaned back in his chair and ran his hands through his hair in a familiar gesture of frustration. Dropping his arms to his side with a sigh, he repeated the painful and embarrassing explanation. "When Mendoza realized that Martinez and Barrios had nearly completed the translation, he decided not to share the treasure with those two crooks. So Friday evening when he left the hacienda he simply took the map with him. Of course he wasn't safe as long as the other two knew about the map and the treasure. Therefore phase two of his plan was simple. All he had to do was hire an amateur private investigator who is smart enough to find them and dumb enough to believe the story.

"Since Octavio is a pharmacist, he knew how quickly and effectively the wrong mixture of drugs could simulate a heart attack. Once I'd led him to his victims, he raced past on a bicycle with his blowpipe and cactus needle. It was just plain chance that we discovered the deaths weren't heart attacks. Octavio Mendoza is gone. I don't know what I'm going to do next."

Miranda looked up at the clock. "What you're going to do next is get to the airport in Mexico City. If you leave right now, you'll be just in time to meet Chauncy Rollock's plane."

CHAPTER ELEVEN

It seemed to take an eternity to find a parking space at the airport. Gustavo sprinted through the crowded airport mall. He arrived at the gate just in time to see Chauncy stroll into the lobby with a small carry-on bag in his hand.

Gustavo waved to get Chauncy's attention.

Chauncy approached and reached out to shake De Leon's hand and was surprised when the investigator instead greeted him with a big hug. "Well, *amigo*, we finally meet! Welcome to Mexico, again."

"It's good to see you in the flesh! Last time I saw you, you were a big movie star on television."

Gustavo laughed out loud. "The last time I saw you, you were swinging like a monkey from a helicopter!"

As they drove, De Leon brought Chauncy up to date. From there the conversation drifted into Chauncy's wistful comments about Dr. Sova and Gustavo's frustrations over the case.

Once they reached Cuernavaca, Gustavo turned into his driveway. The both exited and Chauncy greeted Miranda. After they sat in the living room they chatted for a while.

"Gustavo, I can never thank you enough for saving my life. I came here to fulfill your wish for two reasons. The first is my professional obligation to keep archaeological artifacts from being plundered and second for saving my life."

Gustavo waved his hand. "Think nothing of it. To be perfectly honest, it was you who orchestrated the entire event."

"What have you got for us?" Miranda asked Chauncy.

Chauncy took the envelope from his pocket and slid a DVD out. "After my rescue I found this waiting for me when I got home from Mexico. Dr. Sova mailed it before he was murdered and it must have taken weeks to arrive. This disc was his private message to me. This is the answer to the riddle of the treasure of the Mayan king!"

"Let's play it!" an anxious Gustavo blurted out as he sprang from his chair. He motioned for the others to enter his office.

Chauncy inserted the DVD in Gustavo's computer. He navigated his way through the barrage of built-in disc security, and abruptly the image of Dr. Sova appeared on the screen.

Chauncy turned the volume up slightly so they could hear clearly:

Greetings, Chauncy! This DVD was necessary because the answer to our riddle is better told with pictures than with words. I am confident that I have finally discovered the answer to the mysterious riddle that leads to the treasure of King Chac! During one of my visits to Palenque I saw the phenomenon that opened my eyes to the answer of the riddle. I finally understood. This phenomenon was previously known only in Chichen Itza. Twice a year at the equinoxes, when the sun shines on the Pyramid of the Sun, the shadows on the steps resemble a serpent.

The textbooks say "this phenomenon has not been seen in Palenque, only in Chichen Itza." The idiots! Just because it has not been seen does not mean that it could not be seen in Palenque. Please follow my reasoning: K' inich Aha, Quetzalcoatl, K' inich Aha, Xibalba. The "sun god," or literal sun, points the way to the "serpent god" on the steps of Temple #22!

As they watched, the image of Dr. Sova was replaced by computer animation.

Here is Temple #22.

The rotating temple came to a stop and the animation zoomed in on the steps of the pyramid.

The Mayans worshiped many gods. One of the most prominent was the sun god, K' inich Aha. During the spring and fall equinoxes the sun casts an eerie shadow on the steps of the temple.

The animation changed perspective and displayed an undulating shadow on the steps of the pyramid.

As you can see, the shadow on the pyramid looks like a snake slithering on the steps of the temple. The riddle said: The sun god will show you where the winged serpent crawls. The shadow looks like the plumed serpent god, Quetzalcoatl; if you follow the shadow it points to another pyramid.

The animation panned across a courtyard of temples. Following a straight line from the shadow serpent, it stopped at another pyramid and zoomed in.

This is the pyramid of the sun, so we have the next portion of the riddle: The winged serpent will show you the way of the sun god. The next clue can be seen from the top of the Pyramid of the Sun.

The camera moved up the steps, stopping at the top of the pyramid.

And now, follow the sun to where it sets.

The camera followed an animated sun as it set behind a mountain range, with the focus on a peculiarly shaped peak.

The sun sets behind those mountains during the equinox, where there are hidden caves. Caves were also worshiped by the Mayans. They believed that the gods of the underworld were swallowing the sun at each sunset! So the riddle says: But the sun god will be swallowed up by the god of the underground. There you will find it. The treasure is hidden in a cave in that specific mountain! The Mayans were superstitious: they believed that evil spirits dwelt in caves so they were not likely to disturb the treasure.

The animation ended, and Dr. Sova appeared again on the screen.

Chauncy, we will have to contact the Mexican authorities and the director of the Museum of Anthropology of Mexico City. Please call me immediately. I want you to be with me when I announce my find to the world.

As the video ended, Gustavo was already stuffing clothing into a duffel bag. He slipped on his shoulder holster and looked at Chauncy. “Get ready, we're going!”

“What are you talking about?” Chauncy asked, shock evident on his face. He was still assimilating the information from the DVD and now this. “Going where?”

Gustavo leaned forward and hissed through clenched teeth, "You can find that mountain faster than I can. And if I don't find it fast, Mendoza will beat me to the treasure. Let’s go!"

Chauncy shuddered when he recalled he had promised Anita he would not be traipsing through the jungle. "Six months ago I saw more guns than I care to remember. You'll forgive me if I don't join you."

Gustavo zipped up his travel bag and looked intensely at Chauncy. “You don’t get it, do you? Octavio is on his way to the treasure. *You* worked in Palenque—*you* know where the mountain is. I need your help to intercept him or else all is lost and the trip you made here would have been a waste of time. Let’s go!”

Chauncy stared at the floor wishing it would open up and swallow him as he was envisioning his wife’s scowl. "I suppose you're right. I guess I knew this when I agreed to come. Do me a favor will you? Don’t tell my wife about this."

Gustavo smiled. “You got a deal. Don’t worry,” he patted his holster. “I have a gun.”

Five minutes later, Miranda watched from the front door as her husband and Chauncy raced off toward the airport.

CHAPTER TWELVE

Ranchero music blared from Octavio Mendoza's white van as he drove down the dusty jungle road toward Palenque.

It was a sad song, but Octavio was smiling as he sang along. Soon he would be the richest man in Mexico; soon he would find the treasure; soon he would be living on Easy Street.

He was amazed at how well things had turned out; how he had made De Leon believe that one or both of the men must have stolen the map. Poor Gustavo had labored so hard on his behalf to find the two scoundrels. He had paid the investigator handsomely, but the investment had produced fantastic returns.

He came to a fork in the road and pulled over. Turning the music down, he consulted his map, then veered to the right. Now he could make out the tops of the pyramids of Palenque. His heart quickened at the sight.

Parking in a small grassy area set aside for tourists, he walked to the base of Temple #22 with the scroll in his hand. He had been planning this for a long time. It was the perfect day: the spring equinox.

Let's see if I can pick up where Raul left off. No point wasting time climbing the pyramid. I'll see the shadow of the feathered serpent right here.

The temple had four corners. On one corner the sun cast an eerie silhouette that seemed undulate the entire length of the temple steps. Octavio looked around. *Not too many tourists yet; good.* He had to work quickly. *The sun shows me where the winged serpent crawls, but now the winged serpent will have to show me the way of the sun.*

He thought about the documentary film that Raul had mentioned from Dr. Sova's computer. The time-lapse footage of Chichen Itza had made what appeared to be a serpent seen crawling on the steps of the temple.

Octavio followed the line indicated across the great courtyard—to the pyramid of the sun. *It points directly to the Temple of the Sun! "The way of the sun!"*

Getting into his van, he drove off north toward the Temple of the Sun. Parking near its base he stood drinking from his plastic water bottle and looking up at the enormous structure.

The solution to the rest of the riddle was at its top. As much as he hated any kind of work he had to climb it.

By the time he got to the top, he was drenched with sweat. *Just think, Octavio. Soon you'll be so rich you'll never have to sweat again!* He sat down and consulted the scroll. *It says that as the sun crosses the sky, it gets swallowed by the "god of the underground." I'm certainly not waiting until sundown to see where the sun sets!*

He stood and drew an imaginary line through the sky with one arm following the path of the sun. Lifting his binoculars, he studied the spot where his arm had pointed at the western horizon. In the distance he spotted a series of mountain ranges. One peak jutted above all the others. *That's the mountain! "The sun god will be swallowed by the god of the underground, and there you will find it." Of course! Xibalba is a cave. That is where the treasure will be! Oh, Octavio, you are a genius. All I have to do is pluck the treasure like a little boy picking up candy after a piñata party. Thank you Dr. Sova and thank you Raul!*

Octavio made careful note of the mountain's location on his map. Shoving scroll and map into his backpack he made the less arduous descent down the temple steps.

Driving toward the mountain, the jungle pressed in on him, and before long the road was nearly too rough for driving. It was more like a hiking trail. He knocked off several branches as he drove. Just when he thought that he would have to continue on foot he came to a large clearing. He was delighted to see that he was at the foot of the mountain.

Perfect! But now I have to start the hard work.

He pulled a wheelbarrow from the rear of the van and began loading shovels, a pick and containers of water. Pushing the wheelbarrow slowly, he approached the foot of the mountain.

Where in the world do I start digging? The scroll doesn't say. There must be a cave entrance here somewhere.

He left his tools and walked along a sheer rock wall covered with vegetation. Any cave entrance was hidden by centuries of plant growth. He stared at the rock wall for a few minutes before returning to the van to fetch a machete. He began chopping at the vegetation and soon exposed a pile of loose rocks. *This must be it!*

Three hours later he collapsed on the front seat of the van. Drenched with sweat, he swatted at mosquitoes as he chewed on a cold bean burrito and contemplated his fate.

Fool! I may need a week or more to carve into that mountain! What was I thinking?

He finished his burrito and forced himself to get up. He approached the wall, holding his shovel as if it were a javelin. Growling in anger he slammed the point of the shovel into the wall, and it collapsed inward, taking him with it.

He plunged into darkness and tumbled down a dark shaft, rolling over and over with the rocks from the wall. The thud of his head hitting the bottom was followed immediately by the sound of the shovel hitting his head.

Groaning in pain he rolled over and sat up. Nothing seemed to be broken, but his left knee throbbed fiercely and he could feel blood running from a gash in his head. The dim light filtering into the cave showed him the steep staircase he had rolled down. All his equipment—digging tools, lights, first aid kit—was in his van at the top of those stairs. Protecting his injured knee as well as he could, he began crawling back up.

An hour later, bandaged and slightly cleaner, he started back down the stairs using the bright yellow extension cord, which ran from a gas generator behind the van as a guide. When he reached the bottom of the steps he set down the lamps and connected them to the extension cord. Then he gasped in amazement.

Twisted fingers of stalactites hung from the distant ceiling. Looking around, Octavio discovered that the cave was actually an anteroom that led to many other rooms. Picking up a lamp he walked to one of the tunnels that led away from the anteroom.

Down one tunnel was a pile of human skulls among some broken potshards. He shivered at the thought of all the human sacrifices to appease the gods of the underworld. Dragging the extension cord behind him, he had to duck several times to avoid re-opening the wound on his head. After a few minutes of pulling himself along he came to another room and stood up.

He shined the light across the floor and something glinted in its beam. This wasn't just another pile of dusty rocks. It took a moment before his brain accepted the message his eyes were sending.

Then he cried out loud in great jubilation. "I found the treasure of the Mayan king! Oh, Octavio, you did it, you did it!"

He laid the lamp on the floor and approached the pile. He thought of all the work he had gone through. He sank his hands into the treasure pile, pulling out jewelry and ornaments. Precious stones and beautifully handcrafted idols and statues were piled everywhere. Thousands upon thousands of figurines glittered in the darkness: gold, silver, and jade.

Ah, Dr. Sova, too bad you couldn't be here. I'll think of you in my beautiful new home ... homes, perhaps. Yes, I'll need more than one—what was that?

Someone was in the cave. "Who's there?" he shouted as his voice echoed in the empty shadows. *Relax, Octavio, relax. Your mind is playing tricks on you. Are you a child who's afraid of the dark?*

Out of the dark he distinctly heard the sound of shuffling feet. It wasn't his imagination; this was real. He stared wildly into the shadows. Before he could move or shout he heard a *pffft* sound and felt a sting in his neck.

"I've been shot!" he shouted in horror. The pain was incredible. "Who's there? Who are you?" He staggered toward the entrance and fell to the ground. The lamp shone on a man's legs; the rest of his body was hidden in the shadows. "Who are you?" Octavio shouted once more.

A deep voice reverberated through the cave. "I am King Chac."

"What? That's impossible! King Chac died centuries ago! Who are you?"

"I am King Chac! Your companions are dead by my hand, and now you too will follow them to *Xibalba*!"

"But, but ..."

"Your dose is not as strong as the others. You will live—a little longer."

"It was *you* that killed them! Why?"

"You have no right to be here. This is holy-ground, and you have profaned it. I am King Chac, and I am the protector of the artifacts of this holy place!"

Octavio grabbed his chest as his heart began to flutter with pain. "No! I don't believe in ghosts! Show yourself to me!"

The stranger stepped into the light and Octavio's mind reeled with emotional shock. "It can't be—it simply can't!

No, not you!"

"You were a fool to discover this place. It is my job to protect this treasure. No one will desecrate it and live!"

He stepped forward and leaned down, a twisted smile on his face. "And now, you will die for your sins."

Octavio could no longer hear him.

CHAPTER THIRTEEN

"Are you sure you know the way?" Gustavo asked as he drove their rented Jeep. He crashed through the bushes of the jungle, splashed through deep mud puddles and plowed through the thick vegetation.

Chauncy held onto the roll bar and looked straight ahead. "Yes, yes of course I do."

Gustavo talked between bumps. "Now you know why I don't come here. I would rather take my wife to Acapulco. I like luxurious hotels, good food, fine wine and massages."

Chauncy chuckled. "You should spend some time on an archaeological dig. The conditions are wretched, but the thrill of discovery is awesome!"

Gustavo slammed on the brakes as a jaguar crossed their path. He wrenched out his gun and aimed.

Chauncy gently pushed Gustavo's arm down. "What's the matter with you? Let the poor animal cross the road. He isn't going to hurt you."

"Big cats with big claws make me nervous!" Gustavo exclaimed as the cat fled back into the jungle.

Chauncy grinned as he picked up his binoculars. "There it is, just like I said. Temple #22, in all its ancient splendor."

As Gustavo put the Jeep in gear, Chauncy waved a hand at him. "No, no, no. From here we walk."

"Walk? Are you crazy? What about jaguars?"

"These cats are more afraid of us than we should be of them. You're just used to the comfort and safety of a helicopter. We need stealth, not speed," he said. He patted Gustavo's shoulder holster. "You have a gun, remember?

CHAPTER FOURTEEN

The mysterious killer knelt beside Octavio's body. Laying the scroll over the corpse's chest, he crossed Octavio's limp arms over it. Then from the pile of treasure he selected a death mask, one that was decorated with jade and mother-of-pearl, and placed it gently over the dead man's face.

He collected the lights and began pulling the cord up the long staircase. In the harsh light of the sun he piled Octavio's equipment into the white van.

Disappearing between the trees, he returned with a box labeled "Caution - Explosives" and a small hand-activated detonator. He didn't waste much time with careful placement of the dynamite. There was plenty to do the job, even if he was a little careless. He connected the detonating cable to each bundle of dynamite and began walking backward away from the cave's entrance, uncoiling the cable.

Just as he reached the end of it he felt the cold barrel of a gun in his back. "Stop right there! Put your hands up."

The stranger slowly turned around, obeying Gustavo's commands. He had a perplexed look on his face. "Gustavo De Leon and Chauncy Rollock! How did you find me?" Then in a quieter voice, "So close. I was so close."

It was hard to tell who of the three was most surprised. Gustavo barely recognized the face. He wouldn't have recognized the voice at all.

"Miguelito?" Gustavo said.

Chauncy blurted, "You speak Spanish!"

De Leon glanced at Chauncy. "Yes, Chauncy. He speaks Spanish. He's not dimwitted. It was all an act." Then he turned to Miguelito, "Where's Octavio?"

Miguelito sighed and then answered. "He's down in the cave—forever!"

Gustavo's eyes widened. "Octavio didn't kill his partners, you did, just like you killed Octavio."

"Finally the investigator begins to understand just a little. At least now you can stop calling me Miguelito." Smiling, he bowed his head slightly and said, "My name is King Chac."

Gustavo shook his head as if a fly were buzzing in his face. "No, no, no. This makes no sense."

Chauncy acted as if he were waking from a dream. "I think maybe it does, Gustavo. I think there's a story here and maybe we should hear it."

Gustavo gestured toward a shady tree with two large rocks under it. "Let's at least sit in the shade while we listen to it."

King Chac lowered his hands, walked to a boulder and sat down. Gustavo watched him move, thinking how complete the transformation was. He was no longer a sickly old man. A smooth agility had replaced the dragging shuffle and an intelligent light had replaced the glazed look in his eyes. Gustavo and Chauncy sat side-by-side on the other rock.

King Chac looked at the two men. "It seems that I have no choice but to tell you my story, Mr. De Leon and Mr. Rollock. I was on a sacred mission, which I have failed. I was born here in the mountains of the Yucatan peninsula. I am from the Quiche Maya tribe. My parents named me King Chac, because I am a descendant of the great king whose tomb you Mestizos desecrated at the so-called Temple #22, the Temple of Chac.

"Centuries ago we were a mighty people. King Chac was our mightiest king. We sacrificed to our gods and had their protection. We were the most powerful people of the Isthmus of Tehuantepec, and our great temples filled Palenque!

"But King Chac's empire faded, and the Quiche Maya had to migrate to other areas to avoid famine. Most stayed in the mountains and struggled to survive. But then the Spanish conquest came. Oh, how they devastated our people! They destroyed our way of life and our heritage and made us their slaves. They took away our idol gods and gave us new idols to worship. Smallpox and other diseases ruined our race; those who could escaped to the mountains. Like the Lacondon, we hid in the mountains and jungles where the Spanish couldn't find us.

"For generations we hid there. Then the airplanes came. They saw our villages. Others followed who took away our lands and made us live in poverty. Our temples and treasures have been plundered and destroyed. Greedy men with evil intentions have done so much damage, and even those with good intentions sent our treasures away to museums. Little by little our way of life was being destroyed. It was foretold that I would be the one to save our people. I am a descendant of King Chac. From infancy my parents taught me that I would fulfill the prophecies foretelling the great restoration of our people.

"One day news came to the village of the famous French archaeologist who intended to decipher King Chac's riddle. For three weeks I meditated in a small hut far outside our village, seeking the wisdom of the gods.

"I left the mountains and went to the lowland jungles of Merida. Believing that I was a moron, Dr. Sova saved himself a few pesos and hired me to perform simple tasks around his hacienda. Working at the hacienda gave me the opportunity to study Dr. Sova, just as he studied the Great Riddle. Then you came, Mr. Rollock, and after a few weeks you left again.

"Dr. Sova continued to work on the scroll, but over time he became erratic. He would disappear for long periods at a time. About six months ago we realized that he would never return. As you know, his widow sold the house but I stayed on with the other caretakers. They looked down on me as much as you Mestizos. So my disguise fooled them completely. I could wander off any time I wanted. It was easy to disappear long enough to give Barrios and Martinez their invitations to *Xibalba*. Octavio slipped away but I suspected he knew the location of the treasure. So instead of searching for him, I came here. With those three dead and the cave dynamited, no one would ever find it again.

"I have failed. You will reveal this place to the authorities and our treasures will be taken from our people! Nothing will be left for us! Nothing!"

Gustavo shook his head in dismay. Finally, finally everything made sense. And yet, it was not due to his ability as a detective, but because of the story he had just heard. He could see there was only one thing to do. It would be difficult; but doing the right thing so often is. "Come with me," he growled.

King Chac and Chauncy followed him to where the detonator lay. De Leon looked at the gun in his hand as if wondering why he was still holding it. He shoved it back into the holster.

"Pick up the detonator and use it!" he ordered.

"What?" King Chac became rather slack jawed.

"I said press the detonator. Do it before I change my mind!"

Chac dropped to his knees and slammed his hand on the detonator button.

The percussion of the explosion filled the small valley with dust. As it settled the men coughed and sputtered, then stood in silence staring at the dusty rubble that filled the mouth of the cave.

Chac turned toward De Leon and held his arms out, his wrists together, expecting to be handcuffed.

Gustavo shook his head slowly. "I no longer work for the police or the military, King Chac. Let them find you and arrest you. I'm just a private investigator. My client is dead. My job is done. I'm the one who had it all wrong." Gustavo waved his hand at the mountain. "The treasure of the Mayan king does not belong to Mexico or any other government. It belongs to you and your people. I've seen enough greed to last a lifetime and I am simply not interested in letting anyone know about this treasure. Rest assured I'll never share the secret of the Mayan treasure with anyone. And Mr. Rollock has already shown that he wants it to be kept secret."

Chauncy spoke up. "I only revealed the secret to help Gustavo solve this crime. It's over now and I'll never have reason to reveal it again."

"I'm not condoning murder," Gustavo continued. "I have heard that there is a God that will judge the entire earth. But I am not God. Let Him judge you, as he will judge us all someday."

King Chac bowed low. "Gustavo De Leon, you show greater insight than any Mestizo I've ever known."

Gustavo scowled at Chac. "But there are others, Chac. There will always be others. Your secret is safe for now. But mark my words: sometime, somewhere, somehow, someone is going to attempt to find the treasure again and this evil game will start all over. The greed, the treachery, the murder, the madness—one day the treasure of the Mayan king will be found again."

Taking a step back, he returned King Chac's bow, then turned without a word and walked toward the jungle. Chauncy followed suit. Moments later King Chac stood alone in the clearing.

Then the Mayan king turned and disappeared into the jungle.

ABOUT THE AUTHORS

Both Alex Zabala and Dyego Alehandro reside in Arizona. To learn more about them and their other works, as well as to read free short stories, visit:

www.arcaniarts.com

You can contact the authors at:

Alex Zabala: **alexzabala2@gmail.com**
Dyego Alehandro: **arcaniarts@gmail.com**